KNAVE

CANDACE ROBINSON

AMBER R. DUELL

FOR JERICA

CHAPTER ONE

FERRIS
BEFORE

Do something enough times and the body remembers. Brushing teeth, putting on a shirt, tying a shoe—all of it was accomplished without thought. For Ferris, that list included playing drums.

One. Two. Three. And four.

He counted beats in his head, even though he didn't need to. It was just something to fill his thoughts as his arms moved across the drum set in front of him. Sweat dripped down the back of his neck, and flashing lights illuminated the bar. Dozens of people crowded the stage, rocking out to the loud music. The heavy drumbeats, the quick guitar notes, the screaming vocals.

One. Two. Three. And four.

The heart-pounding song poured from him in sync with the rest of the band, Death Remedy. Perfect. Well-practiced. All body memory and no conscious thought. Without his arms knowing the movements, the beats, he wouldn't be able to play anymore. His mind was numb. Empty. Except for the counting…

One. And two. Three. And four.

Ferris's lifeless eyes followed the studs on the back of the lead singer's jacket as he moved energetically across the stage, riling up the crowd. The man had to be sweating his nuts off since Ferris was in a tank with torn-off sleeves and still dripping. Dark hair fell across Ferris's slick forehead and stuck, whereas Oliver kept his short, so at least he had that going for him.

That and the lack of anxiety over getting another hit. Oliver had been suspicious that something was up with Ferris and had searched his stick bag earlier, discovering the dwindling coke stash. Ferris had hidden it in there before the show, deciding to wait until after the gig to take more and relying on hard liquor to get him through the performance. There would be a fight later. Another one. Which only made Ferris need the high all the more. Needed it so he could fucking forget. Forget *everything*.

What the fuck did Oliver care anyway? Ferris had his addiction completely under control. It was *fine*. He just needed something to take the edge off the pain. His bandmates didn't understand—*couldn't* understand. And they were no saints either. They'd all experimented at some point and he'd never given them shit.

One. Two. And three. And four.

Shit. That was wrong. Lucas, their bassist, shot him a sideways look as Ferris stumbled to catch up with them. Maybe he needed to stop counting and just let his body do all the work. Let his mind shut down.

Ferris squeezed his eyes closed. If only it were that easy. Thoughts circled through his brain endlessly, reminding him, blaming him. That was what the drugs were for: *forgetting.*

The cymbal *crashed* against his stick and he flinched.

Images of *that* night came between flickers of the strobe light. Metal crunching. Tires squealing. Flashing blue police lights. Blood. Everywhere … blood. The heat of it streaming down his forehead, into the corner of his right eye. And—

The drumsticks fell from his hands. "Fuck!"

"You okay, mate?" Lucas asked as his fingers kept plucking the string of his bass. Oliver's singing never faltered and Johnny didn't miss a chord on his guitar.

Ferris could barely hear the question over the music. Or perhaps it was the ringing in his ears. The phantom *whoop whoop whoop* of the ambulance as it took away everything important to him. He turned his head just in time to avoid puking all over his snare.

Lucas jumped back as the vomit splattered the stage next to the bassist's custom rainbow-checkered Vans. "Ferris! The fuck?"

Ferris shoved up from his stool and tripped, falling forward. He crashed into the drums, sending them flying, and slammed face first on the old wood floor. The song screeched to a halt. Every eye in the godforsaken room landed on the drummer, the silence deafening, as he struggled to get back on his feet. Embarrassment flushed his face. *Just fucking perfect.* Oliver met his gaze, his eyes hard. Ferris winced.

"Fuuuck," Ferris groaned when he was finally standing again, swaying. He reached for something to steady himself, but found his crash cymbal. The moment he put weight on it, the metal tilted, dumping him back to the floor again.

"Shit," Johnny said as he hurried to catch him.

And failed.

Ferris rolled onto his back and closed his eyes with a disgruntled *hmph.* He could hear his friends now—*loser!* And his family—*such a disgrace!* First, he'd gotten Ellie pregnant before marriage, and now he couldn't function without shooting up. He couldn't function *with* the fucking drugs either. He was too far down the rabbit hole and there was no climbing out. He didn't *want* to climb out. But this… He closed his eyes against the shame and let himself pass the fuck out.

Whomp, whomp, whomp. Ferris groaned, clutching his head as his pulse thrummed in his ears, echoed in his mind. The sounds of the bar boomed, muted, through the walls of… Where was he? Squinting, he took in the off-white metal interior of the van plastered with different band stickers. The band name *The Swingers* carved into a pineapple, a red snake circling a skull, an angry, zombified teddy bear, and on and on. Collected from all the bands that Death Remedy had played with over the years. Some from concerts he and his friends had been to before they'd became popular. And, now that they were popular, the band was phasing Ferris out.

"Fuckers," he wheezed. His band members had dumped him in the back of their van and… He listened harder. And went back to playing? The twats. "See how good you are without a drummer, arseholes," he shouted to the stickered ceiling.

Rubbing his face, Ferris forced himself to sit up, kicking empty beer cans away. His palms were sweaty, hands shaking, and he ground his teeth against the urge to scratch his face. He needed his fix *now*. Oliver could go fuck himself. Except… *Damn.* His stick bag was inside with the rest of the equipment.

He stared at the stickers above him and focused on the one of a penguin holding an iced coffee. Stars rested in its overly large eyes and a smile lingered on its beak. *Ellie.* His girlfriend had been just as excited, just as happy, as that stupid bird. About nearly everything. It was what made Ferris fall in love with her when they were sixteen and stay in love with her for the last four years. Her optimism was contagious, her smile more addictive than the drugs his body now craved. If he could, he would trade anything to hear her laugh again. Give up his damn soul to bring her back.

But he couldn't.

No one could.

Because she was dead. And their unborn daughter had been ripped from the earth along with her.

Ferris and Ellie had danced in the rain on their fourth date, then cuddled in the van when lightning struck at the park. She'd seen the band's paltry sticker collection at the time and fished out the penguin from her purse. When he'd asked her why she was carrying it around, she said she'd bought it on a whim that morning. Where she randomly found it was a mystery and he regretted not asking her, not that it really mattered. He was sorry he hadn't asked a million things over their three-year-long relationship. Little things he would never know now, things that anyone else would call irrelevant. But when someone died, *everything* was relevant about them—it was just too late to realize it.

Pressing the heels of his hands against his eyes, Ferris willed away the building tears. It had been eleven months since the accident. The one where *he* had been driving. Where *he* hadn't swerved in time to avoid the car driving down the wrong side of the road. Eleven months and thirteen days.

Every day since had been a complete and total spiral into hell.

"Damn," he croaked.

He needed to get high before his thoughts went any further. Like to the list of baby names in Ellie's handwriting that he still carried in his wallet even though they'd eventually decided on Luna, or to the plant she'd kept in their shoddy flat that was now withering because he was apparently shit at keeping anything alive.

No. He scrambled to unlatch the back door and flung it open, practically falling to the pavement. Drugs were exactly what he needed to forget *them*. The fact that they were gone. He needed—

"Ferris!" a deep masculine voice called.

He squinted down the alleyway, catching sight of someone he'd painted houses with a couple years ago. Roger? Or Richard? Something like that. He looked the same as he did back when he was sacked for showing up to a job while tripping. Ferris grinned.

"Hey, man." He stood up straight and smiled. *Raymond!* That was it. "How you been?"

"Good, good," Raymond said. "Looks like you're having a rough night, though. Did you hit your head up on stage?"

A wave of shame washed over Ferris but vanished as quickly as it had come. "Nothing a little pick-me-up wouldn't fix."

Raymond smiled knowingly. "I thought as much. You got cash?"

Ferris stumbled up to him, hands shaking with need, and cast a quick glance over his shoulder to make sure they were alone. Pulling his wallet from his back pocket, he drew two fifties out—his last banknotes—and handed them over. "What will this get me?"

"What's your poison? Pills? Powder?"

"Coke." Ferris licked his lips, aching for a hit.

"For a hundred?" he asked, brow raised.

"Come on. As you said, it's been a rough night." First Oliver finding his stash, then the stress of the impending fight, and the whole falling over his own drums…

Raymond studied him for a moment. "I've got something new tonight. Not sure what it's cut with, but it should do the trick."

"I'll take it," Ferris blurted. As long as it made his mind shut the fuck up.

His old acquaintance dipped his fingers into his pocket, taking his sweet time as Ferris's heart beat anxiously, then reached out to shake hands. "Have fun, mate."

Ferris glanced down at the bag of white powder. His needles were in the stick bag, but that was fine. Tapping a messy line out on the back of his hand, he quickly snorted it, then repeated the process. The burning inside his nostrils faded to numbness. Ferris sighed, eager for the full effects of the high to kick in, and stumbled through the backdoor of the bar.

The world spun for a moment. Florescent lights in the hallway became starbursts and it felt as if the ground tilted beneath him. Ferris collapsed to the dingy floor with just enough time to realize how badly he'd fucked up.

Soft lyrical voices drifted around him. Dreaming. Dying. Images of Ellie floated across the back of his eyelids. Her long blonde hair danced around her oval face, her dark eyes glittering as she smiled. She cradled the baby bump that grew beneath her shirt and held her hand out to him. He stretched to grasp it…

Pain lanced his arm and he tried to pull back, but couldn't. His fingers twitched, unable to reach Ellie with his free hand or move the other away. A scream built in the back of his throat, trapped, captured by his unconsciousness. Then the pain faded. Pleasure replaced it.

Every inch of his body hummed with life. His skin tingled, a warming sensation spreading through him, through every cell, just right. He imagined himself floating. Up, up, up. Toward something better. Something sublime.

The smile fell from Ellie's face and the image of her blurred. Faded. Disappeared. He fought to pry himself away from the pleasure clouding his thoughts, anchoring him. To follow Ellie and their daughter.

Let me go, he pleaded.

Let him join them, wherever they may be. He wanted the pain to stop, to end it all. Overdosing like this had been an accident, but maybe it was for the better. Then he wouldn't be such a burden to everyone around him. He wouldn't have to suffer this loneliness anymore…

Come back, he begged Ellie. *Don't leave me here without you.*

"Is it working?" asked a woman.

An intense pressure came against his arm as someone sucked. He gasped and his eyes fluttered open. The pale-yellow walls were bright, too bright, around him. The tiles too hard. His arm lowered on its own.

No. Not on its own. Someone gently placed it on his stomach and patted him. "There now, you're all right."

Ferris forced his eyes to focus. A woman leaned over him, her head haloed by the ceiling light, her face in shadows. He dragged in a ragged breath. The woman shifted to where her face was visible. Delicate features with a spattering of freckles across her nose and cheeks. Violet eyes and soft lips. A pink plait draped over one shoulder. He'd never seen anyone so beautiful before … so *inhuman.* Perhaps he was dead after all.

"Are you an angel?" he rasped.

The young woman blinked, a smile slowly spreading across her cheeks. "Me? Gracious, no."

Ferris sat up slowly, his head throbbing, body shaking. Another figure with purple curls and a bowler hat atop her head moved behind his angel. The second woman looked similar, except her features were a bit sharper. A sister, maybe. "Looks as if this is your lucky night," she sang, grinning as she adjusted her hat.

Sure, if bad luck counted as luck... Ferris thought for a moment, letting what had happened sink in. He'd had a horrible reaction to whatever Raymond sold him, had been dying, had *wanted* to die for a moment. Because Ellie was… He swallowed hard. Somehow, he was awake now. Not only awake but clear headed.

"I…" His body ached with a soreness that ran bone-deep.

"I think we have different definitions of *lucky*."

"He looks like a newly-hatched baby bird." The purple-haired one poked his arm.

"At least he's sober now," the angel replied.

Sober. When was the last time he'd been that way? *Eleven months and fourteen days ago.* "I don't understand." Ferris lifted his arm, his gaze locking onto two puncture wounds with a trickle of blood running from each. What kind of strange ass shit were these two into? "The fuck?"

"I drank the poison from you," the angel said softly.

Did she say *drank*? As in pierced him with something, then drank his *blood* to sober him up?

"Good thing, too. You'd be dead if Mouse hadn't found you." The purple-haired woman waved her hand in the air.

Dead. Yes, he'd been dying, but hearing someone else speak the word was jarring. Ellie and their daughter were gone, but he wasn't ready to join them. Not really. Not yet.

The angel—Mouse—knelt beside him, a comforting gardenia scent drifting around him. What sort of name was Mouse, anyway? As she leaned in to whisper, Ferris forgot the question. "You look as though you need a friend. And perhaps I can help you, if you help us. If not, I can make you forget."

Ferris arched a brow. He wouldn't easily forget this night, no matter how much coke he snorted in the future. "What do you mean exactly?" The ache in his temples throbbed harder, distracting him from gathering proper thoughts.

A faint smile twitched at Mouse's lips as she drew closer, caressing his ear with her voice, her warm breath brushing his skin. "You want a high and we want to feed. So would you like to make a deal with a vampire?"

CHAPTER TWO

MOUSE

PRESENT DAY

A mouse was a quiet thing, one that hovered, listening, waiting for its moment. Although small, the creature wasn't helpless—it could terrify if it so chose.

And waiting was precisely what Mouse was doing.

Waiting for her moment to strike.

Loud techno beats boomed around her while white lights shimmered through the smoke inside the mortal club. Mouse easily blended in, wearing her black gothic frock and dark platform boots, her pink plait resting over her shoulder. She sat at the bottom of the stairs, peering out at the crowd as the mortals' bodies gyrated. Their blood called to her, pulsing, *slamming*, in their veins, begging her to rip their flesh open and take her fill.

Breathe, Mouse.

The front pocket of Mouse's dress wiggled. "Just a little

longer, Des," she said over the loud music, lightly patting her chest. The caterpillar had been with her each night, calming her, keeping her from massacring innocents, the way she'd done that day in the donor building in Ivory when she'd murdered twenty mortals. The donors were supposed to be safe in Wonderland. But she'd been so incredibly *hungry*.

Since returning to the Ivory Palace after Ever reclaimed her throne, Mouse had been feeding on humans—those who deserved it—almost every night. Her hunger never satiated. Her sister, Maddie, didn't know about Mouse's appetite, and she couldn't either.

A warm body, smelling of cigarettes and luscious blood, sank down beside her on the stairs. The rows of steps stretched across the back wall in the dance room, and at the top rested a stage with several tables and chairs. On some nights, bands would play up there but tonight it was couples drinking, kissing, and groping.

Mouse ignored the mortal, but the brazen male shifted closer so his arm was pressed to hers. She again inhaled his intoxicating scent buried within his flesh when he finally spoke, "What's a pretty girl like you doing here?"

"I've come to satisfy my appetite," she said, not meeting his gaze.

His index finger brushed her hand, delicately stroking, and the urge to rip it off flowed through her. Bold, touchy mortals didn't sit well with her. Not since that day long ago when a mortal man forced Mouse against a library shelf, hiked up her skirts, and had his way with her. Even after fighting against him, she'd been silent through it all, until she'd gotten home and finally cried, truly screamed.

"You look a little young to be here," the man purred in her ear.

Mouse clenched her jaw as she met his dark irises. He wasn't unattractive—his chestnut hair was parted on the side and his chiseled cheeks were sharp under the lights. He wore a black fishnet shirt and dark trousers with too many buckles. She'd been twenty when she was turned, but the majority of humans believed she was much younger.

"Do you *like* young girls?" she cooed, then bit her lip, setting the trap.

He grinned, wolfish, his white teeth shining too brightly. "That depends."

"I'm sixteen," she lied, waiting to see if he took the bait.

"That's older than I'm used to."

Rage filled Mouse, her veins throbbing hot. She wanted to rip off this mortal's head, tear out his heart, break him into pieces, lap up all his blood. "Follow me to the back alley," she said softly, calmly, "and I'll do anything you'd like."

"Maybe you should get my name first." He licked his lower lip. "I'm Liam."

"I'm Margo." She used her real name most of the time with humans because she didn't want them to have the one that felt more like her.

Liam stood and Mouse led the way through the dancing crowd toward the back door. She tried not to breathe too much as the bodies pressed against her, begging her to taste them.

Outside, lamps along the building lit up the area. Several people lingered, smoking and laughing. Mouse glanced over her shoulder when Liam's hand clasped her arm. Her rage only intensified at his touch. Since having her virginity ripped away, she hadn't allowed a male or female to get close to her in a sexual sense, not even a kiss besides pressing her lips to a throat, a wrist, a thigh, to sink her teeth into their flesh to sate her appetite.

They walked to the side of the building and entered a dark, damp alley that reeked of the rubbish bin.

"You said you would do anything I like?" Liam's breath was hot on Mouse's neck as he backed her into the brick wall while unbuckling his trousers. "Suck my dick."

Mouse blinked and pressed her lips into a tight line.

"Bollocks, I changed my mind." She leapt forward, slamming his back against the opposite wall. Her fangs dropped and she pierced his throat as he sucked in a sharp breath. Before he could feel any pleasure from her bite, she tore out his throat and drank. The thick liquid against her tongue tasted like the richest of heavens. So good, so *good*. Mouse couldn't stop, not even to rip out his heart and drink that dry too. She wanted more and more, and *more*. Wanted it to block out *everything* that had happened at the Ruby Heart Palace…

After every speck of the mortal's blood was inside her, she dropped his body, letting it collapse against the ground. Another murder that would go unsolved. A well-deserved one.

Her pocket wiggled once more, and Mouse sighed, taking out her blue and yellow caterpillar. Des, head tilted to the side, peered up at Mouse with beady black eyes.

"He deserved it, and I think you agree because you didn't try to stop me as you did in the donor building."

The caterpillar wrapped her body around Mouse's index finger, giving it a hug.

Mouse glanced down at herself, soaked in scarlet. She needed to stop making a mess out of her meals, but she wanted it to hurt. However, now she couldn't very well go traipsing into the club looking like an axe murderer.

Placing Des back into her pocket, Mouse darted out from the alley and away from the club, using her immortal speed. Rav's old portal was the nearest one, but she hadn't been back to Scarlet since her escape. Chess was there, preparing for the new palace that he and Ever would share on the border between Scarlet and Ivory. The construction had already begun, yet it would still be a while before they all moved in.

Gripping the skirts of her dress, Mouse bolted into the woods. She ran through the night, unable to ignore her unwanted thoughts that always managed to slip in. In that blasted Queen of Hearts' palace, every weapon imaginable had pierced Mouse's heart. Numerous blades had carved bloody smiles across her throat. Thorned whips had flogged her back, tearing her flesh over and over again. Her head shoved into a bucket full of water, in and out, in and out, until she drowned. Bled dry with Rav's scientific contraptions. After tortures such as those, a vampire needed fresh human blood to fully heal on the inside, but Mouse had never been given any. Only the same cold blood bags day in and day out. It caused her cravings to intensify, and the effects lingered. Maddie couldn't know—Mouse didn't want her sister to feel any more guilt. The Hatter had been through enough.

Mouse had always been a bit vicious when it came to her appetite. Unlike Maddie, she had killed some of her prey. Liked it. *Loved it*. But those humans had deserved it, just as her mortal abuser had when Maddie slowly killed him with hatpins and knives. Regret still haunted Mouse that she hadn't been the one to break him apart all those years ago.

Instead, she'd recently killed the twenty donors.

Rav had created a monster.

Her.

Mouse shoved that day away, the humans' screams, the way her teeth had plunged into their throats, shredding them, how she'd sucked every drop of their blood from her fingertips.

A light fog covered the cemetery and cracked headstones littered the area, not a fresh grave in decades.

Mouse knelt by one of the trees and crawled through the gaping hole. Before her, a mirror-like surface appeared, a glistening sheen reflecting her image. She pressed a hand forward, and a floral scent ignited as she was tugged through then spat out in the middle of a pathway, the stone medallion now across from her.

Rising to her feet, Mouse dusted off her hands. In front of her, the Ivory Palace loomed, beautiful and gothic, its towers massive with a silvery moat surrounding the castle. Once the new castle was built, she would miss the Ivory Palace dearly.

But maybe she could still return here sometimes when she needed an escape.

The white daisies were in full bloom and a troop of bats beat their wings overhead. Mouse hurried around the palace to the back and slipped inside with her key.

Mock, a guard with dark irises and yellow hair just past his shoulders, stood at the foot of the stairs beside Didi, a newer guard. Her silver and orange locks were drawn back in a bun, and she smiled warmly at Mouse.

"The coast is clear." Mock grinned, seeming to have noticed how she preferred sneaking in.

Taking a breath, Mouse nodded while staring at the floor, then bounded up the stairs to her room before someone else could round the corner. She didn't want to answer questions, and she shouldn't have to either.

Mouse should've been at the Ivory Palace, but she'd snuck away, claiming she was still tired. However, the truth was she hadn't been able to sleep, not in months. Maddie always believed herself to be the strange one of the sisters, but perhaps it was Mouse because with each passing day, she'd found it harder to know what to say to anyone.

Except for the once-Knave of the Ruby Heart Palace. Her friend, Ferris.

Yet, she'd kept recent things from him too. She wasn't ashamed—she didn't know what she was. Most certainly she wasn't that female who'd saved his life back at the club. The one who would dance to his music, the one who would laugh at his sarcasm. Two years in a prison cell could change someone, but two years tortured by Rav and Imogen would make a monster out of anyone. Even though she'd already been one.

But she was *fine*.

Mouse left her door cracked open as she'd been doing since leaving her prison cell. On her bed rested a pale-yellow envelope. Mouse's heart inflated at the sight, and with a smile, she scooped it up. She opened the envelope and fished out the paper. A rosewood scent drifted to her nose, and she inhaled the comforting smell as she unfolded it. Drawn across the page was a feminine hand holding several gems. At the bottom was a single sentence: *You're stronger than any diamond.*

She smiled at it. *Ferris.*

Mouse refolded the paper and stashed it with the others beneath her bed. He'd snuck her drawings while she'd been in the prison cell and continued to give them to her afterward. She set Des on top of a green leaf on the bedside table then went inside her bathing chambers to wash.

The warm water calmed her until it turned cold—icy like it had been in the Ruby Heart Palace when Rav would poke and prod her with needles, drawing her blood.

Clenching her teeth, trying to forget those memories, Mouse toweled off and put on a fresh dress. She then padded to her bed and slipped beneath the silk covers.

It was still night and she shouldn't be lying in bed, but all she'd been wanting to do was feed and rest. Des lifted her head for a moment before falling back asleep on top of her half-eaten leaf.

Imogen digging her nails into Mouse's flesh, then shoving her head into a bucket filled with water drifted through her mind. Mouse hummed to make it stop, to go *away*—it was something she'd started while inside the prison cell. She couldn't breathe, the water filling her lungs.

Shakespeare. Shakespeare. Shakespeare. She thought about his plays, as she always did in times like these. Des had been named after Desdemona, after all. But Mouse had always felt something for Ophelia from *Hamlet.* What would have happened if Ophelia hadn't killed herself? Sometimes Mouse thought about going to the mortal world and waiting for the sun to rise to see if she truly would die.

A light knock came at her cracked door, and Ferris's hulking shadow crept up the wall. "Mouse?"

"Come in," she whispered, inhaling his calming rosewood scent as he approached. Ferris looked striking, dressed in the white and silver Ivory guard uniform, the clothing hugging his strong arms, chest, and legs. His short dark hair was swept back, and his brown gaze latched onto hers.

"Hello, luv." Ferris smiled softly. She loved that smile, loved seeing it on his handsome face. "Maddie returned from Scarlet."

Her sister. She still didn't know Mouse had slaughtered the donors. Ever and Chess had agreed to keep what she'd done a secret, as long as it didn't happen again. "I'll meet with her later." She bit her bottom lip. "Thank you for the drawing."

Ferris shrugged and stepped forward. "Do you want company?"

Mouse knew what that meant—he needed company but didn't want to ask it of her and put pressure on her. Neither of them liked asking for things, yet she did want the company, *his* company. She nodded, opening her arms to him. "Are you having a tedious day too?"

He took off his boots and his large frame slipped beneath the covers beside her. "It's better now."

She circled her arms around his neck and held him close. Ferris was her best friend. For centuries, it had always been Maddie and Ever—she'd never wanted to let anyone else in. Not until him.

As she breathed Ferris in, she remembered the days at the club when she would feed off him, giving him the high he needed, giving her the food she craved. Since the day they'd met, they'd never talked about their pasts, only the present, the future. But back then, Mouse had known he'd wanted to escape his demons, just as she'd needed to feed. The day she'd found him, almost dead, there was something about him she'd wanted to save. He'd thought her an angel while most mortals had believed her to be a demon.

As she listened to the rhythmic sound of his pulse, her

fangs threatened to drop at the thought of what his blood would taste like in his vampire state. What would the high feel like to each other now that he was a vampire? She'd never tasted the blood of an immortal since being turned by Maddie. The hunger swirled in her stomach, her eyelids fluttering.

The sound of his voice snapped her out of the moment. "Are you all right, luv?"

"I still feel everything from inside that palace." She rested her head in the crook of his shoulder, her chest heaving, not wanting to discuss how she craved to taste him. That would be another of her secrets, one that would have to go away.

He ran a hand through her wet hair. "I know. So do I."

CHAPTER THREE

FERRIS

"Ferris?" Mouse whispered.

Ferris stirred from sleep and cracked open his eyes to find a halo of pink hair framing Mouse's face as she looked down at him. She'd come into his room this time, which she did whenever she needed him. "What's wrong?" he asked, his voice thick with sleep.

"Nothing really." She set her head back down on his pillow and snuggled closer.

A sheet was between them, kept there so his naked flesh touched no part of her body. Mouse knew he slept without clothes and never once tried to crawl beneath the blankets. An unspoken agreement between them so their nights together didn't get awkward. It was especially important now that he couldn't stop wondering what it would be like to settle between her legs. To have her naked body beneath him. Ferris shoved the thoughts away before blood could rush to his cock.

This was *Mouse*.

"Nothing?" he repeated.

"I just wanted to hear your voice," she replied quietly.

"Ah." Ferris draped an arm over Mouse and tugged her closer, giving her what she needed. "Should I tell you a story to help you fall back asleep?"

She sighed against his chest, relieved. "Yes, please."

Ferris set his chin atop her head and thought for a moment. "Have I ever told you about when I learned to play drums?"

A gentle shake of her head.

"Well, I was only ten when I begged my mom for lessons, but she was dead-set against it because it would be a racket. My dad though? He only winked. A week later there was a drum set in my room when I came home from school. My first lesson wasn't until later in the month, but of course I was too impatient to wait. I wailed on those things, smashing the cymbals as loud as I could. It was complete chaos. My mother nearly went mad listening to it.

"But once the lessons started, I practiced everything I'd learned over and over. Which, I'm fairly certain, only made things worse." Ferris chuckled, remembering his mother's exasperated stares. "Soon enough, I understood how to read music and the noise became songs. It took a while for them to be *good*, but at least they were recognizable."

On and on Ferris went. Talking about his different drum sticks, about the first time he'd played through one of his lessons without any mistakes, his mother's growing acceptance of never having a moment's peace. The story wasn't riveting by any means, but it wasn't meant to be. It was simply a way to soothe Mouse and, he supposed, relive a memory or two.

Once Mouse's breaths were soft and steady again, Ferris slowly slipped from the bed. He was no longer tired, and he ached to play the set Ever had given him. He glanced wistfully at the drums in the corner. It was far too late to play now unless he wanted the whole palace to wake up.

Instead, he grabbed a pair of loose gray sweatpants and settled into the chair beside the bed with his sketchbook. The pencil was still between the pages where he'd left off, the last drawing of a rose bush covered in blooms that made him think of Mouse. Not quite as beautiful as her, but delicate, soft. And her hair matched the petals almost exactly.

He quietly pressed the pencil tip to the next blank page and began drawing the outlines of Mouse's face. Her features were smoothed in sleep, her plump lips parted slightly, her long lashes caressing her cheeks. A few strands of pink hair slipped over her temple and down her cheek, over her chin to rest against her neck.

The drawing took shape slowly as he tried to capture her essence with a simple piece of lead. He erased, retrying parts until his muscles ached before setting the book and pencil on his lap to stretch his back. The pencil fell to the carpet and, as he bent to reclaim it, the book followed. When he opened it again, it was to a sketch of Ellie, and his chest tightened. He didn't have the heart to tear the image from the spiral binding, but he'd made a point of *never* looking past a certain point in the notebook.

Practically flinging the sketch pad back onto his bedside table, he grabbed a black T-shirt from the floor and left before he could wake Mouse. He needed to expel some energy and, if he couldn't play drums, he needed to do something else. But what? What could *possibly* stop the memories from overwhelming him? Swallowing him whole?

Ellie. Their daughter. The crash. Crunching metal. Flashing lights. Sirens. A funeral.

Ferris shook his head violently to rid himself of the thoughts building without permission. There was only one thing that had ever helped him cope. *Two things.* But he could never ask Mouse to feed from him now. He knew what happened when two vampires indulged in sharing blood—a practical fuck fest followed. After everything he and Mouse had lived through in the Ruby Heart Palace, he didn't want to use her like that. Not that he didn't think she was the sexiest vampire in Wonderland.

"Shite," he swore under his breath. Some time away from the palace might do him good, help him clear his head. And maybe he needed a little bit of help managing it. He scribbled a quick note to leave on his bedside table in case Mouse woke up to find him gone, then he fled the Ivory Palace.

When he stepped through the main doors without running into anyone, Ferris breathed a sigh of relief. The cool air filled his lungs but did nothing to help the frantic edge building in his head. He needed to go … just *go*. What he needed could only be found in the mortal world.

Ferris ran his trembling finger along the crack in the outer wall and dropped through the portal, landing unceremoniously on his knees in an old cemetery. He stared up at the night sky, purposely avoiding looking at any gravestones, and stood. A heaviness thumped in his chest in time with his heart. The sorrow of losing Ellie and their unborn daughter had never left him, but sometimes it was easier to live with the pain. He could've lived without the reminder of death at the moment though.

Rushing from the cemetery, he let his feet carry him away from the portal. A slight drizzle fell from the sky, just enough to make everything damp and smell musty. He'd missed this place, though he didn't want to admit it. But Wonderland was his home. It was where he could be himself, live his life without judgment—at least now that he was no longer forced to slave away for the Queen of Hearts. He had played his part as the love-struck Knave well, but he'd always belonged to Mouse. Saving her was worth the torment he'd suffered. He'd do it again in a moment if he had to, but sometimes he still felt like a true knave for not telling Mouse about his past. The death of Ellie and their unborn daughter, Luna, set off a chain of events that led to him in the back hallway where he'd nearly died.

His mother and father had refused to speak to him for months after he'd gotten Ellie pregnant. They were strict Catholics and he wasn't married. Even after Ellie died, things remained strained with his parents. So, he'd tried drugs to cope with Ellie and Luna's deaths and found they worked—almost too well. Ferris had only ever been an embarrassment to his parents. And his bandmates...

After Mouse saved him, he'd refocused, found a new high to thrive on—her bite. Getting clean was enough for his bandmates to forgive him, but that hadn't meant they'd trusted him anymore.

He slowed to a walk once he reached a sketchy, run-down bar and stuffed his hands into his trouser pockets. The cold, misty rain landed on his face, clung to his hair. Inside, the stench of alcohol assaulted him. His trainers stuck to the dirty floor, each footstep going *scritch* until he plonked himself down on a stool at the bar. He'd been here before. Knew the bartender, Ken, would have what he needed.

"Hey," Ken said, peeling himself away from a couple of older women at the opposite end of the bar. "Haven't seen you in a long time."

"I've been busy," he grumbled. "Do you have anything?"

Ken nodded once. "Not been out of town at rehab, have you?"

Ferris snorted. If only that were true. "What does that matter to you?"

"It doesn't." Ken shrugged. "Just trying not to personally kick anyone off the wagon."

"Ken," Ferris said, compelling him. "Give me the coke on the house and, when I walk back out of this bar, forget you ever saw me."

With stiff, robotic movements, Ken fiddled around beneath the bar and finally slid him over a can of beer. Beneath it would be the hit Ferris desperately needed. Using his vampiric speed, he snorted the white powder before anyone could notice. The burn was instant, faded quickly, and was replaced with the tingle of a high.

Only it stopped there.

His body no longer reacted the same. Mouse and Maddie had spoken about how drugs didn't affect vampires, but he hadn't really wanted to believe it.

"Fuck," he growled to himself.

"Something on your mind?" Ken asked, tossing a cloth over his shoulder. "There's got to be a reason you came looking for a hit tonight."

"Sure there is," Ferris said through his teeth. "I remembered my girlfriend and daughter are dead. I just spent two years groveling to the power-couple from Hell, plucking body parts off monsters to be used in horrible experiments, and falling asleep to screams of tortured souls. Also had to fuck the bitch and pretend I wanted to do it again, when I hated myself for doing it at all. Of course, the reason was worth it, but I'd only ever been with Ellie before that and—" He dragged in a deep breath. The fuck was he doing, spouting off like this to one of his old drug dealers, of all people? But he couldn't seem to stop himself now. "I finally got out of that toxic as fuck palace, only to hide away with some newly-turned female who asked *why* more times than a damn toddler. But at the end of the day, what good was I, really? I saved Alice, sure, but I had to let Mouse be tortured for two years. I couldn't even help kill the arseholes who'd held her captive. I'm as useless as an old fucking shoe."

"Wow." Ken grimaced. "I don't understand a single thing you just said. Are you sure you should've taken another hit?"

Another. He thought Ferris was already high and speaking nonsense. "I'm fine," he mumbled and let out a long breath. Just saying that out loud made him feel better. Or did he feel worse now? Calmer, either way. Resigned to his life and the fact that he needed to pull himself together without reverting to old habits. "See you around."

Having lost his appetite, Ferris returned to Wonderland and strolled the streets of Ivory instead. Since becoming a vampire, he'd never really gotten the chance to explore this part of his new world—though Scarlet was as familiar as the back of his own hand after all the sneaking about he'd done during the last two years. Over the past couple months, he'd been getting to know the city around the Ivory Palace. A few streets here, a few more there, unwilling to get himself completely lost but enjoying that he wasn't trapped in the Ruby Heart Palace or running from safe house to safe house.

Vampires and humans roamed the streets together, laughing, talking, kissing, feeding. Art shops beckoned him closer with the brilliant works in their display windows, but he kept walking. A new café had even opened that served human food alongside blood so anyone could enjoy a meal together. Good timing too, as the donation center was still temporarily closed. That didn't stop other vampires from keeping their own private donors in Wonderland or bringing them over for a night, of course. Ferris still wasn't hungry after his trip to the mortal world, though he would force down a bag of blood when he returned to the palace to keep himself from regretting not eating tomorrow. He nodded to a young woman as she exited a clothing boutique on the arms of a male with a green streak in his hair. Mouse might like checking out the place once she was feeling up to an outing. Update her wardrobe a bit since it had been years.

The castle rose at the edge of the town and Ferris stopped in his tracks. He wasn't ready to go back, fake a smile for

Mouse's sake so she didn't worry about him. Avoid Maddie's questions. Play a round of cards with Noah. Ever would ignore his current mood as she was always busy with her queenly duties or Chess.

Instead, he turned around and walked back down the streets. Past white and silver store fronts, through waves of jazz music spilling from open windows, and away from the hubbub of the crowd. When a glittering silver lake appeared before him with pearly white gazebos, he smiled to himself. The clearing was scenic in the moonlight as crickets chirped. Eager to see something new, his pace quickened.

Mouse would definitely like to see this, he thought as he rounded the lake to one of the gazebos. It was quiet here. Peaceful. She had probably already visited, though, since she'd lived at the Ivory Palace before. Ferris wanted to show her something to help pull her out of her own head a bit. Distract her. Help her heal.

Ferris wandered through one gazebo, then the next, taking in the feel of the lake. The drums would sound amazing here. Maybe he could put out a notice for other musicians and start up another band here in Wonderland. One just for fun—nothing serious like Death Remedy.

Something to enjoy without the pressure of earning enough money to pay the bills and booking gigs. His lips spread into a grin. *Absolutely going to happen.*

Hopping onto the marble railing, Ferris spread his arms wide and closed his eyes. The light breeze blowing off the lake brushed against his body while the fresh scent of Ivory hit his senses and—

His eyes flew open.

And blood.

Slightly stale blood.

Fangs dropping, he leapt off the railing and darted straight for the metallic scent. It became stronger, overwhelming, as he neared the furthest gazebo. Straining his ears for any hint that he wasn't alone, he prowled closer. A splatter of rust-colored blood decorated one of the pillars holding the gazebo roof. Ferris slowed his steps, casting a glance at the white and silver tree line for danger, before turning his attention back to the blood.

More of it dotted the white grass. Along with a severed finger.

Ferris took another step and froze. The rest of the body was scattered around the ground in a giant pool of dried blood. Or what was left of it. A foot, still wearing a black stiletto, another finger, and a clump of … *fucking hell.* Was that part of their intestines?

Occasionally fights resulted in a severed limb or two, but vampires didn't eat flesh. So where was the rest of the body? Whether the victim was an immortal or a human didn't make any difference. No. This was no vampire attack. A werewolf maybe. They'd been in the woods of Ivory when the group had left the safehouse, though he saw no signs of the beasts here. No beastly footprints in the blood.

A long strand of black poked from the dirt a few yards from the gore. Ferris skirted around the mess and plucked the object from the ground. *A quill.* Did Ivory have porcupines? If it was a porcupine, it was fucking massive, given the quill was nearly as long as his arm.

Twirling the quill between his fingers like one of his drumsticks, he took in the carnage again. Ever needed to know about it. It was too close to the palace grounds not to say anything and he didn't know what could've caused this. Ferris rushed back to the palace, shoved his way inside, and nearly barreled into someone.

"Woah," Chess said, stepping back just in time to avoid the collision. He wore a black vest, his chestnut hair tied back with a cord, and reeked of sex and Scarlet. "Something chasing you, boy-o?"

"What is this?" Ferris asked, ignoring the jab at his youth, and held up the slightly bloodied quill.

"That—" Surprise flashed across the king's face and he quirked a brow. He snatched the quill away and studied it before speaking again. "*That* is bad news. Where did you find it, Knave?"

"Near the lake." Ferris wiped the flakes of dried blood from his hands. "Someone was torn apart there."

"Torn apart?" Chess asked in a low, curious voice. "You saw the body?"

Ferris shrugged. "Parts of it."

Chess snorted. "I'm surprised. The Jabberwocky doesn't usually leave leftovers."

"The Jabberwocky? It rarely ever comes to Ivory and Scarlet." At least, that was what everyone had told him. That, and how loud the beast was, always letting its presence be known. He'd always pictured it as having scales instead of quills, though.

"Ah. This is true." Chess bopped Ferris on the nose with the narrow end of the black quill. "But as you know, Ever and I saw the beast in Ivory when we returned months ago. The lake is too close for comfort though, isn't it? And no one heard the beastie?" Chess gave a sharp *hmm* and dropped the quill into a tall decorative vase in the hallway. "Keep this between us until I speak to Ever. We don't want to create a panic when your female is still recovering from our latest tragedies, do we?"

"I'm not lying to Mouse," Ferris said in a low voice. He'd heard enough stories of the Jabberwocky to know this was no light matter.

"It's not lying if you simply say *nothing*. Consider it a royal secret and keep your mouth shut. I'll tell Ever and she can arrange things on her end as she sees fit." Chess spun on his heel and disappeared down the hall.

Mouse would be pissed when she found out Ferris knew and didn't mention it. Of course, she would. But…

Maybe Chess was right, as much as he hated to admit it. Mouse was still sleeping with her door open, and she was barely speaking to anyone except her caterpillar. Not about important topics, anyway. Nor was she sleeping properly. He wasn't going to give her anything new to fear unless absolutely necessary.

CHAPTER FOUR

MOUSE

Two days had passed since Mouse sated her appetite at the mortal club. She wanted to see how long she could wait to drink fresh blood, but, already, the hunger stirred within her, beating at her like the sound of Ferris on his drums, reverberating through the hallway from behind his closed door. Mouse had remained in her room, and since Maddie had come home, the Hatter hadn't disturbed her besides slipping leaves for Des into the room when she'd pretended to be asleep.

Mouse couldn't keep avoiding her sister, though. She knew if she didn't seek her out today that Maddie would come to her. When her sister returned from the Ruby Heart Palace, Mouse should've gone to her, like she always would've in the past. As much as she was relieved Imogen and Rav hadn't taken her sister, a part of her wondered why they hadn't. Had they believed Mouse didn't love Maddie as much as the Hatter did her? They'd seemed to think both had known where the

White Queen had been hidden. But Maddie was Mouse's weakness just as much as she was her sister's.

Straightening the skirts of her obsidian dress, Mouse descended the marble staircase with Des sleeping in her pocket. Footsteps echoed from below and she caught sight of long white hair flowing down the Queen's back with a plait across the front. A viola case rested in her hand and a short lacy dress with sleeves to her wrists cloaked her slender form. She normally wore her hair up except for when she was around the king of Scarlet. A hint of a smile crossed Mouse's face that Ever was happy, but it vanished when two male guards walked into the room carrying luggage cases.

"Are you leaving for a while?" Mouse asked.

Ever's head jerked to Mouse, a wide smile spreading her lips. "You're so quiet that I didn't even hear you. It won't be that long. I need to help Chess with a few things. He's already left to check on the situation in Scarlet. It's getting better, but occasionally there is a stir of trouble. Everyone needs to know we are truly aligned and that uniting the territories is best for Wonderland."

Mouse nodded and approached her friend. "I can help."

"Once the new palace is built, I will accept your offer. For now, focus on you." Ever stepped closer, a concerned expression forming. "Do you need to talk? I can leave afterward."

Mouse shook her head. She didn't want to make Ever waste time on her over something so important. The queen and Chess had spent enough time apart and she didn't deserve to be wrapped up in Mouse's troubles. Not when there was nothing that could be done.

"It's not good to keep everything bottled inside," she whispered so only Mouse could hear. The guards stood at the front of the room, not seeming to be interested in the conversation. They were committed to Ever and nice enough, but Mouse wasn't ready to let anyone else in. Not even those closest to her.

"I'm fine," Mouse murmured.

Ever released a breath and circled her arms around Mouse. "Take care of yourself and if you need me, come to the Ruby Heart Palace or I can come back. However, please at least see Maddie. She's worried about you."

"I will." Mouse held Ever tight and rested her head on her friend's shoulder. "I'm glad to see you happy again."

Ever drew back and lifted Mouse's chin. "I want to see *you* happy, Mouse. Healing works differently for all of us. I don't know everything that happened to you in that palace, but I believe your feeding habits will return to normal."

Mouse shrugged.

"How about when I come back, we have a game of chess, then I'll play the viola and you can dance like old times?" Ever's deep brown eyes held Mouse's.

"I would love that." It was a lie, but she didn't want to hurt Ever, not with the hope sparking in her friend's gaze. Before being held prisoner, dancing would've been precisely what Mouse would've wanted. But not now. Most likely not ever. Lying was all she seemed to be doing these days. Inside she was screaming, *crying*, but she didn't want anyone to hear it. No one but her.

Mouse bid Ever goodbye, then ventured through the palace toward the drawing room.

Didi turned down the hall, carrying two pouches of blood. "Just grabbed Mock and me a snack." The guard's smile was warm again.

Mouse nodded as usual and focused her gaze back on the marble floor. It wasn't that she was trying to be rude to Didi or the other guards—they were quite lovely—she just couldn't force a simple hello. Perhaps because as they learned more about her, they would see her for what she was. Broken.

The drawing room's door was wide open and a fire crackled. She peered inside, her eyes meeting black combat boots hanging off the side of a chair.

Mouse padded inside and Maddie jerked forward, her purple curls bobbing, a dark hat pinned to the side of her head.

Maddie grinned as she continued to work on a felt beret. "Hello, sister, so lovely for you to join me on this glorious occasion."

"What's the occasion?" Mouse asked, taking out a chair and sinking down at a table for two. A metal chess set rested on top.

"Why for our chess game, of course," Maddie sang, tossing her sewing things on the cushion before plopping down across from Mouse.

"I haven't played you in a while, only Ferris." Even then, she hadn't done that since they'd all been hidden in the safe house together months ago.

"He's shite at the game. You need a real opponent."

Mouse's lips tilted up at the edges. "All right."

"Tea?" Maddie asked, already grabbing a porcelain set and an ice chest from beneath the table.

Mouse took a deep swallow. Once she'd had a taste of fresh blood after being held prisoner, she hadn't wanted to drink any other sort. "Not at the moment. Where's Noah?"

"He'll be back soon. He's visiting Alice."

His sister—the girl from the palace, the one Mouse had told Ferris to save after Alice had unwillingly been turned into a vampire. He'd stopped by Mouse's cell with Alice in his arms before he was supposed to bring her to the dungeon. Mouse had just gotten lashed earlier that day and she'd heard Imogen's favorite, Rine, laughing about the things she was going to do to Ferris, followed by what else she would have him do with his tongue besides clean the rooms. Mouse would've wanted Ferris to save Alice anyway, but it had been an opportunity to get him out of the palace since she hadn't known how much longer Imogen would keep him alive. It was a chance for him to be unchained to the Queen of Hearts. He'd been more than lucky the memories she'd seen in his blood hadn't included Maddie and Mouse or he would've been dead.

"Your move first," Mouse said as Maddie poured herself a cup of blood. The smell drifted to Mouse and her eyelids fluttered at the scent, but the cravings pulsing through her veins weren't for that, but something warmer.

Maddie inched a white chess piece forward, then Mouse went next. With each move, Mouse lost concentration, her thoughts focused on leaving the palace and heading to one of the mortal clubs again.

"Another round?" Maddie asked, taking a sip of blood.

"Perhaps tomorrow."

Her sister sighed. "You can't go on like this forever."

"Oh, I think I can." Mouse blinked, not looking at her sister. She wasn't sure what aspect Maddie meant, and she didn't want to ask either because that would mean discussing it.

"Ah yes, we are immortal." She waved a hand in the air, then reached to softly grasp Mouse's fingers. "I want you to heal at your own time, but with each passing day, you're drifting further and further away."

Mouse drew her hand back, biting the inside of her cheek until it bled. "I'm fine, Madeline."

"You're not." Maddie furrowed her brow, her lips set in a tight line that was very unlike her sister. "I know you weren't treated fine in the palace. You used to tell me everything. I know … I know this is my fault and it should've been me with Imogen and Rav. Not you. Never you."

Mouse's heart lodged in her throat at those words because she never would've wanted her sister in there. Not with Imogen and especially not with Rav. Her sister wouldn't have survived him. "Imogen would come by my cell," Mouse finally said. "Flash me her pathetic cards, predict my future with them, ask me where Ever was. Rav would taunt me about how he would see you, how you were so easy to give yourself to him when you two first met. There, satisfied?"

Maddie let out a breath. "I'm glad those fuckers are both dead, but there's more to it than that. You won't feel better until you talk about what happened. It doesn't have to be with me, just someone."

Biting the inside of her cheek harder, she stood from her seat. "I'm hungry now. I'm going out. Thank you for the game."

"Mouse," her sister pleaded, rising from her chair.

"I love you, Maddie. You don't have to worry about me. Be happy with Noah. You deserve it. I'll play another round of chess with you tomorrow." Mouse walked out of the room, tears pricking her eyes. She ventured down several hallways, humming to herself, staring at the floor, not wanting to meet anyone's heavy stares. As she rounded the corner, she bumped into a broad, *naked*, chest, his abs perfectly sculpted. "Bollocks."

Without glancing up, she knew it was Ferris by his comforting rosewood scent. Not only that, but the raven tattoo he'd designed on the left side of his stomach and the chain necklace with the white gold ring dangling. He only wore his dark jeans slung low, paired with his black boots, just as he always did when he wasn't on guard shift and practicing his drums.

"Why hello there. Fancy running into you here," he teased, grinning as he tilted her chin up, his dark irises meeting hers. "You should keep your eyes up when you walk, luv."

She wrapped her arms around him, holding him, squeezing him too tight. Ferris's heartbeat echoed in her ears, that alluring rhythm drawing her in. With his bare skin pressed to her cheek, his scent became stronger, and as on the previous night, her fangs threatened to fall. There was a need, a drive, to tear into him. His throat, his wrist, then unbuckle and slide down his jeans ever so slowly so she could pierce his thigh with her teeth. She just wanted to taste him, his blood.

What the bloody hell was wrong with her? He wasn't mortal anymore, his blood wouldn't satisfy her hunger. Perhaps it was a different sort of craving she yearned for… She wanted to discover what else rested beneath his jeans. He was so tall, and she wondered how big his length was, how it would fit inside her mouth, slide against her tongue… Horrified at the thought, she drew out of Ferris's grasp—her *friend*—and backed away from him. "I gotta go."

"Mouse, wait—"

Before she could hear the rest of what he was going to say, she dashed from the hallway, past the stringed instruments hanging on the walls, and ran out the back door of the palace. She'd always loved feasting on Ferris, but she hadn't thought about tasting him like this before. This was Rav and Imogen's fault. *Steady, Mouse. You just need a human to drink from.*

Mouse didn't pause as she darted around the daisies and leapt into the mirror portal leading to the mortal world. It spat her out onto her stomach in the cemetery and Des wiggled in her pocket. The night was pitch black with a sliver of the moon in the sky—not a single owl hooted, but a rustling of one stirred in the tree above her. Pushing herself up from the damp grass, she checked on Des, finding her back asleep, before hurrying in the direction of the clubs.

On this night, she would slip into one where mortals pretended to be vampires. Once she made a vicious kill at a club, she would wait a bit before returning to it.

She thought about Ferris, when he'd first come to the palace, how surprise, anger, relief, and fright filled her at seeing him there. He shouldn't have risked his life, shouldn't have bedded Imogen to become a servant at her palace. Mouse didn't deserve what he'd done—she hadn't deserved that sort of friendship. Then there had been the drawings he'd snuck to her, ones that she looked at over and over after each threat, each beating, each death.

As she crossed the street toward the clubs, Mouse dropped

her fangs. She could be her immortal self and easily blend in at the mortal vampire club.

She opened the door to a sleek black building and a broad man with auburn hair to his waist greeted her. "ID," he grunted over the loud music and adjusted his septum piercing.

Cocking her head, Mouse locked gazes with the man, letting her influence seep into him. "I'm old enough. Now let me in."

Eyes glazed, he nodded and she walked down a hall, decorated with framed vampire posters, into the main room where bodies danced against one another. A heavier song took over, its beats pounding like a rapid heart. Blood pulsed in tune inside the crowd's veins, and she wanted to taste each precious throat. A monstrous side of her wanted to shred them apart, drink them dry until nothing was left.

Mouse tightened her fists, steadying her breaths while scanning their attire. Several wore fangs, white or black contacts, bat wings, cloaks, leather, bondage, vinyl.

Her mouth was dry, and the thirst took over. She studied the room, then the bar, deciding who she would feed on tonight. A young man sat at the bar and she was about to just take him when a woman behind him, wearing a leather miniskirt and a fishnet shirt over a black bra, poured a clear liquid into a drink without the mortal seeing, then handed it to him. Mouse's brows rose. She hadn't seen a woman attempt to roofie a male before, and it looked as though it would be a death tonight instead of a feeding.

Mouse took the cup from the man's hand before he could drink from it. "Go dance," she said, persuading him out of his seat with her influence.

"Excuse me, bitch?" the woman spat, her fake fangs exposed.

Mouse stilled, the blood in her veins pulsing hot. Her voice came out quiet, deadly. "I think I've experienced worse than name-calling before. Come with me outside."

The woman's eyes glazed over and she nodded. It wasn't as fun this way, but the mortal wouldn't have followed her outside like the man had the other night.

Tonight she'd planned to feed on numerous mortals until her thirst was quenched, but draining one who'd done wrong would be more fulfilling.

When they got outside, Mouse led the mortal to the back of the building where only the rubbish bin lingered, its decaying stench drifting in the air. She released her influence on the woman to see the horror on her face, then lunged forward, shredding her throat apart as she fed, lapping up the taste, the *feel*, of the blood on her tongue.

"What is this?" a man stuttered.

Mouse jerked her head up to a mortal holding a bag of rubbish. His eyes widened at the blood covering her mouth, her dress. *Monster*, he thought—she could see it in his expression.

His blood caressed her nose—she couldn't control herself and leapt forward, knocking him to the building. Mouse pierced his throat with her fangs, yearning for only a taste.

She needed to stop.

But she was unable to stop.

She tore into him the way she had the woman, drinking all of his essence, relishing in the moment. His body was limp in her arms and she drew back, shaking. Des stirred in her pocket, fully alert. Since the donor building, Mouse had promised herself no more innocents.

What had she *done*?

CHAPTER FIVE

FERRIS

Ferris hadn't intended to follow Mouse. After she ran into him in the hallway, he'd gone back to his room and gotten dressed with the intention of finding himself a meal, but something felt … off. It almost felt like she was nervous to be near him, though he *knew* that wasn't true. Which meant either he'd done something to unintentionally upset her or something else was wrong. Once he found Mouse, he would either join her or go about his night, depending on whether she was all right or not.

Since Mouse had gotten a head start, Ferris used his enhanced speed to track her down. He'd already gone into two clubs that he knew Mouse enjoyed, finding a handful of vampires but none with pink hair. At the third establishment, he stopped dead. The hint of fresh mortal blood tinged the air. The metallic smell didn't mean Mouse was there, of course. It could've been any vampire, but there was only one way to find out.

As he rounded the back of the building, the scent became stronger. Ferris's fangs dropped without warning as the rich, metallic scent practically danced over his tongue. The odor was far *too* strong. This was no simple feeding. He ignored the urges pumping through him to *feed, feed, feed,* and approached the alley with silent steps.

And came to a dead stop.

Mouse held a man with flailing limbs against the building, feasting at his throat, a hand over his mouth. Surrounded by rubbish. She drank and drank as his movements slowed to a near stop, the body limp in her arms as she drew back, trembling with apparent hunger. Her grip on him tightened, and she leaned back down to lick away the remainder of blood still oozing from him.

"Mouse?" Ferris breathed. He'd never seen her like this. So wild. So … *starved.* Just behind her laid the lifeless body of a woman in a mini skirt. She'd drank two mortals to death and still craved more? It was too much. "Mouse!"

She raised her face from the man, her trembling ceasing as a savage glint flickered in her eyes, the dead mortal falling from her arms. Blood ran over her lips, dripped down her chin. And she snarled at him. The sharp twist of her mouth turned her sweet face into something foreign. Something feral.

"I beg your *fucking pardon*?" Disbelief coated his words. What the hell was happening right now? Had he walked into *The Twilight Zone*? Mouse had *snarled?* At *him?*

Her monstrous expression dissolved as recognition settled in. She stumbled back, furiously wiping at her face. "Ferris?" she squeaked. "What are you doing here?"

He took a tentative step forward, his eyes holding Mouse's terrified violet ones, until he reached the man's side. Kneeling in the pool of blood, he felt for the man's pulse, even though he already knew he was dead. There was nothing he could do here. Not for either of the victims. The woman was beyond help, her throat torn as if a ravenous beast had shredded her apart. He'd seen vampires do worse, had seen Imogen rip out hearts, Rav string victims out in the garden that he would break and cut. But not Mouse. Never had he seen her do something like this. She'd always been sweet when she'd drank from him, her touches light, her tongue delicate across his flesh.

"Ferris, I…" Mouse stumbled over a few consonants as she pulled Des from her pocket before falling completely silent. The caterpillar's head lifted to peer from Ferris to Mouse, worried.

"It's okay." Ferris stood and stepped over the man, taking Mouse's scarlet-coated face between his hands. More blood soaked into her dark clothes, leaving wet patches where the splatter had landed. "It's okay, Mouse. We need to feed, yeah?"

"But he was innocent," she whispered. "I couldn't stop myself."

"You didn't mean to, right?" he said in a consoling voice. While he knew she'd been struggling with her inner demons lately, he didn't want to believe Mouse killed without reason. She'd never been one to murder her way through a crowd before.

"Only *her*." Mouse's lips pursed, her nostrils flaring as she studied the dead woman's body.

Ferris froze. He was no stranger to killing. Of course not—he'd spent two years in the Ruby Heart Palace. Mortals had come and gone, either to their grave or onto immortality. But Mouse? *His* Mouse? The same female who had found him nearly dead and saved his life… It was hard to believe she'd murdered the woman just because she'd felt like it.

A rustling came from not far away and Ferris stepped away, grabbing Mouse's slick hand. "Come on. Let's get out of here."

Without waiting for Mouse to agree, he led her through the club, pausing only long enough to compel someone into taking a smoke out back so the bodies were found. After a quick stop in the bathroom to clean Mouse's face and hands—there was nothing they could do about the stained dress—the pair made their way through the gyrating bodies and techno music. It was a den of temptation. Even for Ferris, the scent of their arousals and promise of warm blood made his gums ache as his fangs almost descended. It would be worse for Mouse, who was still licking the corners of her mouth when she thought he wouldn't notice. He should've led her around the building, but they couldn't walk around with blood all over Mouse's face and hands without raising a few brows. At least the crimson-soaked dress wasn't as obvious. It blended well with the black fabric.

Outside, London greeted them. A dark sky, cobbled streets. Brick buildings with flower boxes lined the sidewalk, and people sat at tables set up outside a pub. Ferris held Mouse's hand as they walked, not fully trusting that she wouldn't try to make a beeline for a portal. If they went back to Wonderland, their conversation could be overheard by Maddie or Noah, but here, they had complete privacy.

"Would you like to go home?" he asked anyway, knowing he would never force her to divulge her secrets.

"Not yet. I … can't." Mouse's chest heaved, and he swore he could hear the desperation in her heartbeat.

"Okay," he soothed. "We don't have to go back yet. Let me take you somewhere else."

When she gave him a relieved nod, Ferris led her through streets lined with bars and clubs and down a narrow alley that ended in a small courtyard. Stone buildings rose up around an open-aired space with a dozen folding chairs tucked into rectangular tables. The windows looked into a dimly lit café and the shop door was held open in invitation by a stone. A tall woman with wiry hair popped out of one of the side doors and halted, a smile lighting her face.

"You're right on time!" she said brightly in an American accent. "Take a seat. I was just about to bring out our canvases."

"Oh, I…" Ferris had been expecting a quiet little alcove to talk to Mouse but, according to the sign he'd missed at first glance, he had led them to a paint and sip. *What the fuck is a paint and sip?* "Sorry, we didn't—"

"Oh, please stay!" She rushed forward, hands clasped under her chin. "It's my first-time hosting one and only three people signed up. *Three*," the woman emphasized. "And I'll do half price."

"What is it?" Mouse perked up, peering inside the door.

"A paint and sip." She motioned to the table set up in the small courtyard. "I have all the supplies and they'll bring us out the wine soon. We're painting the magnificence that is the night sky today, hence the late hour. Which, now that I think about it, might be why so few people are coming…" She bit her lip and Mouse squeezed Ferris's hand, her fingers digging in. He cast a glance at the vampire, finding her eyes locked onto the woman's neck. "I'm Linda, by the way."

Ferris drew in a breath. "I don't think—"

"Let us participate for free," Mouse said, using her influence on the mortal woman.

"Of course." The mortal's eyes glazed over. Another couple walked into the alleyway, their arms draped around one another, and drew Linda's attention. "Have a seat," she urged them before going to greet the newcomers.

"Let's go," Ferris whispered at the same time Mouse said, "Let's stay."

He blinked down at her. After she'd killed two people in a back alley, she wanted to stay and paint? There was blood on the knees of his jeans and splashed across her black dress, though it was hard to see on her. And, he supposed, his jeans could look mud-stained in this lighting.

Still, he said, "I'm not sure that's a good idea." He'd wanted to take Mouse somewhere more private, away from small spaces full of humans. Because, while she'd calmed down significantly on their walk here, there was still a slight glimmer of hunger behind her gaze.

"I'll be good," she promised, perking up, and slipped into the nearest seat.

With a silent sigh, Ferris joined her. He couldn't believe they were doing this together, that she was doing something— anything—other than wandering the Ivory Palace like a ghost or lying in bed humming. It almost felt like old times when they would meet in a club before slipping away so she could feed from him. Then they would hang out and talk for hours or watch old movies on his cracked leather couch. She seemed almost *relieved* to be sitting there with him at the moment, which tugged his lips into a slight smile. Maybe she was thinking the same thing…

"You came after me tonight?" Mouse asked as Linda led the others to the opposite end of the table.

Ferris leaned back in his chair and shifted slightly to face her better. The light freckles sprinkled across her nose and cheeks made him want to trace patterns in them, and the curve of her lips held his attention, possibly for a beat too long. "You ran away from me at the palace as though I'd hurt you or something. I wanted to make sure you were all right."

"I'm fine," Mouse whispered. "I'm always fine."

"Sometimes we're not fine." He leaned in closer, lifting her chin, as her gaze locked on his. "Sometimes we have to talk about our demons to someone. You can talk to me, luv. Always." Her gardenia scent caressed his nose and a warm feeling washed over him. Something raw, growing bolder.

Mouse opened her mouth to say something when Linda returned, along with an older woman who sat down opposite them, and began handing out a canvas and paintbrush to everyone. Ferris blinked, dropping his hand from Mouse's chin.

He'd wondered at times where she'd been going so frequently, but he didn't own her, and it wasn't his right to ask.

But maybe she'd been visiting a particular mortal for feedings. Like she had with him. Only, maybe *unlike* him, they would've done more than feed. *Fucking*. A chill of jealousy crept through him and he frowned. "Next time you have an ache to run off, you can ask me to come. I'd go anywhere with you, luv."

"All right. But if I don't ask, don't follow me." She furrowed her brow as though thinking deeply about something.

"So…" He glanced carefully around at the mortals who were all preparing the paint Linda had set into the center of the table. Mouse grabbed a few tubes of blue and set them down between them. Ferris picked up the cerulean and worked the paint from the end, rolling the tube. "What happened back there?"

"Nothing I'm not used to," Mouse answered matter-of-factly.

Ferris arched a brow. They were vampires, so of course she'd killed before, but she hadn't been the Mouse he knew when she snarled at him so viciously over her prey. "I don't know what that means."

She let out a breath. "You don't know everything about my past."

Linda appeared at the end of the table and handed Ferris two small pallets for the paint. "Here you are. Is everyone ready to get started?"

Ferris passed Mouse her pallet and they both silently squeezed a dab of each paint color onto the wood. Mouse and the single woman exchanged tubes once they were finished, giving them all two different shades of blue, black, white, and yellow.

Linda set up her own canvas and started discussing how to make the paintings their own. She was only there to guide them, but they were free to use whatever inspired them about the night sky. As she went on about mixing colors, a waiter brought out a tray with glasses, half of them full of red wine, the other half with white.

"Thanks," Ferris muttered as he and Mouse took theirs. They wouldn't drink them, but they wanted to at least *seem* like they would. As a mortal, he'd drunk enough wine—and vodka and beer and rum—to last ten lifetimes. Any alcohol he could get his hands on after Ellie died. He drank and drank until he blacked out or vomited his guts out.

Mouse tapped the end of her paint brush against her lips in quiet contemplation. They were still a little pinker than usual from her scrubbing the blood away with paper towels in the club bathroom. A little fuller, even. Ferris lifted a hand to smooth out the crease between her brows but stopped himself.

"What?" she whispered, apparently noticing how quickly he'd dropped his hand.

Clearing his throat, he pretended to pluck something from her hair. "You have some lint."

Mouse glanced sideways at him. "Do you know what you'll paint? You know how to get fancy with this sort of thing while you've seen my scribbles. Perhaps I should just follow Linda's instructions."

Her art skills weren't the best, he would admit, but he loved her attempts anyway. Once, when he was still human, she'd found one of his drawings and asked him to teach her. "Fine, luv, but only if you don't tell your sister. I don't need the whole world asking me for lessons," he'd teased.

Mouse had come to his flat for her first and last lesson. The pencil strokes were too light as if she were afraid to make a mistake or commit her vision to paper. In the end, she had a blob that was meant to be a mouse. They'd laughed together, the first full laugh he'd had since he'd lost Ellie and their daughter. Then Mouse had fed from his wrist, his fingers tangled in her hair, while he relished in that high, in her friendship. Ferris had kept that drawing. Hidden it in his room in the Ruby Heart Palace for two years and taken it with him when he fled with Ever's set of keys. Right now, it was tucked into one of his old sketchbooks back in Ivory.

"Let's do what we feel," Ferris said. "And we won't peek at each other's until the end."

"Mmm, so like a present to one another." Mouse smiled and nudged his shoulder with hers, then shifted in her seat so she could hide her canvas better. Ferris grinned and mirrored her movements. They spent the next two hours working on their art as Linda led the group in replicating her own painting. The mortals laughed and drank as they moved their brushes. He and Mouse stayed focused, his gaze every so often sliding to the milky skin of her face, her neck, her shoulder, stirring something within him that had been hidden for so long.

In the end, Ferris had created a sky of blues and blacks. Stars flecked across the landscape where he ran his thumb over the brush, to splatter white paint in a fine mist. In the top corner, he crafted a full moon and spread a cloud over the bottom half. Two more wispy clouds cut across the image. It was his perfect sky—one meant to be gazed at from below in wonder.

"Ready to share?" he asked Mouse.

She remained quiet.

"Mouse?" He shifted to face her. "Do you need more time?"

She shook her head and slid her canvas toward him. Ferris peered down to find the entire square painted black. The paint was thick, the brush strokes choppy and sharp, as if she tried desperately to force the canvas to become even darker. "You said to paint how we feel," she explained.

Fuck. Ferris dropped his canvas to the table and scooped her out of her chair. They needed to get back to Wonderland and away from the prying eyes of mortals. Then she needed to talk to him, tell him exactly what was going on and how he could help her. Doing nothing was obviously not helping. Sleeping beside her. Offering her distractions with games and books. Comforting her. None of that was enough. He needed to do something more, be someone better, to help *her*. More than ever, he was relieved he'd listened to Chess and kept the Jabberwocky quill a secret. She didn't need added pressure.

"What did I do wrong?" she squeaked as he raced away from the pub, heading toward the portal back to Ivory, with her tucked against him.

"Nothing. You did nothing wrong, luv," he whispered. "We should go home now and I'll draw you a bath. Then we're going to leave the Ivory Palace together for a while."

CHAPTER SIX

MOUSE

If Shakespeare were still alive to write Mouse's story, she wondered if it would end up a tragedy or one of his rare, semi-happily ever afters. As the wind rumpled her hair, her face planted against Ferris's strong chest while he ran her home from the paint pub, she took in the darkness behind her closed eyelids. Black. Black. Black. Just as she'd painted across her canvas at the paint pub Ferris had taken her to. Her life, she decided, was leading toward a tragedy, one that Shakespeare's ghost may rise from the dead to write at that very moment. *Woe is me.*

Mouse finally forced herself to open her eyes, pulling herself away from the black oblivion. She peered up at Ferris, his determined gaze focused straight ahead, his hard muscles flexing against her flesh as he moved. The floral scent of Ivory washed over her and a murder of crows cawed high in the night sky. Over the course of her life, she'd been saved on numerous accounts. First by Maddie who'd turned her into a vampire, then by Noah who'd rescued her from her prison, and now by Ferris who'd helped too many times to count. Even in the mortal world, centuries ago, Maddie had always been there to get Mouse out of trouble, except for the one time she wasn't… The thing was, Mouse didn't mind being saved. What did it matter if one wasn't a savior? Did that make them any less worthy in life? In a story? In Hamlet, even though Ophelia was a tragic heroine, that didn't make her *nothing*. Everyone was something.

But Mouse didn't want Ferris to think she *always* required rescuing—he had his own inner demons he needed to face.

"I can walk," Mouse whispered, staring at the hard lines of Ferris's handsome face. She'd always thought him pretty with sharp angles and chiseled features.

As though attuned to her low words, Ferris halted, not arguing as he lowered her to the pale grass. "I didn't mean to go all caveman on you there, but I just wanted to get you home," he said, his chest heaving.

"If I didn't want you taking me home, you would've certainly heard it from my lips." The palace rested ahead, its gothic physique appearing ethereal beneath the moon's glow. "Let's go through the back. Ever's gone, but I had a slight argument with Maddie earlier and I don't want to see her just yet."

"Mmm, so avoid the Hatter. Done." He smirked, grasping her hand and leading her to the back of the palace. They passed tall white daisies that danced with the breeze. A few guards stood in the windows, peering out at them, and gave a brief nod.

Mouse took out her key and unlocked the backdoor. They slipped inside, finding Didi guarding near the stairs. "Good evening," the female said, bowing her head.

"Hey, Didi, hope you're staying out of trouble." Ferris grinned as they passed and Mouse studied the floor. She should finally say hello, too, be friendly, invite her to one of

Maddie's tea parties like she would've in the past, but she just couldn't. There weren't tea parties for Mouse any longer.

"Oh, you know me, just making sure no bastards take over Ivory again," Didi said.

Noah's deep voice echoed down the hall and Mouse hurried up the ivory staircase before he could relay to Maddie that her sister was back. Not that she would shame him for it, but Noah didn't keep anything from Maddie, not after their journey to save his sister … and Mouse.

They ventured down the silent hallway, neither saying a word until they stepped into her room. Mouse left the door cracked open behind her and turned to Ferris, the skirt of her dress swishing. "I'm sorry," she rushed the words out.

His brow furrowed. "What do you have to be sorry for, luv?"

Mouse rolled her gaze to the ceiling. The way she'd acted when she'd first seen him behind the club—it was as though she wasn't herself for a second, as if she didn't recognize him. "Snarling at you earlier. Then we were having a pleasant time at the paint pub and I made more mistakes. Perhaps I should have just painted the night sky or *sunshine* instead."

He bent his knees, lowering himself so they were eye to eye. "Snarl at me and I'll snarl right back," he teased. "And I think we both hate sunshine, so that would've been a horrific choice. As for the canvas, you painted how you felt. You could've hidden it and not shown me. Instead, you let me in. That's fucking brave."

Mouse didn't feel brave. As she stared into his eyes, a curious emotion washed over her. She wanted to know what was hidden behind those dark irises of his—his past—as she'd always reveled in the here and now with him. Yet right then, standing in this room, she wanted to know what had ailed him and how he'd faced those demons. How they could exorcise the gruesome things they'd both dealt with at the Ruby Heart Palace. Perhaps together?

"I'm going to draw a bath for you," Ferris said, "then we can talk."

"I can start my own bath, you know." Her lips tilted up at the edges.

"Not the way *I* can." He smiled and leaned in close. "There will be lots of bubbles."

She couldn't help laughing. A warmth spread through her as Ferris exited toward the bathing chamber, glancing one more time over his shoulder at her before going in.

Her smile faltered as she mulled over the talking part… Ferris was going to dig like Maddie. Dig and dig until there was nothing left to find but her melted, ruined heart. The brokenness. Some vampires murdered relentlessly—she'd killed over the years when she felt the ache of what Mr. Taylor had stolen from her, but what she was doing, what she was starting to become wasn't her—it was Rav's monster. His creation.

Running water echoed from the bathing chamber and Mouse lowered herself to the soft bed. She removed her boots before fishing Des out from her dress pocket.

The caterpillar cocked her head at Mouse, her furry body completely blue, not a sign of yellow in sight. This meant her mood was down too.

"I know. I know, I did a very bad thing tonight. Again." Mouse couldn't get the image of the man she'd killed out of her head. She wanted to believe that he was an awful human being, but most likely he wasn't. What if he had a wife? Children? *Stop it, Mouse. It's done.* A part of her still believed that walking outside into the sun would be the answer, but what came after that? She didn't know if she would end up in a true hell, where Rav and Imogen were.

Des wrapped her furry body around Mouse's finger, giving it a hug.

"Thank you, friend," she murmured, then placed the caterpillar on top of a fresh leaf on the bedside table. Blood lingered on Mouse's dress, the metallic odor brushing her senses. Her body trembled, remembering not only the man's face tonight but all the donors she'd slaughtered in the building. Her teeth diving in, her strength tearing off limbs as she'd fed, blood spraying her flesh...

Humming escaped Mouse's lips while her heart pounded faster, her throat turning dry. Ferris's heavy footsteps behind Mouse drew her out of her bloody reverie. She stood to face him, his eyes growing wide.

"You're shivering." He wrapped an arm around her, the heat radiating from him making her eyes flutter, her body tremble less.

"I know. The bath will warm me up," Mouse said, keeping her voice light, even though she didn't feel cold anymore next to Ferris. "Don't go yet." She walked past him, inhaling his comforting scent once more.

Lavender enveloped her as she kept the door cracked behind her, the bath filled with endless bubbles. The edges of her lips tugged up again, and Ferris was right—he did know how to make a bath. One fit for royalty. She peeled the clothing from her body, unplaited her hair, and stepped into the water. A low moan poured from her mouth as she sank into the bath's depths.

"You can come in now," Mouse called after she was settled beneath the foam.

Ferris cleared his throat and the door opened fully, but she couldn't see him or even his hulking shadow.

"I said come in, Ferris." She laughed, amused. "I'm up to my throat in bubbles and you wanted to talk." As she studied him, her thoughts turned in an unexpected direction—Ferris slipping into the room, her pulling him into the bath with her, clothes and all, his large hands skimming up her naked body, cupping her breasts, then dipping his fingers into her heat.

He stepped inside, yanking her from her not unwanted thoughts, and raked a hand through his dark hair, his eyes darting everywhere but on her. "We do need to talk, but we don't have to talk in *here*."

For a brief moment, the humming left her lips like earlier, just as it had in her prison cell, just as it would when wandering the Ivory Palace halls. She wanted to keep her thoughts inside her, not bombard anyone, but she couldn't. Not any longer.

"I don't want you to see me differently…" she whispered, twirling her finger through the bubbles.

"I see you, Mouse. *You*. Only you. That won't change." Ferris's gaze trained on hers as he sat on the floor, propping his back against the pale cabinets.

"You know that Rav and Imogen would bring me behind closed doors for interrogations," she said slowly, taking calming breaths. "It wasn't only chatting or taunting—it was more than that. They would break me apart. Whip me, drown me, remove my eyes, drain me of blood. So much and too much. And the times when I would see you in my cell, I wanted to forget, and I did. By you being there, it was as though everything was fine."

"They *what*?" Ferris inhaled sharply, his hand covering his mouth. "You didn't tell me any of that. I thought—"

"You thought it was bad but not this bad. Chess was there sometimes and—"

"That fucking bastard." Ferris pushed himself from the floor. "I'm going to kill him."

"No." She leaned forward, holding a hand up. "No. You know he helped me with Des."

"But he did *nothing*," Ferris growled, his fangs dropped.

"He did the best he could and he's done so much now." Mouse paused, taking a deep swallow. "I haven't told anyone. Not even Maddie. And it wasn't only me who faced Rav and Imogen's wraths—you did as well."

Ferris gripped the back of his neck, his face twisted in pain. "Mouse, it was hell for me there, but nothing like that. Imogen's taunts about my past? Cleaning the palace with my tongue? Rav being an arsehole? Seeing all that awful shit? That is nothing compared to this. I would spend a damn eternity doing all that for them not to have touched a hair on your body."

Ferris was being a savior, but perhaps she was, too, because she would've dealt with it for an eternity if he was safe. "We can't compare our experiences. They were both equally life-changing. It's why I had to get you out of there."

Ferris narrowed his eyes. "What do you mean get *me* out of there?"

Bollocks, he wasn't going to like this. "It's why I told you to save Alice."

"Motherfucker." He clenched his jaw. "I should've known."

He wouldn't have saved himself, otherwise. "It all worked out," she said, cocking her head, the frown still on his face but slowly dissolving.

"But what if it hadn't?"

"It did, though."

"You have the best heart, you know that?" He inched closer to her.

"No, Ferris, I don't." Mouse reclined in the water, leaning her head against the back of the bathtub as she stared at the ceiling. "Once I was free, everything hit me at once. The memories. The hunger. To go without feeding straight from the source while enduring Rav's abuse did *something* to me. I'm just so blasted hungry all the time."

"You have been feeding more than normal. But it will have to level out soon, right?" It sounded more like a question, one that she had no answer to.

"There's something else you don't know about me," she said softly. "Because of something in my past, I kill mortals differently. Over the centuries, when I feel the hunger stir, when I'm having a rough day, I venture out into the mortal world and take someone's life who I believe deserves it. Today it was the woman you saw—she'd been trying to drug another mortal. But recently it's become more frequent, less controllable, and I … I did something awful not long ago."

"Go on." Ferris knelt at the bathtub, not a single sign of fear shining in his eyes. He wasn't as old as her and had only been a vampire for two years, so he would have a much stronger human side than she did.

"I'm the reason the donor building is temporarily closed. I killed everyone inside with my bloodlust." Tears pricked her eyes and she wanted to sink beneath the water, drown herself for a second before her breaths returned, but she kept her gaze locked on his.

His brows rose, his throat bobbing. "That's why it's closed?"

"Yes, only Ever and Chess know."

"Chess again?" Ferris said between gritted teeth, the muscle feathering along his jaw.

"He was with Ever when they spotted me returning here drenched in blood. Since that day, I sometimes lose control of my hunger and I'm trying not to unravel. But I don't know what's happening."

"I promise I'll help you, luv, and I won't tell anyone." Ferris's soft gaze turned hard. "If Rav wasn't dead, I would murder the fucker. Piece by piece. Over and over."

Mouse could feel the ghosts of Rav's needles piercing her flesh, taking and taking and taking not only her blood but her essence. She couldn't confess anymore, not right then. "Can we talk more tomorrow?"

Ferris nodded, pushing a lock of wet hair behind her ear, and her stomach fluttered at the gentle movement. "Get some rest and we'll decide our next step then."

Mouse watched him leave, keeping the door cracked behind him, and a little weight lifted off her chest after her confessions. But as she sat in the bath for a long while, hours passing, the weight started to build back on her lungs, her bones, like an anchor wanting to tug her below the freezing water's surface. Her breathing came out quick, her body shivering from the cold water, and she needed to see someone. It had to be Ferris because she still couldn't go to Maddie and talk about everything again. Not right now.

Mouse threw on a long black skirt and silky shirt, then padded down the hall to Ferris's room. She just needed to slide in bed beside him and hold onto him.

As the door creaked open, her gaze settled on a muscular form resting on the bed. Smooth, naked tan skin. Mouse blinked and blinked. Ferris was usually under the covers… But not now. He lay face down, his firm buttocks on display, his taut back covered in the tattoo she'd always been drawn to. A piece that made it look like his skin had been peeled away, revealing a mechanical system beneath the layers. He'd sketched it himself for the artist to tattoo the design on him. Her eyes drifted back down to his arse, lingering on the delectable curves of it. Why couldn't she take her eyes from that body part? Her fangs threatened to drop, to sink into his taut muscles.

Ferris stirred, rolling over, his gaze meeting hers. "Mouse? Shit, let me get dressed."

Mouse spun around from him, but not before she caught a quick peek at his length—thick, long and perfect with a shiny silver piercing at its tip. "I know you thought you wouldn't see me until tomorrow…"

"No, it's fine." The rustle of clothing sounded.

She studied the poster on the wall, a black and white scene of a drum set covered in fog, trying to distract herself from what she'd just seen. A heat spread through her, drifting lower, and she liked it a bit too much. She thought about Maddie and how her sister would use sex in the past to take away her pain. For the first time in her life, Mouse truly wanted to give in to that lust, trail her tongue down Ferris's abs, then run it up his cock. Mr. Taylor had taken that want from her. He'd been courting Mouse and they'd done things … but she'd wanted to wait until marriage to make love and the bastard hadn't. But this wasn't about covering up pain. She wanted to see what it would feel like for Ferris to slide himself inside her.

No. He's your friend. Emphasis on friend. A friend she wanted to—

"You can turn around now." Ferris's voice came out thick with sleep.

She slowly spun to face him, finding him now dressed in only dark trousers. "I was just seeing if you wanted to take a walk." There was no way she could lay beside him at the moment, in a bed, where she would either be thinking of what it would be like to sink her teeth into him to taste his blood or what it would feel like to have his length inside her. *What in the world was happening?*

"Of course, wake me up for a nightly stroll any time."

Or a nightly fuck. Mouse's eyes widened at her own inner thought, but she schooled her features and nodded.

As they walked out of the palace, the fresh air circling her, Mouse was starting to feel back to herself instead of focusing on Ferris's naked body.

"So, luv, should we discuss our top-secret plan to curb your appetite?" He waggled his brows, making it so she knew he was there for her, despite what she'd done.

"Ah yes, the lovely plan." She smiled, nudging his arm with hers. "Do tell me more about it."

"Imagine this." He smiled wide, tiptoeing his fingers across his palm. "We get the fuck out of here for a week and—"

In the distance, a piercing wail reverberated, interrupting Ferris. They both stopped and Mouse squinted, catching sight of arrows soaring through the sky from the city. The next roar shook the trees, followed by blood-curdling screams. And then she saw the creature darting through the sky, its leather wings cracking like thunder.

The Jabberwocky.

CHAPTER SEVEN

FERRIS

Mouse tensed beside Ferris as the massive beast circled closer, practically overhead, its leather wings beating so hard the wind whipped the branches of trees. He could practically feel the predatory gaze scrape against him where they stood on the far side of the moat outside the palace. It sent a shiver down his spine and he reached out to touch Mouse, to remind himself she was beside him and safe. Knowing she was okay allowed him to steel himself against the danger. To be the guard he was trained to be.

This is the Jabberwocky. The roaring beast could be nothing else—especially with the quills poking out from its fur. The same as the one he'd found near the lake.

A volley of arrows soared through the sky from the palace turrets just as screams rose up from the streets. The Jabberwocky tilted, avoiding being hit, and dove for the center of the city, landing with a boisterous thud. Ferris remembered the quill hidden inside the large vase just inside the main doors. Remembered and regretted listening to that bastard Chess. Ferris had seen what happened to someone who was killed by the creature. Seen that practically nothing was left of them with bits and pieces strewn about the blood-soaked grass.

"We have to stop it from destroying the city," Maddie called, bursting from the palace and racing across the bridge to them.

As Ferris looked again toward the hideous beast with its deep green, almost black, fur, quills rows of sharp teeth, talons, wings, and barbed tail, he had only one thought: *How?* He'd seen many things in the Ruby Heart Palace. All sorts of torture. Brutal murders. Everything in between and beyond. But he'd only heard tales of the Jabberwocky—and everyone seemed to agree on one thing. If you see the legendary monster of Wonderland, run … and hope your friends are slower than you.

"Mouse!" Maddie cried and swept her into a quick hug. "I'm sorry for earlier, but we have other matters to deal with as you can see. Here."

Ferris forced his gaze away from the monster to find Maddie handing Mouse a bow and arrows. "Do you know how to use that thing?" he asked.

"Of course." Mouse swung the quiver of arrows over her shoulder. "I should already know, but what weapon are you best with?"

"Preferably a gun." Swords and arrows were fine, but he was more of a modern-weapon guy.

Maddie produced a gun, having seemed to suspect his answer, and held it out to him. "Silver bullets won't save our arses like they did with the werewolves, but they'll still hurt like hell."

Ferris took it from her and flicked off the safety. The weight felt good in his hand, powerful. Deadly. When he looked up, he noticed Maddie and Noah each held a matching gun as well.

"Hurry," Maddie urged the group.

Guards were already filing from other palace entrances, swords drawn, arrows nocked, and Maddie and Noah raced after them. Didi and Mock led the group, their bright white uniforms soft in the moonlight. Following suit, Ferris took off for the city where screams seemed to rattle the windows. The sound mingled with the monstrous roars and his racing pulse, creating chaos inside his head.

"Come on, slowcoaches!" Didi yelled back at them, and Mouse smirked.

Running against the crowd, Ferris pivoted and jumped to avoid colliding with those fleeing. It was every vampire for themself as they tore down the streets. A blonde female fell and curled onto her side when a male stepped on her chest. More feet pummeled against her lithe body, marring her white suit. Ferris shifted between vampires with the intent to help her up, but she beat him to the punch the moment a pocket formed between citizens. Blood trickled down her forehead, the sweet copper scent quickly filling the air, but she wasted no time disappearing between shops.

The ground vibrated with another growl when Ferris and his friends neared the city center. Quills poked above the tops of buildings as the Jabberwocky reared up. Its wings stood high and proud. And the stench… *Bloody hell, the smell.* A mixture of wet dog and rot permeated the air, burning his nostrils. Ferris drew in a shallow, steadying breath. *Damn.* The beast was even bigger up close.

When they reached the edge of the town center to fully face the Jabberwocky, Mouse released an arrow. The projectile hit its back leg and bounced away, but the Jabberwocky didn't even flinch. Just turned slowly, eyes narrowed, and slammed a taloned furred foot down on the granite fountain.

A loud *crunch* sounded as the stone crumbled to dust. Water flowed between the cobblestones, carrying away rivulets of blood that dripped from a mangled body clutched in the beast's talons. He hadn't noticed it until just then—the top of the head was barely visible between the beast's claws, strands of dark hair trailing over the beast's fur.

Another arrow flew, singing through the air as a dozen more followed from the guards that had caught up. All projectiles hit. All bounced harmlessly away. Mock aligned two arrows onto his bowstring at once and let them soar. "This isn't working," he called out.

"Bollocks," Mouse mumbled. "We need something stronger."

"Fuck," Noah hissed.

Mock was right—the Jabberwocky didn't even seem to care they were attacking it. They were no match against this bloody thing. Not without better weapons, not without strategy. He raised the gun Maddie had given him. Aimed. Shot.

The blast echoed through the city center, vibrations running up his arm, and the Jabberwocky whipped its head to face them. A low growl rumbled out from between jagged teeth, its foul breath carrying all the way to them. But its fierce orange eyes only flickered over them as if they were fucking insects. Instead, the monster turned its gaze to the surrounding buildings. The streets. The sky. Its nostrils flared, quills bristling. It was almost like the beast was searching for something…

"Fuck this," Didi shouted, shoving her plait over her shoulder. She bolted forward with her sword raised and released a battle cry.

The Jabberwocky spun, its body a blur. It was much faster than Ferris expected something its size to be. One second, Didi was racing forward, the next, she was between its teeth. She didn't even have enough time to scream. With one grinding *crunch*, Didi's lower half fell to the ground with a wet *thwack*.

Mock screamed her name and Ferris's breath caught in his

throat. Didi … was dead. His eyes had witnessed it happen, but his brain rejected the idea. She was too full of life for it to be snuffed out so easily. They'd only just become friends…

Fuck this, Didi had yelled. And Ferris couldn't have agreed more. He raised his gun as the beast chewed. Fired his weapon again and again. One of the bullets slammed into the Jabberwocky's soft upper lip and a small spot of blood shot outward. The Jabberwocky reared back, half-howled, half-screeched, and threw the unknown dead body from its talons at Ferris.

Leaping backward, the mangled, dark-haired corpse splattered at his feet. The head was completely flattened, making it impossible to know who it might have been, and a large hole pierced straight through their chest cavity, exposing snapped ribs and torn intestines.

"Fucking hell," he breathed. Images of Rav's experiments flashed through his mind. The bodies Ferris had to dispose of. The brain matter he had to mop up…

Mouse sucked in a sharp breath and he snapped his gaze to her, hoping she wasn't thinking about the same thing. *Rav's room of horror*. But no, it wasn't that, not as something darker filled her eyes—*hunger*. Her fangs dropped, piercing her bottom lip where she'd bitten it, and she shifted her feet back. Whether it was about stepping away from the vampire's body or away from the Jabberwocky wasn't clear, but Ferris grabbed her arm to steady her as she swayed.

The Jabberwocky scanned the city center once more as Mock fired uselessly at its face, screaming his rage. Then, Ferris could've sworn intelligence flickered in the beast's eyes. Throwing its head back, the beast released a high-pitched screech and leapt into the sky. The Jabberwocky pounded against the air to gain momentum for its massive body, dipping a few times before soaring away.

With the crack of the Jabberwocky's wings fading, silence descended, heavy and cloying. Ferris tucked the gun into his waistband and turned to Mouse. Her eyes were wide as she stared at the blood on the ground, her breaths coming too fast. "Luv," he said slowly. "Let's get you back to the palace."

She jerked at the sound of his voice and lifted a hand to hide her fangs. "I'm fine. We need to clean up the city."

Ferris took in the carnage, the crumbled fountain, pieces of debris knocked from surrounding buildings. Shattered glass lay in front of windows, their awnings in tatters. Shingles from roofs littered the ground. But none of that mattered. Either the guards or the people who lived in the city could take care of it. It was more important that Mouse didn't lose her self-control and attack a guard. Worse yet if she tried to drink the blood from the cobblestones. She was considering it—he could see the thought in her eyes as her gaze flicked back to the blood on the ground.

"We can handle it," Maddie said. Her tone was strained, her shoulders stiff, but she offered Mouse a comforting smile. "I'll see you in a little bit, all right? Ever is already being summoned to return."

"I can help clean up," Mouse insisted.

"No," the Hatter said with a sigh. She looked over her shoulder and sighed a second time at the sight of Noah holding Mock back from Didi's half-corpse. "Please, go inside. We'll take care of Mock, but you need to take care of yourself."

"Fine." Mouse relented.

Ferris released a breath and guided her away from the gore. Vampires were already creeping back from their hiding places. *Cowards.* Not that Ferris blamed them. It wasn't fair to ask most of Wonderland to take up arms when they weren't trained to fight. A chill ran down his spine as he thought about the massive wings, claws, and teeth. The damned thing was built to kill.

"Are you all right?" Mouse asked when they entered the palace through the main doors.

Ferris furrowed his brow. "Me?"

"You look a little horrified," she said.

"Well, yeah," he admitted. "But what about you?"

She bit her bottom lip. "I'm … hungry."

"I know." He gave her a small smile and turned them toward the storage rooms where the blood was kept. Aware that Mouse craved it fresh from the source, he wasn't sure how much good the powdered stuff would do to take her edge off. There was little to be done about that tonight, though. Anyone she fed off of would probably end up like that bloke behind the club. *Dead.*

"The Jabberwocky has never attacked anyone here before," Mouse wondered aloud, seeming to speak to herself.

Yes, it has.

"I'm going to get Des," she added before scampering up the nearby staircase.

Ferris opened the door to the small kitchen where meals would sometimes be cooked for human visitors. Pops of blue in the tile backsplash accented the gray quartz countertops and white cupboards. A small sink, narrow icebox, and gas-powered burner made it functional. He ran his hands down his face and released a sigh. Things couldn't be calm for two fucking seconds? He had to jump right back into the fire and lie to Mouse on top of it?

Mouse entered the kitchen, steps light as air, and took a seat on one of the tall barstools along the peninsula. She set Des on the cool marble in front of her. "So, what do you think could've changed? To bring the Jabberwocky so far into Ivory, I mean."

"Damned if I know," Ferris muttered. He poured some of the powered blood into a water bottle, shook it, and guzzled it down to ward off the hunger that always followed a battle.

With Imogen and Rav dead, and Chess and Ever merging territories, it was possible the upheaval set the beast off. Ferris set about collecting a few packs of powdered blood and water bottles, his mind wandering. The Jabberwocky had been at the lake, so very near the palace, only days ago. Had killed someone then too. Chess had a point about not creating panic over the quill Ferris had found, but now? The Jabberwocky had done that all on his own.

Ferris ran a hand through his hair. "Mouse?"

"Yes?" She eyed the red liquid he'd absentmindedly prepared, and he slid it toward her.

"I need to tell you something."

CHAPTER EIGHT

MOUSE

"The other day I—"

Ferris was cut off when two sets of loud footsteps echoed down the marble hallway and Mouse turned from him to find Ever and Chess rushing toward them.

"Are you two all right?" Ever asked, her nostrils flaring and her plaited hair disheveled. "One of the guards came through the portal to Scarlet as soon as he heard the Jabberwocky, but it seems we're too late. I shouldn't have left." She sighed, flexing her hands.

"No," Mouse whispered. "The guards were prepared, but the Jabberwocky hasn't been in Ivory since the day when I…" Slaughtered all those innocent donors. Lost control of herself instead of continuing to fight it.

Chess let out a low whistle, observing his nails, then arched a brow at Ever and Ferris. The queen pursed her lips and Ferris's throat bobbed while they all exchanged a knowing look.

"What is it?" Mouse stepped toward Ever as she gently placed Des in her pocket. "I should've been more observant, been ready if the Jabberwocky had returned. But perhaps I didn't expect for the beast to do something like this since it hasn't made an appearance in months."

"The Jabberwocky has been here recently," Ever said slowly. "Once for certain. And made a kill."

Mouse tensed, her gaze drifting from face to face. Her chest tightened as their knowing looks seemed to make sense. "No one told me?"

"About that..." Chess ran his thumb across his lower lip, glancing over his shoulder down the hallway. "After the Knave found a quill from the Jabberwocky, I ordered him to stay quiet about it until I spoke to Ever."

Mouse glanced at Ferris and he narrowed his eyes at Chess.

"So Maddie didn't know either?" Mouse murmured.

Chess scratched the side of his face while peering at Ever. "This is going to get a bit messy now, Queenie."

"No, Maddie knows," Ever said. "I informed all the guards before I left for Scarlet."

Mouse's heart sped up, the white room seeming to pulse in sync with her blasted organ. "But I saw you before you left, and I went to Maddie right after that. *No one* said anything to me."

Ever placed a hand on Mouse's shoulder. "We felt it was best not to until we learned more. We didn't believe the Jabberwocky was an immediate threat, and not only did I leave Maddie in charge while I was away, but I prepared guards to warn me if I needed to return from Scarlet immediately. You've been going through a lot. More so lately. It just didn't feel right to make you worry."

Inhaling a sharp breath, Mouse drew out of Ever's grasp. "So is everyone going to tiptoe around me? Hide important matters from me? We talked about the Jabberwocky months ago in the garden. You didn't mind then."

"That's because you'd heard the beast," Chess pointed out. "You were outside, remember?" Outside and covered in the donors' blood…

"Hush." Ever elbowed him in the arm.

As Mouse opened her mouth to speak, more footsteps sounded, vibrating across the floor. She glanced toward the hallway just as Maddie and Noah entered the room with a few guards behind them, including Mock. Their clothing was spotted with a mixture of blood and dirt, the reek of death. She pushed away the alluring metal odor that started to overpower the rest.

"Wait." Mouse held a hand up and focused back on Chess. "Did Noah know the Jabberwocky was here before you left for Scarlet?"

"Not from me—Maddie's boy toy has a big mouth. But after Ever told the Hatter…" Chess trailed off.

"I did tell him." Maddie skirted around Chess while biting her lip. "But he's—"

"I don't care if he's one of the guards. He's been in Wonderland for barely any time at all." Mouse balled her hands into fists, then pointed at herself. "*I've* been here for centuries, *Madeline*. I don't care if you think I'm the actual *mad* one—I deserved the truth. I deserved to be warned."

"Mouse, you need to understand," Ferris said, his voice pleading.

"No!" Mouse cut him off. "You're the worst one of all." Even though it may have seemed childish to everyone there, she turned on her heel and raced from the room, darting up the stairs with her sister shouting behind her as she followed.

She pounded down the hallway, wishing she had chosen to flee the palace instead. But there was nowhere in this direction left to go except for her room. She didn't want to see anyone, feel the embarrassment rising around her when she looked at their faces, knowing they were walking on eggshells around her.

Maddie caught her by the arm and spun Mouse around. "You're being unreasonable."

"*I'm* being unreasonable!" Mouse shouted. "You want to be secretive just because I haven't confessed my truth to you on my own terms? Fine! You want to know what I experienced so you can have as many nightmares as I do? Fine! Fine, fine, fine! Every week in the Ruby Heart Palace, I got to have my bloody fun with Imogen and Rav. Her, with whips to my back or drowning me. Him tearing me apart from the inside out or bleeding me dry. You name it, they did it. And ever since then, I've been growing hungrier, more ravenous, wanting to eat and tear apart every human in sight. So much so that I murdered everyone in the donor building. It was *me*! *There*, damn it!" Her voice cracked on the last word as spittle flew from her mouth.

A horrified expression crossed Maddie's face, tears filling her eyes while she slowly released her arm. "Mouse, I—"

Mouse shook her head, batting her sister's arms away when they reached forward to draw her into a hug. "No, I don't want your pity. Because no matter what mindset you were in, no matter how much you felt like you were drowning, I would've warned you about the Jabberwocky, about *danger*. That would be *protecting* you. Not keeping it a secret, which in turn, could've destroyed me. If I had known, I could've been helping instead of being caught off guard like I was today."

Maddie took a step forward, not looking at her any differently. "It's just … you're my little sister and—"

"*And* you're my sister. Nothing can change that, but for now, leave me alone." Mouse gripped the knob to her room and opened the door, then slammed it behind her, closing herself inside.

Mouse pressed her forehead to the door and ran her hand against the wood. Even though Maddie didn't call out for her,

Mouse knew she was still there, heard the rustling of her sister's dress as she must've lowered herself to the floor and the press of her back against the door. Always her big sister. Always her protector. Mouse had said exactly how she felt, so why did shame, regret, and guilt wash over her at once, pleading with her to apologize for her words?

Slowly backing away from the door, Mouse sank down on the edge of her bed and drew Des from her pocket. The caterpillar rested in the palm of her hand, lengthening her body upward so their eyes met.

"Am I?" Mouse asked in a hushed tone. "Am I being unreasonable?"

Des cocked her head side to side as if she wasn't sure who to agree with. The caterpillar was still entirely blue, not a speck of yellow visible. Perhaps it was her moods that had made Des this way, perhaps she was better off before befriending Mouse too.

Mouse placed Des atop her leaf on the night table, then stood from the bed, pacing back and forth. The day crashed into her … the Jabberwocky's destruction. She hadn't known the beast would be there today, but Ever had informed the guards about its previous prowling. Didi would've been informed. And even then, the caring guard had died. A guard who had been nothing but kind to Mouse every time she passed her in the Ivory Palace's halls, even though Mouse had been aloof, staring at the floor instead of the vampire's eyes, not able to say a simple hello. What the bloody hell was wrong with her? And now she would never be able to. She would never get to invite Didi to a lavish tea party.

"But there are no tea parties for me anymore," Mouse reminded herself.

And then she looked at the door … the *closed* door. Her hands trembled and her body quaked, hot tears like lava pricking her eyes. All she had to do was walk to the door, turn the knob, and pull it open. But her body stood frozen, trapped,

trapped like she'd been in her dank, dark prison cell. Blood. She could smell all the blood that Rav and Imogen had stolen from inside her. So much spilled from the whips, the slices, the—

Mouse dropped to her knees, releasing an ear-shattering scream as she rocked against the hard marble. "Maddie, I'm sorry!" she cried, her body racking from her sobs. The door flew open and a tall form rushed in, scooping her into his lap.

"She left to clean herself up so she asked me to keep watch," Ferris said softly. "She'll be back, I promise."

Mouse thrashed, fighting him. She didn't want him. He'd hid important things from her. And she was mad at him most of all because she'd believed he was the one person who would never lie.

"You didn't tell me!" she screeched, shoving at his hard chest.

"I know," he whispered, his dark eyes locking on hers. "I was fucking stupid and shouldn't have listened to anyone, much less Chess's dumb ass. But I was about to tell you before the whole troop burst in there and made everything worse."

"You could've told me sooner." Mouse stopped fighting, her body relaxing slightly as she grasped the collar of his shirt. "I told you so many things today. You were the first I told about what went on inside the palace..."

"I know, luv," Ferris rasped. "I know." Their gazes locked, and his lower lip trembled. For the first time, Ferris truly looked afraid. Was it of her?

"I overreacted," she said, her chest heaving. "It's been happening a lot lately. I'll make it stop." Fear crawled through her that she could lose him, that he would get exhausted of her antics.

"No, you didn't." He brought her plait over her shoulder and toyed with the ends of her hair. "I-I had a girlfriend."

Mouse furrowed her brow, a sinking feeling churning within her stomach. "What are you talking about?"

"She ... Ellie died," he whispered. "It was when I was nineteen, before I met you. She was pregnant with our daughter, Luna. There was a car crash, and I was driving. It wasn't my fault, but it felt like it was. Still does at times. That's why I started using drugs. Even after nearly a year with her gone, I just couldn't deal with life. Not until I met you."

Mouse took a deep swallow, letting his words echo in her mind. She'd known Ferris for a little over four years and they'd never talked about depressing aspects of their pasts, yet this... He'd lost not only a girlfriend but his unborn child too. She couldn't imagine losing two things so dear at once.

There were a handful of people she could never live without, including the one holding her now. Mouse thought about if something horrific were to happen to him, if he were to die. What if the Jabberwocky had gobbled him up or chewed him in half like it had with Didi? Her lungs ached, and she couldn't breathe, couldn't find the air she desperately needed. She cupped his beautiful face, his soft cheeks, and pulled his mouth to hers, their lips molding together. That was the only thing that could save her in this moment, the air she needed.

Mouse closed her eyes and allowed her lips to move against his, drinking him in, his breaths calming her as he kissed her back. Slow and gentle, his hands drifted to her hips, holding her steady.

Safe.

Ferris was her safe place.

Mouse drew back, finally opening her eyes, his meeting hers, both of their gazes wide as they studied one another. A smile played across his lips and she mirrored it as she rested her head against his chest, then wrapped her arms around him, not regretting the first real kiss she'd had in centuries. Her smile fell as the world came back into focus. "I'm so sorry, Ferris. I'm so sorry you didn't get your family and now you're stuck being a babysitter to me in this life."

"You have nothing to be sorry about. I would follow you

anywhere, to *any* life, luv."

She wished she could go back to the days at the mortal club. Happy. Carefree. Listening to Ferris on his drums while dancing to the music.

Yet this felt more real than anything, especially with her lips still tingling from their kiss. A comforting kiss from one friend to another.

But her heart told her otherwise, that it was more than that, as did the heated warmth spreading through her, traveling lower and lower. Her fangs dropped, begging her to taste him, to taste every inch of him. Because she would follow him anywhere too.

CHAPTER NINE

FERRIS

Mouse's fangs scraped over Ferris's neck, ending with a light nip. It didn't break the skin, but it *did* send a shock straight to his cock. Her weight shifted on his lap. And then she was straddling him, a knee pressed against either side of his hips. His pulse sped at the sensation of her breath on his skin. Her fangs. The slip of a tongue as if she were tasting him.

Shit. He wanted that tongue somewhere else. Somewhere lower.

The thought snapped through him and his grip tightened on her hips, bunching the black fabric of her dress. They were friends… *Just* friends. So he shouldn't be imagining her licking his cock, the sounds she would make if he ran his own tongue up her core. Mouse moved her mouth up his neck to skate along his jawline until she found his lips again.

Fuck it. There was no reason they couldn't indulge each other a little. Was that his dick talking? Probably. But two years of hell in the Ruby Heart Palace left him with a need his own hand couldn't satisfy.

He pressed his lips to Mouse's, met her tongue with his own, careful not to prick himself on her fangs. One of his hands drifted higher. Up her back. To her hair. Gripping her plait gently at the base of her skull and holding her close.

A moan filled his mouth—*her* moan. A sweet, seductive sound that had his cock straining in his trousers. Then she *moved*. Slid herself against the bulge beneath her. Tentatively at first. The layers of fabric separating them were a damned curse. Ferris wanted to feel her. Wanted her to feel him. She must've sensed his desire as their tongues slid over one another because the next time she moved her hips, it wasn't shy. Her mound ground against his length and he groaned.

Mouse broke away from his mouth with a gasp, pupils blown wide, and kissed his neck again. Ferris let his head fall back to give her better access. His breaths turned shallow as she explored his chest with her hands. Somewhere deep in his mind, he wondered if he should stop her, but—

Fangs settled against his artery. He froze as the air took on a slight edge. There was nothing wrong with a bite and a fuck—in fact, it sounded damned amazing. He wanted to experience it himself, preferably with Mouse, but not when she was having control issues.

"Stop," he whispered.

He tugged her back where he was still holding her hair. The space between them crackled with arousal and he wanted nothing more than to indulge but … not right now. Not until she was better in control of her hunger. If she took too much and killed him, he knew Mouse would never forgive herself.

"I should…" He swallowed hard. "I should go take a shower."

A crease formed between Mouse's brows, but she nodded slowly before climbing from his lap. He sat a moment longer to try to compose himself, but his length was too stiff, too demanding, to even think about waiting until his hard-on was gone.

He nearly groaned when he stood and walked from the room. The piercing at the ridge of his cock pressed at an odd, almost painful angle against his zipper. *Shit.* He rushed into the bathroom and removed his trousers with a relieved huff.

The relief didn't last long, however. His hard length swelled, begging for attention. Grinding his teeth, he turned on the shower, removed the rest of his clothes and stepped under the warm spray.

But he could still feel Mouse's mouth on his, her tongue on his neck, the way she moved on top of him. Phantom sensations that throbbed through his veins had him gripping himself. Ferris stroked his cock and rubbed his thumb over the tip. The barbell piercing had two small silver balls at the edge of his head. One above the ridge. The other just below, next to his shaft. He stroked again and set his forehead on the glass door, his heavy breaths fogging it.

Holding back a groan, he imagined Mouse doing this instead. Imagined her on top of him exactly like she had been, her clothes gone. With her wet folds gliding over his length. He moved his hand faster. Harder. Ferris squeezed his eyes shut and imagined her gripping him, guiding him to her soaked entrance. Sinking down on him.

"Shit!" he growled as his cum spilled against the glass door. His legs trembled slightly when he pushed himself upright again and angled the showerhead to wash away the evidence. Just as he shoved away the pang of guilt he felt for thinking of his best friend riding him.

She *had* initiated it though. Kissed him first. Straddled him. Teased his neck with her fangs. Still—better not to tempt fate and ruin their friendship because he was horny as fuck. Maybe he needed to get out of the Ivory Palace for a bit. Out of *any* palace and learn who he was as a vampire. He hadn't gotten the chance before becoming Imogen's toy. And it would help clear his head. But he needed a purpose. A goal.

He didn't want to wander aimlessly around Wonderland.

The Jabberwocky.

It was perfect. The beast needed to be stopped and no one knew how to achieve that. He could find out. Fueled by his new idea, Ferris quickly washed himself and made his way back to his bedroom in only a towel.

To find Mouse sitting on his bed with an empty bottle of blood.

"I ate," she whispered, seeming to have followed his gaze. "Sorry about almost biting you."

He smirked. "It wouldn't be the first time. And I never minded before, did I?"

She shook her head and Ferris slipped on a pair of loose black shorts before tossing his towel over the back of a chair. "Are you going to wear those to bed?" she asked with a tilt to the head, her gaze trailing down his bare chest. "I can turn around if you'd like to get under the covers and be comfortable."

"I'm not going to bed yet," he admitted. As Ever's guard, he would need permission to leave his post. The sound of her viola music drifted through the palace so he knew she was still awake and he'd like to leave as soon as possible. "I need to talk to the queen."

Mouse looked up at him in surprise. "Why? Is something wrong?"

"No." He hesitated. Mouse wouldn't like him risking himself alone… "I want to go to Red and see if I can find anything to help us fight the Jabberwocky."

"What?" The word was a mere breath. "You're leaving?"

"I hope to," he said as he rummaged for a T-shirt.

"What do you want to find in Red?" Mouse pressed. "There's nothing left. It's a wasteland."

The royals were dead and the citizens had either moved to Scarlet or Ivory, but that didn't mean *nothing* was left. "Some sort of clue might still be there. Or I'll go to the library—I heard talk about one inside the Red Palace. Maybe there's a painting on a cave wall or something, I don't know. But I should try, shouldn't I? Before more vampires get hurt."

"It doesn't have to be you," she said after a long, thought-out moment.

"It doesn't have to, no. I would like it to be, though." He needed to do *something* other than roam the hallways.

"Then I'm coming with you." Mouse stood and squared her shoulders. "We'll talk to Ever together."

"No," he said, slightly harsher than he intended.

"What do you mean, *no*?" She scowled at him. "I will go wherever I like."

He released a sigh. "You should stay here with Maddie."

"I love my sister, but that doesn't mean I need to be attached to her every moment for all eternity." She folded her arms. "I'm coming."

"You need to feed," he reminded her. "Red is a wasteland. What will you do for blood?"

She scoffed and held up the empty bottle. "I *can* survive off of this, just like you can."

Just more of it. *A lot* more, that they would need to carry with them. And what if she snapped? Ferris didn't want to have to pin her down until the bloodlust ceased. "No," was all he said, and brushed passed her into the hallway.

"Before the Jabberwocky rudely interrupted, you were planning to take me somewhere for a week anyway," Mouse said, following on his heels, feet practically stomping as they followed the quiet, complex melody of Ever's viola to the empty ballroom. She stood in the center with the instrument up to her chin, eyes closed, looking regal and every bit the queen. Decorative pillars lined the room, carved with climbing ivy, and a massive crystal chandelier hung overhead. The white grand piano in the corner gleamed.

"Hello, Ferris," she said without stopping the song. "Mouse."

"I didn't mean to intrude," he started.

"You're not." She lowered the instrument and looked over at him. "Chess is still taking note of the damage in the city, so I thought I'd try and relax with a song while I waited for him to finish." Ever tilted her head. "What brings you two here?"

"Grant me permission to go to Red," Ferris blurted.

Her brows rose. "Red? It's been a desolate wasteland ever since—"

"The Red Queen died, I know," he said. The stories he'd heard of the monster's murderous rampages in Red had sounded terrifying as fuck when he'd first arrived in Wonderland, and he didn't want Ivory to become like that. "Everyone left because of the Jabberwocky, but that's exactly why I need to go."

"I'm not sure I understand," she replied slowly.

He took a deep breath and let it out, glancing sideways at Mouse. "That's where the Jabberwocky is from, right?"

"We want to see if we can find any clues on how to defeat it," Mouse chimed in.

Ever glanced between them. "I'm already gathering a group of guards to travel to Red for that purpose. I want to know how to kill it, but I'm just surprised the two of you want to take on the task."

"It killed Didi," Mouse said quietly.

"And I need some time…" *Away.* He kept the last word to himself, but he could see the understanding in Ever's softening expression. Clearing his throat, he continued, "The Jabberwocky is a one-of-a-kind monster which has to mean something. If Red dealt with it for centuries, there has to be something. Someone must've documented it." Like Bigfoot back in the mortal world, with conspiracy theories and all that shit, only real.

Ever studied them for a long moment. "I agree to it. It will draw less attention if the two of you go in place of an entire group of guards first anyway."

"Mouse should stay," Ferris added firmly, though he couldn't stop the wince. He knew Mouse would hate him making choices for her.

"I'm going," Mouse snarled.

Ever played one long, drawn out note and stared at Ferris. "Will you leave her here alone?"

He couldn't distract himself, couldn't run from his problems, if they followed him. He wanted to kiss her again. Sink his fangs into her, drink her blood, see what she tasted like, the way she used to taste him when he was human. Touch her. Listen to her moan his name as he— *Shit. No.* Friends. They were *friends.* "She won't be alone. You and Maddie are here."

"Yes, but it's not me or Maddie who she creeps in bed with almost every night, is it?" Ever raised a brow in challenge, then focused on Mouse, color filling her cheeks, before the queen looked back at him. "I think she should go. Getting out of Ivory might be good for her bloodlust. Besides, I know what a strong fighter she is, how vicious she can be, how smart, and how well she can help you hide if you encounter the Jabberwocky."

Ferris clenched his jaw. Ever had a point though—Mouse was strong and clever. "All right," he agreed.

Mouse raised her chin and stared at him with an unreadable expression. *No.* Perhaps not unreadable. Part pride, part hurt. Part something else.

Ever smiled and ran her bow across the strings, playing another song, deep and hopeful. They left the queen there to play and he forced his thoughts away from being completely alone with Mouse on a probably-perilous journey as he jogged up the stairs. Mouse moved slower, taking the steps one at a time.

If there wasn't a fresh mortal to feed from, it wouldn't really be good for her problem, but Ever had known Mouse longer than him, had been a vampire even longer than that. He would trust that she knew what she was talking about.

"We should get a good sleep in before we leave." Ferris rubbed the back of his neck, unsure if Mouse would want to join him in his room now that he'd pissed her off. He wanted her to—he *always* wanted her to. He was even willing to keep his clothes on tonight. After their kiss, he didn't want to sleep next to Mouse naked. Though maybe she wouldn't mind it. Maybe she wouldn't even mind crawling under the covers with him now… Damn it, *no*.

"I'll pack in the morning," she said in a cool tone. "We can talk about our strategy as we travel."

Ferris nodded and Mouse appeared pacified as she strode around him, into his room. He hesitated in the hallway, the memory of her grinding against him flashing through his mind.

"Coming?" she called from inside the room.

"Yes, sorry," he replied as he walked toward his doorway. *Though, not in the way I'd like to be coming.*

CHAPTER TEN

MOUSE

Red was a deserted wasteland that Mouse had only ventured to a handful of times. Neither Ever nor Imogen had been interested in claiming that part of Wonderland as their own, but now that Ever was working with Chess to unite their territories, that might change one day. However, they didn't want to revive the desolate territory if the Jabberwocky was constantly a threat. The Jabberwocky needed to be eliminated for the safety of all of Wonderland, but how could one destroy a beast with a body like iron?

A mystery indeed.

A mystery that was in dire need of being solved.

What Mouse needed were the witches from *Macbeth*. If witches were real, she would have one cast a spell on the Jabberwocky or at least offer a prophecy on how to kill the wretched monster.

Mouse hummed lightly while she finished packing her bag with a few changes of clothes, dried packets of blood, a few canteens of water, and daggers. She'd gotten plenty of sleep with Ferris and she was supposed to meet him at the palace's entrance once she finished. But she tried not to focus on what had happened the night before—his hot mouth on hers, the way she'd ground her hips into his, how delicious his flesh tasted against her tongue, how his hard length had nestled into her softness, even with clothing on. If he hadn't stopped, she knew she wouldn't have. And she wished he wouldn't have either.

Pushing away the heat that was spreading to her center, she slipped her gun in her boot, then straightened. The main reason Ever had agreed for Mouse to journey with Ferris was because the queen didn't want to keep her trapped like Imogen had. It was one thing for Ever to say she wasn't ready to be a guard, but a whole different matter to forbid her to go somewhere entirely. Ferris hadn't wanted her to go at first, but she'd forgiven him since he hadn't fought her on it again.

A nagging sensation tugged at Mouse—there had to be something valuable in Red, some sort of clue that would hint at a way to destroy the Jabberwocky. The Red Queen had been a vicious twat from what Mouse had heard over the centuries, even Imogen and Rav had agreed on that. What was suspicious, though, was why such a tyrant allowed a terrifying beast to live in her territory if she'd possibly had a way to destroy it herself?

Mouse peered at Des, who lay curled on top of the mostly-eaten leaf, her mouth parted as she lightly snored. Selfishly, Mouse wanted to bring her good luck charm on the journey for her own comfort, but she needed to learn she couldn't drag the caterpillar everywhere, especially since she wasn't certain when she would return. The only one of their group who had been to Red in recent years was Chess, back when Maddie led him on a wild goose chase in search of Ever. But he'd returned just fine, not even spotting the Jabberwocky while there, so Maddie shouldn't get her panties in a twist when Mouse informed her what she was about to do.

Adjusting her backpack, Mouse then scooped up Des's sleeping form, tucking the caterpillar into the front pocket of her dress to bring to her sister.

Mouse stepped into the hallway and walked to Maddie's room and knocked on the door. Her sister didn't answer, so she headed downstairs to the drawing room where she found her sister asleep on the chaise, thread and felt in her lap. Maddie's purple curls were mussed and her black and white striped hat rested on the velvet cushion beside her head.

Mouse's heart ached at the sight. Before she met up with Ferris, she needed to discuss a few matters with Maddie. She couldn't leave Ivory after the last few outbursts she'd had with her sister—she needed a clear conscience so she could focus on the task at hand.

Kneeling beside the chaise, she cupped Maddie's cheek. "Big sister, wake up."

Maddie's eyes flew open, her honey-colored irises shining from sleep. "Mouse." She sat up, patting the cushion for her hat.

"I have to tell you something," Mouse whispered. "Remember the stories Mama used to tell us when we were younger? You always wanted to be the hero and I wanted to be saved?"

"Ah, yes, Mama's glorious tales." Maddie grinned, placing the hat on her head. "It made our roleplaying decisions easy."

Mouse folded her hands in her lap. "I don't want to be the hero of this story, but I do want to make it easier for you and the others."

Maddie furrowed her brow. "I don't like the sound of this, Margo."

Mouse studied her sister's concerned face and she couldn't hold back her emotions. She threw her arms around Maddie, squeezing her tight. "I'm sorry for earlier. I'm sorry for the past few months."

"You don't have to apologize for anything," Maddie murmured, brushing a loose tendril from Mouse's plait behind her ear. "If I had known what that sick bastard had done to you, I would've left the safe house and slaughtered his arse myself. Stabbed him with a thousand hatpins, then cut him into the smallest of pieces before setting them on fire."

"That was one reason I didn't tell you—I didn't want you to risk yourself again. But most of all, I thought it would be easier to keep everything inside, that it would go away." Things never truly went away, though—they just lessened over time. Even after Mr. Taylor ripped away her virginity, she was still haunted by the good times they'd had when he'd courted her. And she *hated* that.

"Think of a hat," Maddie said. "There is only so much fabric and pins you can place on and in it before it will tip over and bleed to death."

"I love your analogies." Mouse smiled softly. "That would be quite the bloody predicament."

"The bloodiest," Maddie sang, then she drew back, her expression serious. "Now tell me what you're planning. I assume I won't want to throw a tea party in celebration of it."

Mouse stood and adjusted her skirts to avoid her sister's staring, then took a seat on the chaise. "You certainly won't. But I need you to do me a favor."

Maddie pressed closer to her sister. "No more beating around the bush," she sang.

"I need you to take care of Des." Mouse took the sleeping caterpillar from inside her pocket and placed her in the center of Maddie's palm. "I'm going on a little adventure with Ferris."

Maddie's lips tilted up at the edges in delight, one of her eyebrows quirking as she tucked Des into the pocket of her skirt. "A sexy adventure? It's about damn time. This will be good for you, sister."

"*What?*" Mouse shrilled, her blood coursing through her

veins, straight to her heart where the blasted organ was *agreeing*. "Ferris is my *friend*." A friend who she liked kissing. A friend whose salty skin she wanted to feel her teeth on. A friend who she wanted to see naked on his bed again. Or preferably her lips on his *while* he was naked, then pleasuring one another, taking him in between her lips, her tongue swirling around that piercing of his. *Oh, heavens…* Her body was growing warm, too warm.

Maddie cocked her head, her eyebrow still arched, disbelieving.

"I'm going with him to Red!" Mouse hissed.

"Red!" Maddie screeched back. "No. No, no, no. Are you mad?"

"Maybe we're all a bit mad here." Mouse laughed softly and lifted a brow in return.

"This is no laughing matter, Margo! The Jabberwocky is venturing wherever the hell it wants to now. It isn't as if the fucker is nestled away like before!"

"Then it may not even be in Red." Mouse shrugged. "Besides, Red's a big place. We've been there together, *remember*? Before Ever sends guards in search of the beast there, I want to see if we can find a hidden way to kill it so they don't get themselves slaughtered. It would be beneficial for the guards to remain here for the time being after the recent attack anyway."

Maddie scowled and Mouse could see in her sister's gaze that she knew she was right about the guards. "Wouldn't someone have found an answer already if one existed?"

"I don't believe anyone has *looked* before." Mouse folded her arms. "Remember when we had a tea party in the abandoned palace? You, me, and…" Her voice trailed off before she could say March's name. He'd asked Ever to kill him and she had to accept his decision.

"Ever was so mad!" Maddie laughed.

"Yes, mad we didn't invite her," Mouse pointed out.

"Anyway, we never thoroughly searched the palace. Maybe there is something hidden?"

"You know what? You're right." Maddie waved a hand in the air and stood from the chaise. "I'm coming with you."

She then spun on her heel and Mouse hauled her back by the arm. "You will do no such thing."

"And whyever not?"

"You went to werewolf territory to save Alice, where hundreds and *hundreds* of snarling beasts live. This is only one monster. Let me do this alone with Ferris. I know how to hide well. The more people go, the more chance of being spotted." She held up a finger. "And hush. You will not go with Ferris. *Me*. I'm going to meet him at the entrance now. This might be a way to find myself again. Not sit in the palace and dwell or drink blood in the mortal world day after day."

Maddie pursed her lips while holding Mouse's gaze, then relented. "Fine. You deserve to do this, to make your own choices. But you do need to be careful since you've been craving fresh blood even more so lately. When you return, if you want me to come with you while you feed, I can make sure you don't get carried away. I'm your big sister and I'm always here for you."

"I would like that." She released a breath. "But I'm going to drink powdered blood every day, and Ferris is going to have cold bags right when we leave." Mouse ignored the hunger churning in her stomach at the thought of blood.

"If you start feeling unwell, please don't push yourself." Maddie tugged Mouse's arm. "Let me at least take you to Ferris."

"Thank you."

Mouse walked beside her sister down the halls leading to the stairs near the palace's entrance. Mock lingered at the door in his white uniform, his yellow hair pulled back, and his eyes no longer red-rimmed but still puffy. Beside him stood Ferris with his backpack strewn across one arm. He looked positively delicious wearing a tight dark T-shirt and jeans that hugged his thighs perfectly. Mouse's heart accelerated as she met Ferris's heavy stare. Did the blasted thing always do that at the sight of him before?

"You might want to give into temptation," Maddie whispered in her ear.

Mouse shot her sister a glare. "Quiet."

Maddie drew Ferris and Mouse into a hug on each side. "You watch her with your life," her sister said to Ferris, then glanced back at Mouse. "And you watch him with yours. Once you find the beastie's secret, I'll go after it with the others."

"That's fair," Mouse agreed. "Don't forget Des likes the leaves from the trees near the lake."

"She won't be a happy caterpillar when she wakes."

Des would understand. Mouse couldn't stop her stomach from sinking as she peered beneath her lashes at Mock. "I'm sorry about Didi." Her voice came out louder than usual.

Mock's brows shot up, his eyes widening. "Thank you, Mouse." It was the first time she'd spoken to him, and it was a start.

With a final goodbye, Mouse and Ferris walked outside, the cool air rustling the ends of her plait.

"Here you go," Ferris said, handing her two cold blood bags. She drank the first one down in seconds, then forced herself to go slower with the second.

Mouse noticed his empty hands and he didn't have any for himself. "Drink some?" She held it out to Ferris. When he didn't take it, she said more firmly. "I demand it."

"Well, in that case." He smirked, taking it from her hands, his fingers brushing hers. Again, the butterflies swarmed in her stomach at the contact.

As she watched him drink from where her mouth had been, his tongue licking the tip clean, she shoved down the urge to press her lips to his, to taste not only the blood there but *him*, just like she had last night.

Mouse turned her focus to the portal as they approached, and the flowery scent hit her senses when they crossed through the barrier to the cemetery in the mortal world. There wasn't a portal directly to Red that she knew of—the queen had somehow kept those a secret, even after her death. But there was one not far away from the cemetery that would take them to the edge of an Ivory forest, next to where Red's territory began.

"Would you have truly wanted to go to Red without me?" Mouse asked.

"I think you know that answer, luv." Ferris winked.

She wanted to talk about what they'd done the night before, but that would mean she would need to discuss how badly she'd wanted to taste his blood too. Her gaze fell to the chain around Ferris's neck, and her chest tightened when she realized what the ring was for. It had to have belonged to Ellie, not just an heirloom or to wear for fashion…

"How about you teach me?" Mouse said as they walked through the cemetery, her gaze trained on his hands to avoid the necklace.

"Teach you what?" he asked, his voice raspy.

Her breath caught, unable to stop the images crawling into her mind of him doing *other things* to her with his hands. "Drums," she finally answered.

He grinned, bumping his shoulder with hers. "You want to learn? I'll teach you any song you'd like."

"How about that AC/DC song you once played for me at your place?" She could still see how fast his hands had moved, hear how the heavy beats had sounded, watch how he'd bit his lip when he closed his eyes, relishing in the music.

"'Riff Raff?'" He chuckled, his infectious laugh echoing through the cemetery. "You know how long it took me to play *that*?"

"I'm a fast learner."

"I bet you are." The edges of his lips stayed tilted up as his gaze trained on her mouth.

An urge to draw his face to hers, run her tongue across the seam of those shapely lips, tugged at Mouse. Her hunger was craving both his blood and his body, and she chewed on the inside of her cheek to tame the lust-filled sensations down. These thoughts were becoming out of control, but more so, welcoming…

Mouse walked beside him in comfortable silence, though her body was still coiled tight, as she led him through the woods and the city until they reached the closest bridge over the Thames. "There." She pointed downward as cars sped past them.

"The river, luv?" Ferris asked. "Where our bodies will collide with water? Are you sure a portal is there?"

"Follow me and find out," Mouse taunted. With that, she leapt from the bridge while Ferris cursed above her. A sparkling white light flashed, the portal sucking her inside, her body falling through glittering darkness. Mouse's stomach rose to her throat as she plummeted, the adrenaline rush singing in her veins until the portal opened, spitting her out on the soft white earth of Ivory.

Ferris grunted when he landed on his stomach beside her. "That was fucking awful."

"Saved us time though, didn't it? Another good reason I came." Mouse smiled, pushing herself up from the ground. She brushed off her hands on her dress and stared straight ahead to where silver and white trees turned to ones of red. But not like the trunks in Scarlet. These were a deep red that was almost black with not a single leaf growing from any of their gnarled branches.

"So, this is Red? It looks positively lovely," Ferris said with sarcasm.

"It is, isn't it?" She laughed softly.

As they crossed into the forest, the scent of rain enveloped her. It was known as the Broken Forest of Shattered Blood because it was where the Red Queen had brought whoever she desired to die. She would break them into pieces, then hang their body parts in the trees as decorations. In many ways, the Red Queen was like Imogen.

The ground below their feet was a sandy red texture and squished as they walked. Up in the branches, bald owls hissed, their beaks filled with sharp black fangs.

"Well, aren't *they* friendly?" Ferris rolled his eyes.

"They're like the crows in Scarlet. Leave them alone and you'll be fine." She shrugged. "Otherwise, they'll peck away and eat your flesh."

The rainy scent of the forest changed to something else… A metal smell wafted through the air, caressing her nose. *Fresh*. A mixture of vampire, human, and werewolf.

Mouse's fangs dropped on instinct and when she peered at Ferris, his were too. They took a few steps forward while surveying the area. A rustling came behind her, accompanied by a deep growl. She yanked out her gun from her boot, whirling around just as Ferris's went off. The werewolf thrashed, its obsidian fur turning gray and orange as its body disintegrated to fiery ash. Another growl sounded, shaking the trees surrounding her.

A twig snapped to Mouse's left and she pulled the gun's trigger, blasting a white-furred werewolf with its fangs bared. Its form changed to ash just as another came barreling from her right. But Ferris gunned it down, its body quaking to the ground while falling to pieces.

"Should've expected rogue werewolves to slum it up here," Ferris grumbled.

Mouse listened closely for a sign of any others. Werewolves weren't ones to stay hiding—if there was a threat, they would all come. But only bugs and small animals made any noise. Through the silence, the scent of blood became stronger.

She walked a few steps behind Ferris as they padded past

thick tree trunks to where several piles of bones rested, licked clean of any remains. Blood splattered the ground, a vampire's head on its side, but the rest of the body was gone.

A gurgling sound caught her attention and she crept behind a tree to find a male form beside another pile of bones. He was without one arm and both his legs had been ripped off. *Human.*

By the sounds of his uneven breathing, he wasn't going to make it. Mouse's hunger stormed through her veins, her eyes fluttering.

Ferris lowered himself and whispered in her ear, his hot breath tickling her neck, "Go on, luv. We are what we are." Her eyes fluttered more, but for a different reason. He then gently nudged her forward. "The mortal won't make it anyway."

Taking a deep swallow, Mouse nodded and peered down at the human, his wide blue eyes. His words came out garbled and she couldn't make out what he was saying. Her hunger grew ravenous as she knelt beside him, but she attempted to rein it in, to control herself. Not be Rav's monster and tear the mortal apart even more.

"Sleep. There will be no more pain after this," she murmured, then lowered her teeth to his neck, piercing his flesh, giving in to her instincts. Warm blood flooded over her tongue and she drank, giving the man what he needed.

Death.

CHAPTER ELEVEN

FERRIS

When vampires referred to Red as a wasteland, they weren't full of shit. Burnt patches and brittle, dead brush dotted the red clay. Even the distant sky was tinted red with the amount of dust the wind blew into the air. Ferris, with a hand on Mouse's lower back, steered her around the skeleton of a large cat-like creature while reveling in her warmth, wishing he could take more of it. But Mouse assured him that they were almost at the palace and he needed to focus. *Skeleton,* he thought to himself, staring at the dead animal to keep his mind on track. These weren't the first remains they'd come across—small birds had been littered about too. Even a human—or a vampire—curled up against the trunk of a decaying tree. Mansions had caved in on themselves while other buildings were completely gone, leaving nothing behind but their foundation.

Despite the obvious disrepair of the entire territory, Ferris wasn't prepared for the sorry state of the palace. He paused, Mouse beside him, and they stared at the polished red sandstone. What *used* to be polished, anyway. Now it sat in crumbling heaps and gold flecks glittered up from the larger chunks. Two stories still stood with what looked to be at least two more having partially collapsed.

Shattered glass crunched underfoot as Ferris picked his way through what once must've been a glorious courtyard. Bricks in varying shades of red were laid in massive overlapping circles with the base of a huge statue at the center of the largest. The base was carved from black stone and only three marble feet were left attached to it. One woman's heel and two old-fashioned men's shoes with broad buckles. Whoever the statue was of—likely the dead king and queen of Red—had been reduced to pebbles. The king had died long before the queen, so Ferris absently wondered if this was her monument to him or if it was created before his death.

"Do you think there's anything worth salvaging?" Mouse asked quietly.

Ferris scowled at the palace. It wasn't like Red was overrun with bandits. Everyone was dead or gone, but there was no telling what happened as soon as the royals had died. If the grounds *were* raided, it would've been for jewels or other nice ass shit—not conspiracy theories about the fucking Jabberwocky.

"Only one way to find out," he answered.

Mouse slipped her hand in his and his heart gave a little jump. The memory of holding her hips as she ground on top of him rushed to the surface. The urge to have her on top of him again pulsed through his body. He wanted his mouth on hers, to feel the weight of her breasts in his hands, to slide into her. To thrust. Hard. *So* hard that she would know how much he wanted her. *Needed* her.

He swallowed, pushing away his reckless desire, and gave Mouse's hand a squeeze before leading her to the main entrance. There was no longer a door, but a round opening where it would've been. The entrance chamber was blacker than sin, not that it mattered much with their ability to see in the dark. He'd seen much more terrifying shit done in brighter places while inside the Ruby Heart Palace. Red's castle smelled stale and dry with the sweet hint of death.

"We should try to find the library first and any rooms along the way," Ferris mused. "If that doesn't turn up anything on the beast, we can search somewhere else."

Mouse scowled, then nodded once. "There's a private library that belonged to the king and queen. If they held secrets about the Jabberwocky, they might have kept them hidden there."

"I wonder why they didn't send someone to kill the monster." Ferris peeked inside the palace and found it empty, save for the layer of red dust. The floors were made of the same sandstone as the walls, the stones laid in a careful herringbone design. The gold flecks in the material were dulled but still visible. Overhead, strands of chains linked five chandeliers made of antlers. Black candles were still imbedded on the points, dried wax running down the bone. "*If* they knew how to kill it, I mean."

He'd wondered about this as they traveled to the palace, but hadn't brought it up because it would mean this might be a wild goose chase. It made no sense to keep the Jabberwocky alive if they could've rid themselves of it. Unless killing it was a lot harder than living with it…

"We can worry about that later," Mouse whispered, seeming to feel how he'd tensed. "Follow me. I think I remember where the library was, but it's been a while since I was here."

Ferris let Mouse take the lead, pulling him down dark hallways by the hand. Even the simple contact, her skin on his, had his body buzzing with desire. Dragging her into the nearest bedroom was a looping thought, but they had a job to do. Jabberwocky first. Fucking second, if she wanted to. So, he studied his surroundings in a desperate attempt to get his dick to behave.

The walls of the palace were all bare—whether it was because any artwork had been stolen or if it was a style choice, he wasn't sure. Dust, leaves, and bramble had blown inside through the open doors. Tattered shreds of fabric clung to the empty window frames and splintered pieces of wood were shoved against the wall under a layer of dust.

They passed by rooms in disarray, finding nothing of use there—chairs toppled over, tables missing legs, chandeliers dangling precariously from the ceilings. Doors hung from the hinges, if there were still doors at all. Rust-colored blood stains splashed against paneled walls and on porcelain tile.

A skeleton sprawled in the middle of a large sitting room caused Ferris to slow his steps. The skull, however, was displayed on an iron sconce hanging from the wall. Judging by the powdered wig still framing the face, it had been a male.

"Interesting décor," he joked.

Mouse followed his gaze, giving a snort, and led him away from the display. A few more rooms down, Mouse stopped in front of a set of open double doors. "We're here," she said and hesitated before stepping into a massive library.

Shelves were toppled, books spilling from them, loose pages scattered about. A pair of green sofas still sat across from each other with a round table between. Directly above was a domed ceiling made of glass with cracks webbing across it. In its glory, this must've been fucking badass. Even Ferris might've considered reading there. *Nah.* But maybe he would've dragged his drum set in.

He gave Mouse's hand another squeeze and dropped it. "Where should we start?"

"This side? We can work our way across," she suggested while chewing on her lip.

Together, they made their way to the far left and scanned book titles. Mouse used her fingertips to trail over them, pushing the ones on the shelf until they sat in even rows. He imagined those fingers trailing over him instead. Starting on his chest, skating down. Tracing the lines of his abs and down the V to unbutton his jeans. Those fingers wrapping around his cock. Stroking him. Ferris drew in a deep breath and let it out slowly. He ran his knuckles over the rows of books to even them, knowing it would please Mouse to see his shelves in proper order too. And also as a distraction to tamp down his damn lust.

The Balance of Life.

The Ballad of a Lady.

Bartholomew's Theories.

Ferris ran a hand through his hair. The titles were arranged, seemingly, in alphabetical order but with no thought to what they were about. Romance novels were beside scientific tomes and poetry. He glanced over at Mouse, holding a weathered black book in her hands, opened to a diagram. She sucked on her bottom lip as she studied it, and he stared at her perfect mouth. Remembered how it felt on his. The way her lips moved over his neck. Holy shit, they had searching to do and all he could focus on was pleasing her and his dick.

"What do you have there?" he asked, clearing his throat, pushing himself to fucking *focus*. The old sketches on the page were too hard to see from where he stood.

Mouse jumped and snapped the book shut. "Nothing."

Before she could place it back on the shelf, Ferris plucked it from her hands with a laugh. She bounced onto the balls of her feet to try getting it back, but Ferris held it over his head, curiosity piqued. The spine of the book was too worn to read so he flipped it open to find page after page of sketches with notations at the bottom.

Sketches of people fucking, their bodies in various sexual poses.

"This is definitely *something*," he said with a grin.

Mouse sighed and crossed her arms. "I only looked inside because I couldn't read the name of the book."

He glanced at her, his grin widening. That might've been why she opened it, but she was most definitely interested in the contents based on how hard she'd stared at the pages a moment ago. "This one looks fun," he said, and held the page open so she could see.

The woman laid on her back with one leg wrapped around the man's thigh, the other draped over his shoulder, as he fucked her. A basic position, but given the year this book was made, maybe it was more intriguing. Still, it *was* a fun one, and he felt himself stiffen slightly, throwing all his focus on searching out the damn window.

"Maybe add a blindfold to the mix for a little extra spice," he suggested, watching her carefully. Their eyes met and he imagined having Mouse beneath him just like the drawing. Her pink plait wrapped around his hand, his cock sliding inside her, the sounds she would make. When he spoke again, his voice was husky. "He should be kissing her, at least. Showing her breasts a little love."

When a blush tinged her cheeks, he closed the book and set it on the shelf behind her. She didn't move as he leaned closer to do so. Only held her breath. He breathed her in, the light floral scent going straight to his cock. Ferris lowered his hand to tuck her hair behind her ear and she let out a small gasp.

"I liked what you did the other night," he whispered. They were friends—adding benefits could fuck everything up. Especially since he *knew* feelings were involved on his end. But damn, he wanted more. He wanted to slip into her heat and fuck her like every single one of those pictures, make love to her so she would be ruined for anyone else, so it was only him tearing orgasm after orgasm from her. "How you kissed me. How you *moved*."

"Ferris," she breathed.

His pulse sped, his cock stiffening even more at the thought of tasting her again. Of plunging his tongue into her mouth to dance with hers. He wanted to lift her off the ground, wrap her legs around his waist, and fuck her against the broken bookshelves. Feel her quiver around him. *Fuck.* He was getting ahead of himself, but the idea of it made him crazy.

"If I wanted to kiss you right now, what would you say?" he rasped in her ear.

"N—no." Mouse spoke in the smallest of voices.

Ferris's chest tightened and he ripped himself away from her, his desire fading. "Fuck. I'm sorry. I didn't mean—"

"It's not that I don't want to kiss you. I enjoyed the other night too," she added quickly, and turned to face the shelves instead of him. Her hand shook as she resumed lining the books up perfectly.

Shit. He'd done something wrong. Was he too forward? Had she wanted the other night to be a once-off? "I'm sorry," he said again.

This time Mouse shot him a sad smile over her shoulder. "If you had asked me in any other room, I would've had a different answer."

Ferris frowned. So it *wasn't* him—it was the library? "I don't understand."

"Did Maddie ever tell you about my past? I doubt she did, but maybe…?" She looked slightly hopeful at the idea, yet when Ferris shook his head, she sighed. A long silence filled the room as Ferris watched her fidget with spines. Finally, she whispered, "It happened in a library."

A crease formed between his brows. He stepped closer and she tensed, so he moved back to his side of the row. "*What* happened?"

"When I was still mortal, my neighbor, Mr. Taylor, courted me." Her voice was emotionless, dead. "We were friends growing up and got along well. He spoiled me, actually. Buying me trinkets and picking wildflowers for my hair. His family had a lot more money than mine, yet it never mattered to him. Our families were even talking of us getting engaged soon. It wasn't a love match, but back then, we were lucky to marry someone we genuinely cared for. Maddie had been missing for a while, and they wanted me to be well taken care of in life. Mr. Taylor seemed to check every box."

Ferris reached unconsciously to play with Ellie's ring hanging around his neck. He was an idiot to think Mouse had never been in a relationship before—she was hundreds of years old. *Of course* she'd been with men. Maybe even women for all he knew.

"What happened?" he asked gently when she didn't continue.

Mouse shifted nervously. "Well, we did things together. You know? Kissed and touched. We even used our mouths on each other a few times. None of it was like I'd expected it to be, but no one really talked about sex back then. It was taboo. Something to be done between a man and wife and never spoken about in good company. But he wasn't my husband yet. Our families hadn't even come to an actual agreement that he would *ever* be my husband. It was still being discussed…"

Ferris curled his fist around Ellie's ring, his chest twisting uncomfortably as he realized where things were likely going with this story. Anger rose, hovering just beneath the surface, waiting for her to confirm the worst. "What did he do to you?" he growled.

Mouse's body shook slightly as she stopped fussing with the books. "One night after dinner, he wanted to show me something in the library. Our fathers had gone off to smoke cigars and our mothers were distracted, so we snuck off alone. Something told me there wasn't anything he wanted to show me, but I figured we would do what we'd always done. I told him I wanted to save myself for marriage, but… He demanded more than I wanted to give."

Ferris's fangs dropped. "He took you unwillingly?"

Mouse hesitated, then slowly nodded.

"I'll fucking kill him," Ferris snarled. His vision went red, his pulse roaring in his ears. *How dare that man?* How *dare* he take that from her?

"He's dead, Ferris," she said matter-of-factly. "Maddie killed him."

"Then I'll dig up his grave and kill the fucker again." He lunged forward and pulled Mouse against his chest in a tight hug. "I'll grind his bones to dust and scatter them in the sewer."

Mouse laughed. Actually fucking laughed. How could she be laughing when he was being consumed by rage? His mind was swirling with ways to resurrect a corpse so he could torture the fucking shit out of it. Now he understood why she fed off of and killed those who hurt others.

"Ferris, you're squishing me." She patted his arms.

"Sorry," he snapped without meaning to. His anger wasn't directed at her in the least bit. "Sorry!"

"It's fine, but let me breathe," she said with another small laugh.

Ferris loosened his arms and inhaled her scent. It filled him, calmed him. He held her until his fangs retracted. Until he could see straight again. Then placed a kiss on top of her head.

"I'm sorry that happened to you," he whispered.

"Me too," Mouse murmured. "But it was a long time ago and I don't like to dwell on it. I just wanted you to know, it's not you. It's the library. That's the only time I'm truly bothered by it anymore."

Ferris stepped away from her, and she glanced up at him. His heart gave a painful thump when their gazes met. Brushing a loose tendril of her hair behind her ear again, he offered a soft smile. "You never have to explain your *no* to me, luv."

"Well," she bit her lip and blushed. "I do, if it's *not* a no. It's just a *somewhere else.*"

"Right now?" he asked. After a revelation like that, he wasn't sure it was right to be lusting after her. But, if she wanted it, he would worship her like the queen she was.

Mouse quietly took the book of sexual positions off the shelf and headed for the door, leaving him to follow.

CHAPTER TWELVE

MOUSE

As soon as Mouse stepped out of the library and into the hallway, relief washed over her. She'd wanted to believe she'd gotten over her fear of libraries after Mr. Taylor, but deep down, a shadow of that night still lingered inside of her, just as the acts inside the Ruby Heart Palace did. Both places always would, but she needed to face her fears. One step at a time. Shakespeare had helped her in the past, during the dark moments, when she still had to live next door to Mr. Taylor, when her mother had held her, comforting her but had also told her to be quiet about it. Back then it was different.

But now, she didn't need the protection—she didn't *need* a Shakespeare play for distraction, or for Des to be her comfort companion, or for Ferris to be her savior. She wanted them because she *chose* them, just as she was tired of trapping her desires away, pretending as if she didn't want anyone, when she sure as hell yearned for Ferris.

"We don't need this." Dropping the book of sexual desires,

Mouse whirled around and leapt into Ferris's arms. He caught her and crashed back into the wall. Her instinct was raw, driven. Lust burned within her, waiting to unleash.

"No, we don't," he rasped. "I can make you feel so good, if you'll let me."

"When did you first see me differently?" Mouse asked, her heart accelerating.

Ferris spun around so she was planted against the wall, his hard cock deliciously pressed against her. "When you were taken by Rav and Imogen, I realized what you meant to me. Then once you were safe, I let myself wonder… And now, I fucking want you like I've never wanted anyone. I don't know if that makes me a piece of shit because of my past."

"It doesn't, and I want you just as much. You're the first person I've ever truly wanted." She ran her hand down his cheek, and he leaned into her touch. "You don't need to be careful with me and you don't have to worry about being too rough. I want it all with you, Ferris."

His lips came to her neck, trailing kisses to just below her ear, his fingers digging into her hips. "If you ever want me to stop or slow down, just say the word."

"Likewise." Mouse skimmed the tip of her finger across his plump bottom lip. "Now, let's go to a room. I don't care how filthy it is." It didn't matter if they were in a crumbling palace—they were together and that was all she needed in that moment.

"Let's see what we can find, then." He chuckled, holding her close as he started walking down the bare hallway.

She loosened her arms around his neck. "I can walk if it's easier on you."

"No, I like you right where you are." Ferris grinned, the tip of his tongue moistening his bottom lip. He halted at a door that wasn't all the way shut and used his boot to kick it open. Before she had a chance to peek in, he spun around, and started walking again. "We don't need an audience."

She laughed louder this time, glimpsing the skeletal remains over his shoulder. "I suppose we could've just turned the guests around if we had to."

"Mmm, we may have to if we can't find anything better." Ferris chuckled.

Broken items littered most of the rooms on the second floor, and black smudges and cracks covered the walls. Due to the rotting wood, the rail around the interior balcony looked like it would collapse to the shattered marble below at any moment.

Ferris opened a crooked door that was falling off its hinges. He carried Mouse inside the mostly clean room and sat them both on a torn chair. The room wasn't as eroded as the main areas of the palace, only layers of dust clinging to everything. A large bed, lower on one side than the other, was pressed against the wall, an empty wardrobe rested in the corner with its doors missing, and the two chairs were beside a writing desk, where a stack of worn books was collected on top.

Mouse studied Ferris's pretty features, her heart still beating like the drums he played. He knew the darkest parts of her that had remained hidden and he didn't look at her differently, just as he hadn't when she'd confessed to him about her past in the Ruby Heart Palace and her visits to the mortal clubs.

She pressed her forehead to his. "You truly don't see me differently now? I don't want you to think of me as broken."

"No, luv. We're all broken pieces just trying to find a way to fit back together again. And our jagged edges line up perfectly."

Mouse grinned and crashed her mouth to his. He didn't hesitate to kiss her back with equal hunger, his hands sliding down her sides to her hips, urging her to move against him. She rolled her hips forward, picking up where they'd left off the other night. He growled and she liked the taste of that sound, the way his tongue dipped into her mouth, flicking against hers.

Ferris trailed kisses down her jaw and whispered in her ear, "Even when I left your room the other night, I couldn't stop thinking about you."

A thrill shot through her. "What did you do?"

"Do you really want to know?"

"Every detail," she said, grinding against his hardness.

"I fucked my hand," he said in a gruff voice. "I pretended it was you stroking me, your mouth sucking, me thrusting inside you." His hands drifted to the curve of her buttocks, and she ground harder into him. "How wet are you now?"

A heat spread through Mouse, sinking lower and lower, her body coiled tight. "Very." She hadn't touched a cock since Mr. Taylor's, and her thoughts turned to Ferris when she'd found him naked in his bed, how much she wanted to see his length again, only this time, *hard*. Ferris wasn't prim and proper the way men were back in her century, and she liked that he was both sweet and daring.

Mouse wanted to be adventurous too, wanted to show her bold side. For now, she would start by making him feel good. "Stand up and show me how you took care of yourself the other night," she murmured.

"As you wish." Ferris grinned seductively and Mouse helped him peel his shirt over his head. Her heart pounded as he lifted and placed her into the chair before rising in front of her. He kicked off his boots, then she unfastened his jeans and drew them down, freeing his large cock, the silver piercing at the tip shining. Hunger swirled in her as she studied his broad chest, his defined muscles, the raven tattoo on the left side of his stomach.

Ferris brought his hand to his hard cock, stroking, and a pearl glistened at the head. The bead seemed to beg for her to lick it away, see how good he tasted.

"What are you thinking?" he rasped as his hand moved at

an enticingly slow pace.

She pushed up from the chair and stepped closer, her gaze locked on his. "That I want to sink my teeth into you."

"Then do it, luv."

Mouse's body grew hotter at his words, her heart slamming against her ribs. She stood on her tiptoes and pressed her lips to his collar bone, her fangs dropping. But she didn't want to pierce him there—she wanted the place she'd been thinking about for a while. It had always been his neck and wrists in the past.

Mouse kissed down his chest to his nipple, circling it with her tongue before gliding her fangs lightly across his flesh, all while he continued to stroke himself faster. Her hand met his and they pumped his cock together, his breaths ragged. Lowering herself to her knees, she took over for him.

She ran her free fingers up his thigh, then sank her teeth into his salty flesh there. A rush of euphoria swept through her as his blood burst onto her tongue. *Heavenly.*

"Fuck," Ferris growled. "That feels so damn good."

Mouse's eyes fluttered as she drank in the taste of him. A part of her wanted to drink him in forever, but she fought that ravenous appetite of hers. Her desire for blood turned toward the need to taste something else. She drew her fangs from his thigh, then shifted her position to collect the pearl from his tip with her tongue, tasting the delectable saltiness. A quiet moan left her and she leaned in to lick from the base of his length to the crown. She circled the warm metal of his piercing before taking him into her mouth completely.

Mouse gripped his buttocks, and he gently thrust into her mouth while his hands fisted her hair. She liked this, the being in control, and she worked him in between her lips, loving how he felt in her mouth. Then his cock pulsed. It had been so long since she'd done this, but it felt natural—all of it.

"I'm about to come," Ferris groaned. But she didn't leave his velvety cock, only continued to take her fill until her name fell from his lips on an inhale and he spilled himself inside her mouth.

Mouse swallowed his delicious flavor, then rose off her knees to stand in front of him. He lifted her chin, his chest heaving. "Tell me what you want now."

"For tonight, I just want to feel your fangs inside me." Mouse unbuttoned the front of her dress and drew it down her shoulders, letting the top fall to her waist, so her breasts were exposed. "And for your hands and tongue to touch me here."

In one swift motion, Ferris hoisted Mouse up, making her laugh while carrying her to the bed. She sat in his lap once more, her legs cradling his hips. His hand slid up her spine as he leaned down, bringing her closer to his face. His warm tongue circled her peaked nipple, then he took it into his mouth, his hand kneading her other breast.

She moaned as he released her nipple and trailed his tongue to the top of her breast, his fangs brushing her skin. Ferris sank his teeth in to the crook of her neck and she arched in pleasure, his fingers caressing her skin as he drank her. Mouse's eyes fluttered and she wanted more. More. More. More. "More," she demanded, her voice breathy.

He flipped her onto her back, caging her in. A loud creak came from the bed before it collapsed to the floor. Mouse squeaked and Ferris's shoulders quaked with laughter.

"I think that's our cue to search the palace like we're supposed to be doing." Mouse smiled.

Ferris smirked, licking the blood from his lips. "We'll continue this *soon*." He crawled off of Mouse and helped her to her feet.

She had never felt this way about anyone, the anticipation flowing through her. For the first time, she wasn't distracted by the need to feed, even though it swirled in her stomach. After searching a little longer, she would drink from their provisions.

Ferris slipped his clothing on while Mouse buttoned her

dress, neither removing their gazes from the other.

She bit the inside of her cheek. "We do need to go back to the library since we didn't finish searching it."

Ferris lifted her chin, his dark eyes fastened to hers. "How about in the morning? That will give you time to prepare for it. If you want, I can even search it myself. For now, we can check other rooms in the palace."

Mouse let out a relieved breath. "I like that plan."

As they explored the palace, there were so many rooms to go through, and her eyes started to close as tiredness swept over her. But she wanted to look a little longer since they were almost finished with this wing.

Mouse opened a door that led to a large chamber and she knew right away that this had once belonged to the royals. The bed was large enough for four people and the faded artwork painted across the walls gave it away, along with the words *Bitch Queen* written everywhere. A potent metal smell enveloped her as she entered. Even centuries after the royals had died, the stench of blood still lingered in the bedroom.

Most of the room appeared to have been raided at some point, not a single jewel was anywhere in sight and near-empty dresser drawers were strewn on the floor.

"Looks like the Red Queen was rather popular," Ferris said sarcastically and slipped inside the bathing chamber.

Mouse crept beside him, peering down at the bathtub filled with black sludgy muck and two dingy skulls at the edge. A rib cage rested on the floor in the corner, dried blood beneath it. The mirror was broken with shattered pieces on the cracked marble.

Imogen was known as the Queen of Hearts for her passion of taking hearts while the Red Queen was known not only for hanging body parts in the forest, but for basking in blood.

"If you didn't know already, the Red Queen liked to bathe in blood like Elizabeth Báthory," Mouse said.

"So, Elizabeth wasn't the first to actually do that then?"

Ferris arched a brow.

Mouse sent him a sly look. "No, the queen would've easily bathed in Elizabeth's blood."

He smirked. "Check the floors in the other room for loose secret compartments while I go through them in here."

Mouse nodded and went to the desk in the bedroom. Even though the drawers were on the floor, she pressed her hands inside the open slots of the desk, patting around for anything unusual. Besides a few quills that had fallen to the bottom, it was empty.

The wardrobe was empty as well, but she stepped into the large space, feeling over the ornate wood, looking for a sign of uneven texture. Yet she found only smooth surfaces.

Mouse lifted a decaying rug from the floor, but no secret compartment rested there. She shoved the bed to the side, searching beneath. It would have been rather cliché for the queen to have kept anything there, but it was commonplace.

A gut feeling coursed through her as though she was missing something. Mouse glanced at the wardrobe again, frowning, then she pushed it to the side and knelt on the floor. Biting the inside of her cheek, she knocked along the marble until a different, hollower, sound answered.

Eyes wide, she dug her nails into the thin edges of the tile and lifted it. Inside rested an old black book and a velvet crimson bag. "Jackpot!" Mouse yelled.

"You found something?" Ferris asked, rushing into the room.

"We'll see." Mouse handed Ferris the velvet bag while she flipped through the yellowed pages of the book. A musky odor invaded her nostrils while she read over the pages, discovering it did indeed belong to the Red Queen. There weren't many entries inside as if the queen had gotten bored with writing in it.

No longer tired, but wide awake, Mouse settled in, poring over the pages. Most of the entries were about how the Red

Queen hated her king and how he'd fucked females behind her back. Her jealousy of the White King and White Queen grew because of their genuine love for one another. She found a way to kill her king and make it look like an accident by feeding him to the Jabberwocky. Her last entry was how she'd plotted to kill the White Royals and had succeeded.

"Well, now we know the queen had a secret about her king," Ferris said.

"There's nothing else about the Jabberwocky in here besides the one mention." Mouse shut the book and sighed.

"You'll be really intrigued by what's in the bag," Ferris purred.

"What is it?" She perked up, finding a small yellow scroll in Ferris's palm.

He cleared his throat and straightened, then changed his voice to a proper accent as he read it aloud. "I cut off pieces of my king before feeding him to the Jabberwocky so he couldn't touch another properly, even in death."

Mouse blinked, waiting for more. "That's it?"

"No. Wait for it." Ferris smirked, then emptied the bag on the floor. Ten bone fingers clacked against the marble.

"And still"—Mouse pursed her lips—"she didn't seem as awful as Rav and Imogen."

"Definitely second place for Wonderland's psychopaths."

Mouse opened her mouth to speak when a boisterous rumbling filled the palace.

CHAPTER THIRTEEN

FERRIS

The palace shook, the king's finger bones rattling against the floor. Glass clinking against glass followed by a shattering in the distance. Booms echoed in a steady rhythm—a drum beat, slow and even. Then a guttural roar ripped through the air, too loud for a werewolf. It sounded more like … *the Jabberwocky.*

"It's the fucking Jabberwocky," Ferris whispered.

Mouse tossed her plait over her shoulder and tiptoed to the window. "It certainly sounds like it."

A low chuffing reverberated from the opposite direction— through the doorway, muffled. "It's coming from over there." Ferris crept out the door and glanced down to the first floor from the railing that overlooked the front entrance. A large shadow passed outside the main doorway, the dark silhouette spilling into the palace. "Oh, shit."

"What?" Mouse asked, peeking over his shoulder.

"It's outside." He snuck down the hallway, his back against the wall. When Mouse followed, he extended an arm in front of her, so he could easily pull her behind him if anything attacked, and peered over the balcony railing.

The shadow moved again, the tip of a tail swishing across the dusty ground outside. Then a sharp, surprised roar echoed into the broken palace. Ferris froze, pressing Mouse against the wall beside him. A furred, darkened snout shoved into the doorway. Nostrils flared on a long inhale. Once. Twice. Then its lips wrinkled into a snarl. Razor-sharp teeth bared. A low growl burst through the front entrance carrying the stench of death.

Fuck.

The beast withdrew from the doorway and replaced its snout with a large furred foot. It reached inside, dragging its talons along the floor with a resounding *screech* that left cavernous gouges in the stone. Ferris swallowed hard. Why hadn't he kept a weapon on him? Not that they were very helpful against the monster back in Ivory, but he needed to make sure Mouse didn't fucking die.

After moving its clawed foot around in search of something that wasn't there, the Jabberwocky growled, deep and guttural, before pulling back. The cracking of wings reverberated, piercing Ferris's ears. He let out a long breath and dropped his arm from in front of Mouse.

Ferris listened hard to the sound of wings as they drifted farther away. Searching the rest of the palace wasn't as important as safeguarding their lives and he wouldn't let anything happen to Mouse. He took her hand in his. "Come on."

Mouse followed close behind him as he led the way down the stairs to the main floor. They needed to find a safe place to hide. Somewhere they wouldn't be seen, heard, or smelled until the Jabberwocky left.

A heavy *boom* came from the roof. He froze as dust rained down from the ceiling, his body tense, waiting. Scrapes and thuds echoed through the palace. As if someone—or some*thing* was punching the ceiling.

"Ah, fuck," he hissed. They were no match for this thing alone. "Do you know if there's a basement?" If they could close themselves off below ground, it might hide their scent long enough for the beast to leave in search of another meal.

"Tunnels, like in … in the Ruby Heart Palace," she said with a wince. "Maddie and I found them when we snuck in for a tea party once."

He ran a hand through his hair and released a short breath. "Okay, I'm sure there are other places to hide. Do you—"

"It's fine. Rav never took me down there to…" Mouse trailed off as the Jabberwocky let out a frustrated screech overhead, the palace walls shaking. "I only know about the tunnels because I visited Imogen with Ever before and… And that's how Rav brought me to his palace the day he locked me up."

Ferris shook his head. No matter the time she'd spent in the tunnels, he didn't want to remind her of that damn place. Didn't want to remind himself of it either, though he knew he could disassociate from it long enough to keep them safe. He'd become an expert at it over the last couple years.

"Ferris, it's okay. If it's safest there, let's go," she said softly.

"All right, luv," he conceded. A portal might even be hidden down there which could get them the fuck out of here. They could check in with Ever and come back later.

Mouse jogged down hallways, glancing inside doors and taking turns with hesitation. Ferris kept an eye on the ceiling as the stone fractured overhead. The Jabberwocky seemed to be following their movements on the roof, but that would be impossible since it couldn't see them. Maybe it could track their footsteps. A *crack* filled the air, stone splitting, and the hair on Ferris's arms stood up. He lifted his gaze upward. They were out of the main part of the palace and the ceiling beneath the roof wasn't visible.

"Are we getting close, luv?" he asked, attempting to keep his voice steady, but he was sure the Jabberwocky was making progress.

"Here!" Mouse called and bolted through an open doorway, down a narrow staircase with spiderwebs crisscrossing.

Ferris glanced over his shoulder as a series of louder cracks tore from above. Then a moment of silence filled the air before chaos descended. The booms and crashes of falling stone and glass. The victorious cry of the beast. A single heavy beat of its wings. Quick, heavy footfalls as it barreled in their direction.

"Fuck!" Ferris shouted, and squeezed into the stairwell.

Mouse made it to the bottom of the steps just as the stench of the beast wafted down behind him. It was far too narrow for the monster to follow, but if it could break through the ceiling, what was stopping it from going through the floor?

Ferris joined Mouse, wrapping an arm around her and propelling her farther into the cavernous room. "Where are the tunnels?" he asked, scanning the circular room.

The walls were rough red stone, just like the floor, but there was no exit. Above, thick metal bars made a tight grid over the ceiling with a large, unlocked padlock dangling over what looked to be a gate.

"Mouse, where are the tunnels?" he asked again when she remained quiet.

Still, she didn't answer. He turned her to face him and froze at the horror in her expression. Eyes wide. Mouth parted. Breaths coming too fast.

"Shit." He took her cheeks in his hands. "Luv, look at me."

Her violet gaze lifted to his. "I was wrong."

"It's okay," Ferris soothed. He knew the tunnels would be a struggle for her, but now there was something on the ceiling that reminded him of the bars of a cage. She wasn't wrong about being able to handle it, though—she was stronger than she knew. And he was going to get her out. "I'm right here. We're fine, yeah? Not trapped. You just need to tell me where the tunnels are and I'll get us out of here."

"No." The word wobbled between them and she looked over his shoulder to where the Jabberwocky now snarled down the stairwell, clawing at the walls with its thick talons in an attempt to fit its body through. "I was wrong, Ferris. These aren't the tunnels."

The muscle in his jaw tightened. Looking around again, his gaze fell on something white. *Bones.* Scattered across the ground, gouged by teeth and claws. He registered the old, faint scent of blood. The pile of dead leaves and sticks off to the side and the scattered trinkets.

"Okay." He inhaled slowly, trying to keep his concentration despite the beast clawing its way into the narrow stairwell. The Ruby Heart Palace had a few places like this too. One where Rav dumped the remains of his experiments, which were then carted outside by unlucky guards. Another that had held humans before they were brought up to feed vampires during parties. They had been tossed inside from a chute at the base of the palace. "It's okay. Trust me. Tell me where we are and I'll figure a way out of this."

"There's no way out." Her voice cracked, barely audible over the continued roars of the beast hunting them. "I've heard tales about this that I didn't believe were true, but I think this is where they kept the Jabberwocky when they managed to trap it."

"Trap it…"

"The Red Queen had supposedly caught the Jabberwocky once long ago, kept it in this lair to try to tame it but it escaped. The tale Ever told me said the Red Queen wasn't able to trap it a second time, but she had fortified it just in case." Tears welled in Mouse's eyes as she stared up at where the beast was. "There's no other way out."

"Fuck that," Ferris growled. He ran his thumbs over her

cheekbones, wiping away the tears. "There's always more than one way out."

"There's not." She grabbed onto his wrists. Held on tightly. "There's not, Ferris. I know there's not. I… I can't…"

There wasn't another way out of her cell. He pulled her close and held her against his chest. "We aren't there, luv. I'm here with you and we *will* get out of this. I've got you."

"Ferris," she sobbed. "Please."

His heart cracked, his head frantically searching for a solution. He'd punch his way out of this place just like the animal threatening them if he had to. Mouse would never be trapped or feel this way again. Not if he could help it.

"Shh," he whispered into her ear. "It's okay."

It was not okay. But he would take the burden of knowing that from her.

The door to the lair flew down the stairs as if the Jabberwocky was calling him a liar. Mouse shook in his arms while the beast slammed into the stairwell over and over. *Fuck.* He saw nothing. No way out. *Think, think, think.*

A low, frustrated grunt poured out from the monster. Then stone blew inward. Blasted down the stairs. And the Jabberwocky tumbled into the underground room, the floor shaking.

Ferris shoved Mouse behind him and pushed her back. Kept himself between her and the beast.

"Shit," he hissed. They were so extremely fucked. "Mouse, hide," he urged. She could disguise herself in the leaves, maybe. Or when the Jabberwocky attacked him, she could run back up the stairs and escape. His pulse thundered, but he held onto the rhythm of it, letting it lead him into the readiness of battle. "Leave me as soon as you get the chance."

"I'm not leaving you," she said, clutching the back of his shirt.

He opened his mouth to argue when the monster rose to its full height, its hulking shadow crawling across his body. Ferris backed away and it advanced. Snarling. Thick saliva dripped from its jagged teeth.

"Nice monster," he tried. "You don't want to eat us."

It opened its jaws wider, as if to say it *very much* wanted to devour them, and took one step closer on those massive furred feet. The ground shifted. Another step. Prowling. The ground cracked beneath its weight. The beast paused and narrowed its orange eyes.

Something was wrong. The lair was built to trap it and yet...

Ferris sucked in a breath. The royals had fortified it to keep the Jabberwocky *better* trapped. What if this wasn't the real lair? What if they'd set this up with the trinkets and the nest as bait? What if the real lair was beneath...

"What's wrong, pretty beastie?" Ferris taunted. He could be wrong—very wrong—but if he was, they weren't any less fucked. "Not so hungry after all?"

The Jabberwocky snarled and took two more slow steps. The ground caved in with a loud crunch, dragging it down. Panic flashed in the Jabberwocky's fiery orange eyes as it fell, clawing at the air to save itself. Ferris sucked in a shocked breath, expecting the creature to fly back up at him and Mouse. But crumbling chunks of stone smacked against its wings, preventing them from opening to save itself.

Ferris breathed a sigh of relief and turned to Mouse. An unreadable expression filled her wide eyes. "We have to get out of here," he said. They could skirt around the gaping hole in the floor and flee before the beast freed itself. With any luck, they could be halfway to Ivory before the fucker escaped.

Mouse nodded and he spun, holding her tightly by the hand. The ground wavered with each careful step they took, threatening to crumble. Then, before it could truly register in Ferris's mind, the threats became reality as a crack ripped through the room.

The floor gave out beneath him, tearing him away from

Mouse. He shouted for her, but she was falling too. Spiraling. Both of them tumbling through the air. He stretched out in a desperate attempt to reach her, but she was too far.

"No! Mouse!" His body slammed into the bottom of the rocky cavern moments before hers, then boulders smashed down between them like a wall. "Mouse! Mouse, can you hear me?"

He shoved up from the ground, feeling every broken rib, as he pounded at the rubble. Behind him, the Jabberwocky stirred.

Motherfucker!

At least Mouse was safe.

But she was trapped. And he refused to let her stay that way.

The beast shook off the stones, its back to Ferris, and shuddered. Pebbles and dust flew outward, slapping Ferris in the face. He winced and pressed himself against the rocks. But the Jabberwocky simply spread its wings and flew out of the pit without noticing him.

Probably gone off to lick its wounds, yet he didn't doubt the beast would be back. They were easy prey now.

"Mouse!" he called again. "Please! *Mouse!*"

CHAPTER FOURTEEN

MOUSE

"*Ah, there's the pretty mouse," a deep voice purred in Mouse's ear, his hot breath tickling her neck, sending chills up her spine. She kept her eyes closed, hoping he would get bored with her, would go the hell away. But no one ever answered her prayers when she silently begged and pleaded, not when the lashings came, not when the drownings occurred, and not when he'd torn out her eyes.*

"Don't play coy. I know you're awake and ready to play." Rav lifted one of her lids, and her gaze met his light brown eyes, the tip of his tongue licking at his lower lip in anticipation of his sick game.

Mouse's pulse spiked, her heart pounding, making the blood rush into her ears. She held back spitting in his face because it would only make things worse, so much worse. When she'd done it last, he peeled off the flesh of her arm with a carving knife and she hadn't known if he would ever stop.

She'd once been strapped in a bed next to one of Rav's victims, privy to watch as he stripped away the vampire's flesh until there was nothing but bone. Then he broke the skeleton into pieces, saving the decapitation of the skull for last so the vampire could feel it all. Mouse could never get those screams out of her head—they haunted her every night in her prison cell.

The door opened and the click of heels sounded. Mouse curled in on herself, yanking at her bindings, but she was strapped down to Rav's laboratory table.

"She truly is quite exquisite for such a little thing," Imogen cooed as she leaned over Mouse, the queen's long, crimson hair spilling over one shoulder. "Perhaps I should keep her in a cage in our room. She can be our precious doll."

Terror coursed through Mouse's veins, panic sewing its way into her heart. Please no. *That would be so much worse than her secluded prison. Ferris couldn't sneak into Imogen's room, and Mouse wouldn't be able to hide Des or the drawings she kept beneath her mattress.*

"No, she would probably get too much pleasure in watching us fuck." Rav smirked, swiping a lock of his red-tipped, white hair behind his ear.

"That reminds me, come to bed when you're done. I want you to fuck my mouth." Imogen's gaze turned hungry and she cupped Rav's length over his trousers, her lips coming to his in a seductive kiss that made him groan. Mouse held back her nausea, staring up at the ceiling. The queen finally pulled away, peering back at Mouse. "But don't stop her lesson too soon."

Rav watched his queen as she swayed her hips, her black and red silk dress swishing behind her. He went and shut the door, then grabbed the chair from his desk, where stacks of paper with drawings of scientific torture designs were strewn across.

Settling into the seat, he placed his chin in his hands as he rested his elbows at the edge of her mattress. His hair brushed her arm and she clenched her teeth to fight the disgust stirring inside her.

Without a word, he studied her for a long while, as if she was his project. Which she supposed she was, as she had been, over and over again. The monster to his Frankenstein.

"You know how easy it was for me to fuck your sister?" Rav finally asked.

Not this again... *"You've told me."*

"Well, let me tell you again." Rav arched a brow, seeming to dare her to try and stop him. "After our very brief exchange, she let me fuck her. I didn't even have to use my influence on her. How pathetic." He paused, perking up in his chair while leaning closer to her. "Here's a secret you don't know. I studied the two of you in your mother's hat shop, deciding who I wanted to take to Wonderland. You were my first choice, but then I knew you wouldn't have been much fun, would've wanted me to court you until marriage before we fucked."

Mouse took a deep swallow, her past creeping in. Mr. Taylor. Him slamming her up against the library shelves, the books crashing to the floor.

"Ah, do you have a secret I don't know about, pretty mouse?" A wicked grin spread across his face. "Perhaps I'll find that out another time." He collected a large silver knife from the drawer of his desk and started sharpening it, the metal scraping metal echoing in the room. As he worked, he hummed a song Ever would sometimes play on her viola. "Dance Of The Sugar Plum Fairy." Except he hummed it darker, viciously.

"Now, let's begin." Halting the movements of his blade, he looked down at her before a sharp pain spread through her leg as he thrust the tip into her thigh.

Mouse jolted, her body shooting upward, the room spinning. A small cry escaped her mouth as a piercing ache traveled through the back of her head and up her spine. She couldn't stand, even though she could feel herself healing. Her breaths came out rapid, her chest heaving, as she searched for Rav. He wasn't there. She wasn't back in his horrific torturous palace. He and Imogen were both dead, and Mouse was in Red with Ferris.

Darkness cloaked Mouse, and even though she could see well without light, she still had to squint. Red sandstone walls surrounded her except for one where large boulders blocked her way out. Mouse's very real dream came back to her once more—her strapped down on the table... The Ruby Heart Palace where her prison cell bars prevented her from escaping...

Mouse's chest tightened and a scream built in her throat, sticking there when a scuffling stirred from the other side of the boulders. Her eyes widened, the dizziness fading, as hope filled her.

"Ferris!" she tried to shout, but it came out a rasp as if she hadn't drunk anything in a while, which she supposed she hadn't. But she didn't know how long it had been since she'd fed from the man in the forest.

"Thank fuck! I thought you were dead. It's been two days!" Ferris whisper-shouted. "Talk as quietly as you can, though—I don't know if the Jabberwocky is coming back. I've been trying to move these boulders ever since we fell down here."

Two days? "I can't stand yet," Mouse started. "Something in my back is broken, and I think I cracked my skull which may have been why I was passed out for so long. I need blood and we don't have our damn bags." Their backpacks with their blood provisions were still in the library... Her stomach let out a small growl, realizing the same thing.

"It's okay. Save your strength. I'm going to get you out today."

Mouse tried to stand again and a gasp escaped her mouth as agony shot through her spine. Rav's song from her dream played inside her mind and she couldn't get it to stop. The walls seemed to close in on her, the smell of Rav's room coming back to her, so she softly hummed a different song as she'd started to do in her prison cell. It was the only way to stop her from hearing the bastard's awful melodies, to push away the memories of what he'd done to her.

Hours passed and Mouse stopped humming. The only other noises that had accompanied her was Ferris grunting, cursing, and hitting things. She didn't think he'd slept at all.

Mouse's spine still wasn't fused. It was healing slower than it should've since she'd been without blood. Her stomach ached, *needing* to feed, but she thought of anything else to push the hunger aside. Maddie. Ever. Des. Home. *Ferris…*

As if hearing her thoughts, a loud clang reverberated from the other side of the boulders. "Ferris?" she said.

"I'm here," he answered in a gruff voice. "How are you doing, luv?"

As long as she continued to talk to him, not focusing on the fact that she was trapped or ravenous, she would tell herself she was fine. "I'm alive."

"Always a good sign." He chuckled.

Mouse closed her eyes, pretending she wasn't in the small space as she spoke to him. "I think you need to leave, save yourself. You don't know if or when the Jabberwocky is coming back."

"Do you really think I'm going to fucking leave you here? I left you behind once at the Ruby Heart Palace upon your request. I'm not doing it again," he said, finality in his voice.

"But if you're dead, I'll still be trapped anyway."

"Don't care. I'm not leaving."

"Stubborn male." She sighed, but her chest warmed at his words. "At least rest a bit. You're wasting strength."

"Not doing that either, luv." He slammed his weight against the boulders and dust rained down from the ceiling.

Bollocks. If her spine would hurry and heal, she could help

instead of feeling like a useless slug on the ground, covered in dust and debris. "So," she said. "Once we get this tedious step out of the way, what will we do next?"

"Well, we won't be able to climb out, I'll tell you that," he grumbled.

Mouse couldn't see the opening now, but she thought about the fall, how far down they'd gone, the smoothness of the walls. She would need a miracle to scale walls like that.

An ache thrummed in her stomach, clenching, her throat parched. She craved a drink, desperate for the taste of blood, *any* blood. Most vampires could go for much longer, but not her, not anymore. She remembered the donor building, the victims she'd slaughtered, how good they'd tasted, their warm blood sliding across her tongue. That was what she needed now—throats ripped apart so she could consume the liquid faster.

Stop! Mouse bit the inside of her cheek until it bled, just so she could taste her own blood. She needed a distraction—she needed to be able to *walk*.

Mouse thought about her and Ferris's time together earlier, his length in her mouth, his lips and tongue on her breast. Their fangs inside one another's flesh. This was what she needed, him with her. "Perhaps," she said slowly, "when we do find a way out and are safe, then we can finish where we left off?"

"Please don't make me fucking hard right now," Ferris growled, his voice deep, seductive.

She laughed softly. "I suppose we can do something different, then?"

"Oh, we will certainly be fucking," he drawled. "We deserve it after this shit, but we need to feed first."

"Feed first," Mouse agreed, her smile widening across her cheeks. But as she peered up at the ceiling, images of the Ruby Heart Palace came back in a rush and she closed her eyes, pretending she was out in the open, not trapped.

And then she hummed once more.

Mouse had fallen asleep at some point, and as she cracked open her eyes, she went to sit up, her spine not hurting any longer. She'd never healed this slow, not even when she was in the Ruby Heart Palace. But her spine had never been broken before. She'd had her neck snapped plenty of times, but even then, she'd healed in less than a day. Yet she'd never fallen this far before either.

As Mouse pushed up from the ground, hunger gnawed at her insides, coursing through her.

"Are you awake?" Ferris asked.

"Yes, and I can finally stand," Mouse whispered.

"Good, because I'm almost there." A scraping sounded, then a small opening appeared as he removed a stone. Mouse walked up to the space and found a dirty, sweat-stained Ferris grinning at her and her stomach dipped at the sight of him.

"Hello, luv." His grin widened further. "I bet you've been dying to see my pretty face, huh?"

"You have no idea." She inhaled his intoxicating scent and wanted to break the rock wall apart to get to him, to pierce her fangs into his flesh. Mouse tightened her fists, digging her nails into her palms to control her urges.

"Let me work on this one." He slipped his hand inside the hole, gripping the boulder, and pulled to create a thin slit.

"Move back," Mouse instructed. Gathering what strength she had, letting her hunger drive her, she lunged forward, shoving her body against the boulder, blowing it wide. Rocks collapsed behind her, but she didn't glance back.

She caught another whiff of Ferris as he stepped in front of her, stronger, alluring. The urge to *devour* him pulsed within her. Mouse's body moved of its own accord, no matter how loud she screamed at herself to not do it. Her fangs dropped and she barreled forward, knocking Ferris to the ground, burying her teeth deep into his throat.

CHAPTER FIFTEEN

FERRIS

Pain shot through Ferris when Mouse knocked him to the ground on the uneven rocks. His vision went black for a moment before the familiar sting of her bite tore into his neck. She buried her fangs in deeper, sucking brutally as she writhed on top of him.

"Mouse," he groaned, arching in to her touch, part pain, part pleasure.

Normally he would welcome the rough treatment, would let her have any control she damn well pleased, but he'd just spent days breaking down a fucking wall without a drop of blood to quench his thirst. Still, his cock responded. How could it not when she gyrated so skillfully against him, teasing him with a hint of what she could do if he were inside her. Circling her hips, sliding along the length of him. As though under her spell, he gripped her hips, tugging her tighter to him. She snarled as she drank from him. The softness of her lips on his flesh and the caress of her tongue pulled a possessive, animalistic sound from his throat.

"Mouse," he growled. As much as he wanted her, as much as he wanted to show her what it was like to be fucked with rawness, with tenderness, to give her what she wanted, *needed*, they had to stop. If she took too much, they'd be screwed. He would pass out and, with no way to replenish himself, they'd never make it out of this shit hole. And there was no telling if or when the Jabberwocky would come back. The bastard hadn't returned for days, so they had no idea if it was even in Red anymore. "Control yourself," he said gently, and reached up, placing a hand to her warm cheek.

She snarled again and clamped her jaw tighter, but slowed her drinking. No longer was she pulling more blood into her mouth, but simply enjoying what was already there. Her tongue slowly lapped up what had oozed from beneath her fangs, enticing him toward something *more*. And he was more than willing to oblige. One hand slid from her hips up to wrap her plait around his fist and his other trailing up her thigh, beneath her dress, reveling in the feel of her smooth skin. She drew in a deep mouthful of his blood and his breath caught.

"Damn, luv," he choked out. Her fingers met his, guiding them to her panties. As she released his hand, he skimmed his digits over the silken fabric, finding her aroused, *wet*. "Bring those beautiful lips of yours to mine."

"Touch me," Mouse whispered, her jaw loosening slightly. Her hips shifted over him, seeking friction. Ferris slipped his fingers beneath the fabric, brushing her bundle of nerves. Her breath caught as he pressed against her core and rubbed slow circles.

"Relax," Ferris urged, picking up his pace. He tightened his grip on her plait and her moan skated along his neck, her fangs gently scraping his skin as if she was fighting not to bury them back in. Her hips found a rhythm with him and he shifted to better feel her. His cock strained to be set free of his jeans. To be stroked and licked and fucked. To be inside her, to feel her heat, to make her scream his damn name.

"Ferris," Mouse begged, voice full of lust. Her tongue swiped the place she'd bit, but she didn't resume sucking his flesh, her attention moving to the other sensations.

"Come for me, luv," he rasped, adding more pressure, dipping two fingers into her heat.

Mouse cried out against him, hips jerking. Her fangs threatened to pierce him as she rode her orgasm out on his hand. Ferris lifted his groin up, desperate for more. When Mouse reeled back with a gasp, he released her hair. When it was safe, he would let her drink and drink from anywhere on his body, feed on him as much as she liked. But he *needed* her to be safe.

"You with me?" His voice was husky with desire, his gaze meeting her violet irises.

She stared back at him with wide eyes. "Ferris, I'm so sorry. I—"

"Hush." He leaned up on his elbows and captured her lips with his. He tasted his own blood on her mouth and hunger rumbled through him. It was important he feed soon, but first, he needed to sate his other appetite so he could focus on getting Mouse out of there and not how hard he was. His kisses grew harsher, his mind clouded by desire.

Mouse dragged her nails down his chest and fumbled with the zipper. When her hand wrapped around his length, he thrust into her touch. *Shit.* Her grip tightened and he was lost to the feel of her. Their lips coasted over one another, their tongues caressing, as she used long strokes up and down his cock, her thumb circling his pierced tip. His release built at the base, his balls tightening.

"Fuck, luv. You feel so good," Ferris growled against her mouth.

His release barreled through him as Mouse continued her perfect pace. "Bloody hell," he groaned. Stars burst behind his eyes. It felt like he came for ages before she let him go.

Muscles aching, he slowly tucked himself away and sat up. A trail of his blood still ran down Mouse's chin. He reached out and wiped it away with his thumb. Even in his wildest dreams, he never expected to experience this with Mouse. She'd drank from him so many times and, though it had turned him on, he'd never explored it with her. Only used his hand over and over again. Now, he wasn't sure how he'd ever resisted asking her if she would want more than blood.

"Are you all right?" His chest heaved.

Mouse nodded, her eyes filling with tears. "I'm a monster. I'm sorry."

"You're not. You were stuck behind a wall of rock for days, luv." Ferris pushed himself to his feet with a pained grunt. He helped her up and lifted her chin, leaning in close. "We both needed it to continue. Besides, I enjoyed it. I *like* it rough."

Mouse's cheeks pinkened. "Still, I shouldn't have attacked you like that."

His lips tilted up, giving her a soft smile. "We'll work on your control, yeah? But we should get the fuck out of here in case the Jabberwocky returns."

Mouse looked up at the broken floor above them and shivered. "Any idea how to do that?"

Ferris blew out a breath. He'd been so preoccupied with getting to Mouse that he hadn't bothered to search for an exit. Without Mouse, he hadn't planned on leaving, so breaking down the wall had been his only priority. It seemed they'd fallen into a cavern of sorts, though. Water dripped onto the newly-fallen debris from stalactites and the walls funneled to one passageway. The ceiling was too high to jump out, the walls smooth and slick, and there was nothing to climb.

"It looks like we only have one option," he said.

"Appears so," she agreed, squinting through the darkness. "Though it seems like a trap, if I say so myself."

Ferris brushed the hair from his face and shrugged. "Seems

to me like we already fell into the trap. If the Red Queen had planned to keep the Jabberwocky down here, she would need access to the beast, right?"

"Perhaps." Mouse picked her way around large fallen boulders toward the passage. "But perhaps not, if she wanted it to wither and die down here instead of train it."

Ferris followed behind Mouse, holding her steady as they crossed over the rocky ground. This all seemed fucking ridiculous if the dead queen only wanted to trap the beast. There was a nest and bones in the original lair which meant the royal cared somewhat. Either way, they needed to at least find where this path led.

They made their way into the dark tunnel and Ferris hoped it would take them to the others. In the Ruby Heart Palace, all the underground tunnels intersected at some point. There was no reason to think they wouldn't do the same here or at least offer an emergency escape. Though there was no reason to think they *would* either.

Keeping quiet, they walked straight ahead. Ferris cocked his head as they traveled down the tunnel, listening harder in case the Jabberwocky made a bloody unwanted return. There was no way in hell its massive body would fit down this pathway, but the beast had already proven itself capable of breaking down walls. Still, he wanted to be clear of this damn place.

"When we find a way out, we need to return to the library," Mouse said after they'd been walking for maybe fifteen minutes. There were no twists or turns to the tunnel. All the debris had given way to smooth stone floors with small puddles of water collected from the dripping ceiling.

"I don't know if we'll find anything there, luv," he admitted. If the Red Queen had gone through all the trouble of trying to capture the Jabberwocky a second time, then maybe she'd wanted to tame it since she didn't know how to kill it.

Mouse shrugged. "We should still check. Besides, our

backpacks are there and we need to drink blood."

"All right." There was nothing to lose by checking, but if he heard so much as a single growl or the beat of wings, they were heading straight for the portal at the edge of Ivory. He would tell Ever they didn't uncover a damn thing, admit their failure. The queen wouldn't give them a hard time as long as they both returned. She had originally planned on sending more vampires anyway. But if they didn't find answers on the Jabberwocky, an entire army might not be enough.

Pausing, Mouse sniffed the air. "Do you smell that?"

"What?" Ferris inhaled and was greeted with warmer, fresher air. His lips curled into a smile. "We're close to an exit."

Mouse sprinted ahead and he easily caught up to her. He scanned the slick walls for any hint of a door, but it was Mouse who saw it first. She skidded to a halt in front of him so fast that he nearly ran into her. Grabbing her waist to steady himself, he glanced over the top of her head.

The tunnel ended with a large grated door. On the other side, another few feet of tunnel stretched with hazy red sky beyond. Ferris slid past Mouse and grabbed onto the metal bars. He shook them and the sound echoed down the path behind them. There were no hinges to know which way it should swing open and the space between the bars was too small to fit between.

"I think it lifts up," Mouse said, pointing at the ceiling.

The rock had been carved out, the metal disappearing inside. Ferris adjusted his grip and pulled upward. The door creaked, tiny pebbles falling. But it was too damn heavy to gain enough space.

"I might need your help," he told Mouse. After days of breaking through a stone wall, then having Mouse feed from him, he wasn't exactly in top form at the moment.

She stepped beside him and latched on. Together, they picked it up inch by inch until there was just enough space for them to squeeze beneath. His muscles quaked under the weight of the gate, coupled with the hunger brewing inside himself, aching.

"Go!" Ferris urged. He couldn't hold the door forever and he wasn't sure she would be able to keep it up alone. But as long as she escaped, she could bring back reinforcements to get him out. If she knew that he was willing to stay behind, she'd never fucking leave—and she needed to be free.

Mouse let go, elongating her body as she rolled beneath the door, then grabbed onto the bars from the other side. "Come on," she said with a relieved smile.

"Can you hold it alone?"

Mouse's smile faded. "It's only for a moment."

If she couldn't hold it, he'd easily be crushed. Then he would be trapped there while she got help, a sitting duck for the Jabberwocky to devour. "Maybe you should go back to Ivory."

Mouse narrowed her eyes. "You didn't leave me and I'm not leaving you. Trust me to hold it long enough. I can do it."

The shaking in Ferris's arms increased and for the first time in a long time, he doubted himself. He never once doubted himself while he was with her in the Ruby Heart Palace, not when they were in the safe house after Mouse's escape, and not even when he was removing the boulders to get to her. But she looked so sure of herself. *Fuck.* He needed to feed and he couldn't hold this piece of shit thing forever. "On the count of three," he said. "One…"

Mouse widened her stance. "Two."

"Three." Ferris used every ounce of his vampire speed to slide under the door.

The sound of Mouse's strained grunt as he passed beneath the heavy metal made his breath catch. But he shoved himself to his feet before it slammed shut. Mouse jumped away from the door, covering her mouth with her hands.

"Bloody hell." Ferris sucked in deep breaths, chest

heaving. If the gate had fallen on him, fuck being trapped, he would've been cut in two. "Now I expect you to help save my arse every time." He chuckled softly as he drew her to him, kissing her temple.

Mouse leaned into him for a moment. "I told you I could do it."

"You sure as fuck did." He set his chin on top of her head and willed his heart to slow. There wasn't enough blood in his veins for it to race like this. He had control of himself for now, but he didn't want to test it either. Mouse had been through too much with Rav and Imogen for him to blindside her with a bite. "We need our bags."

CHAPTER SIXTEEN

MOUSE

Hunger clawed within Mouse but not like it had before she'd drank from Ferris. Back in the alley at the club, she'd *almost* lost control with him. This time she had. It was something she could never let happen again, yet part of her had known to drink from him slowly, savoring his taste, instead of ripping apart his throat.

As they entered the palace through a large hole in the castle wall's side, Ferris's eyelids fluttered. There was no sign of the Jabberwocky or any other danger for that matter. A good thing. But if the beast returned, Mouse would have to do her best to carry Ferris—she didn't think he could make it much farther.

They traveled down several crumbling hallways, then to one with shattered glass littering the floor that opened to the main entrance of the castle. Mouse wrapped her arm around Ferris's waist, searching for a place to hide. *Aha!* A small crevice rested beneath the stairs, the perfect place for Ferris to remain out of view in case danger struck again.

Ferris had saved Mouse, pulling her back from the brink of madness, had touched her in a way that made her see stars. It was more than a distraction from feeding on Ferris, more than him just trying to help her.

She guided him to the stairs and found his gaze trained on her neck, the tip of his tongue sweeping across his lower lip. If Ferris didn't feed soon, he would attack her, the same way she'd done to him. Any other time, Mouse would hold out her wrist, but if she gave him what he wanted in that moment, the monster within her could rise once more. And this time she might not be able to hold back from tearing out his throat. If she did, life wouldn't exist for her any longer.

"Wait under the stairs," Mouse whispered. "I'll collect our backpacks, then we'll drink and get cleaned up at the lake before searching the library." They were both covered in sweat, blood, and grime, and they needed to make certain the Jabberwocky couldn't sniff them out as easily if it did return.

"No," Ferris swayed, his gaze never leaving her throat. "I'll grab them. You shouldn't have to go into the library by yourself."

"I'm fine and can do it quicker." Mouse held both his arms, steadying him as she brought him to a sitting position beneath the stairs. He was too weak to argue with her about it. "Save your strength or we may murder each other, and neither of us wants that now, do we?"

"You smell so fucking good," Ferris slurred, his fangs lowering. He shook his head, sobering himself. "Go and be careful."

Mouse was hesitant to leave him, but she nodded and raced up the staircase, not wanting to waste a drop of any more time. Her movements stayed quiet, her feet barely touching the floor as she used what energy she had left for her enhanced speed. When she came across the library doors, her stomach sank. Pushing away the anxious feeling, she snatched their backpacks and left.

Heart pounding, she stormed to the main entrance just as fast, wishing for the Jabberwocky not to show its monstrous face.

It had only taken her a few seconds to reach Ferris, yet it seemed like an eternity passed. His skin was paler, perspiration dotted his brow, and he clenched his stomach as his breaths came out ragged.

"Hold it together for a little longer," she said quickly, unzipping his backpack first to fish out both his canteens of water.

"I've never been this damn hungry before," he rasped. "I've gone much longer without feeding."

"You've also never worked yourself like this." She opened a pouch of powdered blood and poured it into one of the canteens. As the delicious metal smell struck her nose, she held her breath or else she would pour the powder directly into her mouth. She wouldn't care about the chalkier taste or how much harder it was to swallow—she *craved* it.

Steady, Mouse.

She slowly inhaled as she shook the canteen to mix the powder and water.

"You drink first," Ferris demanded, even though he looked half dead.

"No." She shoved the bottle into his hand.

"Stubborn vampire." He smirked but put the mixture to his lips, growling as he drank, deep and lusty.

Taking a swallow to push away her burning desire, she took the other canteen and poured in the powder. The liquid was warm when it hit her tastebuds, a moan escaping her mouth while the blood slid down her throat, strengthening everything inside of her. Her tiredness dissipated, the hunger lessening.

"Let's drink another," Ferris said, appearing more like himself, his eyelids no longer fluttering and his voice steady. "Just in case we run into some shit again."

"Smart idea." Mouse fixed them both a drink in the last two canteens from her bag, then they finished them off. Only a tiny hint of hunger buried itself in her stomach, and she hadn't felt this full in a while, but with Ferris's blood pulsing in her veins along with the provisions, it should hopefully hold her over for a bit.

"Let's hurry to the lake while the coast is clear." Ferris crawled out from beneath the stairs and rose to his full height. He helped her up and led her to the front door, where he peered out, then waved her to follow. "No sign of the beast."

Her shoulders relaxed and she walked out the door beside him. A light breeze rustled the hem of her dress and the sky was darkening, the half-moon high up in its depths. Above the castle, a large bat flapped its wings while gliding through the air.

As they passed barren trees and the deteriorating statues, Mouse listened for any sign of the Jabberwocky, the crack of its leather wings, or the pounding of its heavy footsteps. But nothing sounded. She prayed the creature wasn't back in Ivory or Scarlet either. If it were in werewolf territory, that would be a dream come true. It could feed on those awful creatures forever.

A dead garden came into view, not a single leaf bloomed from any of the bushes, and they skirted around it. It would take a lot of work to revive this territory, but the potential was there, especially when they rounded the castle to the back. Her gaze settled on a low decorative stone wall that ran around the edge of a glistening crystal-clear lake, forming a walking path along it. Tall trees that weren't completely barren sprouted a few deep purple flowers.

"This area doesn't seem so bad," Ferris said, kneeling in front of the lake to fill up his canteens.

Mouse mirrored his movements with her two, then placed the bottles in her backpack. She zipped up her bag and stood, finding Ferris's gaze trained on her, his dark irises shining.

"Turn around so I can undress," she said softly.

Ferris arched a brow and smirked.

"What?" Mouse placed her hands on her hips.

"You do realize you've seen me naked more than once now, and I've seen you pretty damn close to being so." That deep voice of his pulled at her, making her skin tingle.

Again, the way he'd touched her came to mind, that rush of heat spreading through her veins. But they needed to get cleaned up and hurry back inside the castle. Even though the Jabberwocky had been inside, it was still safer than milling around out in the open.

"Well," she drawled. "Then you can wait until later to see me fully. Now, turn around."

"Until then." He smiled seductively, facing the opposite direction as she took out a black dress from her pack.

Mouse glanced at Ferris's back, her gaze drifting to his buttocks, the way his tight jeans hugged the curve of it, how they showed off his muscular legs. As butterflies swarmed in her stomach, she pulled off her dirt-covered dress and kicked her boots away before slipping naked into the warm water.

"All right, come on," she called, unraveling her plait.

Ferris turned around, his dark gaze studying her as he crossed his arms.

Mouse tilted her head to the side. "What?"

He lifted a finger and slowly spun it in a circle, that perfect digit which had brought her to bliss so easily. "Now, *you* look away, luv."

Fighting a smile, she rolled her eyes and did just that. Even though she couldn't see him, she couldn't stop listening to his every movement, the way his clothing rustled as he peeled them from his body, how the water sloshed against his flesh when he moved through it, *toward her*.

"You can look at me now," Ferris said, his voice gruff.

A blush crept up her face as she found his hair already wet, the beads of water glistening against his strong arms and broad chest.

Neither spoke as they scrubbed the dirt from their bodies, but her gaze continued to drift toward him as if he were her beacon. Smiling to herself, she glanced toward the castle where a pristine balcony rested. Not a single crack or missing piece marred the stone. A trellis woven with dead vines hung beside it, reminding her of the balcony in *Romeo and Juliet*, and how Shakespeare had written the scene so splendidly.

"Are you thinking about Shakespeare?" Ferris asked, running his hands through his wet hair, his lips tilted to one side.

"How did you know?"

"You have that look when you read his plays or talk about him. Should I be jealous?" His grin widened.

"Hmm." She pretended to mull it over. "If the master of plays were alive today, you might have a bit of competition there. He does have a way with words," she teased.

Before she knew what was happening, Ferris's hands were around her waist and her legs circled his hips. "I can have a way with words," he purred in her ear.

"You really like getting me in this position, don't you?" she said, pressing herself into him.

"I do." He tightened his grip on her, somehow bringing her even closer, her softness pressing into his hardness. "And didn't I say we would fuck after we fed?"

As she parted her lips to give into temptation, a roar tore through the air, followed by the cry and howl of a werewolf in the distance. The Jabberwocky must've found a meal...

"Maybe not this second though," Ferris growled, carrying her out of the lake and placing her on her feet.

Mouse shoved on her clothing and boots, not worrying about plaiting her hair. At least the Jabberwocky was taking care of a rogue werewolf so they wouldn't have to use loud bullets again.

Snatching their backpacks, they bolted for the castle,

keeping as close to the trees as possible. Once inside, they darted up the stairs and down the hall toward the library. Her heart slammed against her rib cage, her chest heaving as they reached the room. She bit her lip, staring at the doors of the library for a moment before deciding on shutting and locking them. With the doors closed, it would give them a little more time to hide if they had to.

"You don't have to shut them," Ferris said gently.

To give them more time wasn't the only reason she'd done it. Mouse also needed to face her fears, and perhaps it was being trapped behind the boulders that had done it, or knowing that while being with Ferris, he would always try to get her away from danger. Either way, she now knew she could survive inside a room with the doors shut. They'd been wide open when she'd first left the Ruby Heart Palace, then cracked, and now this was the final step. As for the library, it wasn't the same one where she'd been hurt—these weren't the same books that had surrounded her, and this man … this man was nothing like the one who had broken her. She grasped the strength within her, taking even breaths. "I'm all right. I have you with me in here and I trust you, Ferris."

"I trust you too, luv."

But then she remembered how she'd attacked him, which was more recent—one memory that wouldn't easily go away. "Maybe you shouldn't," she murmured. "I'm still unpredictable."

He cocked his head and blinked at her as if she were mad. "Do you feel like you want to attack me now?"

"No," she said slowly.

"Maybe you should." He took a step toward her, pushing a lock of wet hair behind her ear. "It led to good things, didn't it?"

"Ferris!"

"Shh!" He put his finger over his lips while smiling. "This conversation is over. We have work to do."

Mouse rolled her eyes but couldn't stop grinning as she pored over the spines of decaying books. She didn't know if the queen, king, or both of them had read the tomes, but most were mundane and about building things. A bright blue spine caught her attention with the words *Beast of Wonderland* written on it in gold cursive. She wiped the dust from the cover and flipped through the yellowed pages of the thin book, filled with mostly drawn pictures of the Jabberwocky. Badly, she might add. Her finger followed the lines as she read over a few facts about the creature. The beast had first been spotted in Wonderland centuries ago and was the only one of its kind. It had been caught once by the royals, but was untrainable, even when provided vampires or humans to eat. The Red Queen wanted to use the Jabberwocky against other territories, but the attempt had failed.

So, the Red Queen had truly caught it once then…

"It doesn't make a lick of sense." Mouse wrinkled her nose, showing him the page. "How can the Jabberwocky be the only one? It still had to be born from somewhere, right?"

Ferris shrugged. "Scotland has the Loch Ness Monster. The States have Bigfoot. And Wonderland has the Jabberwocky."

"The what?" She frowned, not understanding what in the world he was talking about.

"Right. You're *older* than me." He smirked. "And you haven't hung around the mortal world enough to hear about those cryptids. But I guess the Jabberwocky wouldn't be considered one anyway since it's proven to be real."

"Our next quest when this is over will be for you to teach me about what a cryptid is," she pointed out, smiling to herself as she returned to scan through the remaining pages. "Bollocks, there's nothing useful in here!"

Mouse went to slide the book back on the shelf, but then the urge to make the row even nagged at her. One of the tomes at the edge of the row continued to stick out a centimeter and she shoved it in when a click sounded. Scowling, she pulled out a stack of books and found what looked to be a small silver key inserted into the inner wall shelf. The metal was about the size of her fingernail and matched something on the back of a wind-up toy.

"There's something here." She beamed, brushing her fingertips against the metal and cranking it to the right.

A grinding noise filtered into the room and the shelf shook, the tomes rattling. Mouse took a step back, the bookshelf opening toward them like a door. Her eyes widened as she met Ferris's gaze.

He rubbed the back of his neck, a satisfied smile on his face. "Let's hope we just struck fucking gold."

CHAPTER SEVENTEEN

FERRIS

Darkness swallowed Ferris and Mouse. The secret door only spilled light into the passageway for so long before they had to rely on their vampiric eyesight. Cobwebs hung down from a white ceiling, crisscrossing along their path. Deep green and gold foil wallpaper lined the walls and a matching carpet softened their footsteps.

"How far do you think this goes?" Mouse asked when they'd been walking for nearly three minutes.

It was impossible to tell which direction they were going anymore—if the floor slanted up or down, made gradual shifts to the right or left. The outline of the door leading back into the library had vanished from view. For a moment, he found himself eager to make it to the other end—not because he was afraid, but because exploring the palace was becoming more like a treasure hunt by the hour. "That's a very good question."

Mouse thought for a moment, sweeping away cobwebs from where they looped across their path. "It almost feels like we're going to the pits of Hell…" She wiggled her fingers in the air and smiled.

"Except without fire." He grinned, plucking another web from her hair. Nothing had ventured down this hallway in ages, judging by the amount of strands weaving across the passageway.

She paused and stepped back from a particularly thick cluster. "I hope there are no living spiders in there."

Ferris chuckled. "You have a caterpillar at home and you're afraid of some spiders?"

"There aren't any spiders—these webs are old." She poked him playfully in the side. "But don't compare Des to them. She doesn't leave a clingy mess behind."

"Sure, luv. I'll go first," he said, laughing again. "Come on."

Ferris entered into a large sitting room and took in six glass cases full of strange objects resting on velvet pillows. One wall held shelves and, on them, what looked to be journals bound with strips of leather. In the middle of everything was a round table between two red armchairs. He paused just inside, Mouse right on his heels, and scanned for threats.

"Seems safe enough," he said. "No skeletons either, which is always nice."

Mouse stepped in front of him and reached up onto her toes. "Let me."

She gathered dusty cobwebs from his face and hair with featherlight touches. He drew in a deep breath, remembering her naked in the lake. Pressed against him. Her soft skin brushing along his. *Shit.* Now was *not* the time for his mind to take a side trip into the gutter, but he couldn't help it. Not when her hands ran down his chest, collecting more webs from him. He wanted to touch her too, wipe her clean … then make her dirty again.

Mouse looked up at him with a coy smile as if she knew exactly what he was thinking. "There you go. Handsome as ever."

"I'm glad you approve," Ferris said in a husky voice and placed a kiss on her forehead. "Now, let's see what goodies we can find." He rubbed his hands together and waggled his eyebrows at her.

Mouse spun around to face the room and gasped. "This looks fun."

Soft, glowing yellow lights flickered to life when they stepped farther into the room. Ferris tugged Mouse back in case they'd triggered a trap. Imogen had them in the Ruby Heart Palace, strategically placed anywhere she didn't want prying eyes. Orbs floated near the ceiling, circling each other and spanning out again to create simple swirling patterns. Shadows danced along the walls from the light but nothing else stirred. No trap doors opened and no arrows soared toward them.

"What is this?" Mouse asked in awe. She lifted a hand toward them, too short to reach, and wiggled her fingers in their light.

"Hell if I know. Let's see what the rest of this shit is." Ferris walked forward carefully in case anything more than orbs appeared, but when he made it to the table unscathed, he released a breath.

Mouse moved around the perimeter of the room, fingers skimming the thick wallpaper. "I wouldn't exactly call this *shit*."

Ferris followed her gaze to the middle display case. Inside was a wide belt inlaid with dozens of gem stones. Large and small. Marquee cut, square, round, pear, princess, all of them gleaming as if the sun were shining brightly overhead. "It's strange," he said quietly.

Mouse inched closer and set her hands on the glass, her lips parting. "It's … humming."

"Even fucking stranger," he said, stepping back. The last thing they needed was to set off a trap. Everything in here was undoubtedly worth a fortune—otherwise, why hide it? A secret door that any vampire could've stumbled upon wasn't likely to be the only security measure in place.

"What do you think this one is?"

Ferris scowled when she ran a finger over the next glass box. Folded red fabric took up a majority of the top shelf. Gold trimmed the edges and a large medallion clasp held the neck together. An overcoat of some kind, he guessed. But it was more than that. The air around the display was thicker, heavier, and scratched against his skin. It didn't hurt but was definitely an uncomfortable sensation. Iron bars surrounded the seams of the glass with engravings in an unknown language. Three pearls were nestled beside it—one blue, one pink, one white. The next shelf contained a golden hourglass encrusted with rubies.

"Oh, a dagger!" Mouse had shifted to the smaller display at the end while he was distracted by the mystery object. "This is what I imagine the dagger would look like that Juliet takes from Romeo to end her life."

Ferris joined her, partially to be near her, to make sure it wasn't rigged against would-be thieves. It *was* a beautiful blade. The point appeared razor sharp, the edges expertly tapered. Halfway up the top of it was harsh serrated edges and a floral design etched along the center. The hilt was gold, inlaid with diamonds and emeralds, scrollwork snaking around it. At the base, the gold flared out into a flower. Another large emerald sat at the center.

"Unless you think it can kill the beast, let's keep looking," he said.

Mouse tsked. "You're no fun."

"Am I not?" He raised a brow. "I'm fairly certain you were singing a different tune when we—"

"We should rest," she said quickly, her cheeks turning pink. "I think it's safe enough in here."

Ferris glanced around the room for any potential triggers

he might've missed—a plank that didn't settle right or an item perfectly out of place. Nothing set off alarm bells. "Let's finish looking around first."

"Ferris," Mouse chided. "You spent days breaking down rocks to free me. Sleep so you can think more clearly."

He reached out and lifted a strand of her pink hair, admiring how soft it was. "I would gladly suffer sleepless years, bloodying my hands, to protect you. You should know that by now."

"I do know." Her breath hitched when he let her hair fall back to her shoulder and traced a line over her neck. "And you should know that I would do the same for you. I'll settle for making you rest though."

He gave her a soft smile. "I'm not sure I'd be able to sleep yet. My mind is too busy."

"Oh?" Mouse bit her bottom lip. "Maybe I can help with that."

Mouse stood on her toes and pressed her lips to his. He slid his hands into her hair and tilted her head back to gain better access. She tasted sweet with the faint hint of blood. His hunger was sated with the powdered drink, but he wanted to taste her. To drink *her*. But neither of them were strong enough for that at the moment.

Her tongue slipped between his lips and Ferris's grip tightened in her hair as he thrust his tongue to meet hers. She tasted like bliss—*his* bliss—and he needed more. He fucked her mouth with his tongue, wishing it was his cock. But he couldn't pull himself away long enough to see if she would drop to her knees for him. Her lips were too delicious, too soft, but he needed *more*. Mouse tilted her chin, forcing his kisses to skate down her neck instead.

"Should we be doing this right now?" he asked against her skin. Everyone was counting on them back in Ivory.

"Probably not," she breathed. "You're not going to be able to help them if you don't rest though."

"And this will help my mind turn off," he agreed. It usually worked when he managed the task alone.

His fangs dropped and he dragged them gently over her skin, eliciting a moan. The sound went straight to his cock, making it hard as fuck. She'd gotten him off when she'd fed from him after being trapped in the cave, but he was nearly desperate with the need to feel her touch again. His hands shook as they drifted from her hair to slide the collar of her dress down.

Mouse inhaled, pressing her chest toward him while he kissed his way across her bare shoulders. "Ferris," she breathed.

"Yes, luv?" He trailed his tongue slowly along her collarbone, hoping to drive her just as mad as him. When he nipped gently at the upper swells of her breasts, she drew her bodice down to expose her peaked nipples. He grinned at her. "So impatient."

"Just making up for the lost time we should've been doing this," she said as desire flickered in her eyes. "Besides, I can lose a little sleep so let's not wait any longer."

Ferris chuckled. "I'm going to teach you the perks of delayed gratification."

"Ferris," she warned. Her hand fell to his, and she guided it up her stomach, ever so slowly until she enfolded it around her breast. "Make me feel good."

Ferris gripped her chin with his free hand, his gaze trained on hers. "Your orgasms are mine now."

"Are they now?" she asked with a wide smile.

Ferris leaned in and sucked her bottom lip between his teeth, careful not to draw any blood. When he released her, he trailed kisses along her jaw to her ear, then whispered, "I want you to touch yourself in front of me, the way I did for you."

Mouse shivered from his words, her heart thrumming with what had to be the same lust that matched his. Playful defiance shimmered in Mouse's eyes as she took a step back. She peeled the dress from her hips, taking her panties down with it, until the fabric pooled at her feet. His pulse thundered as he raked over every glorious inch of her naked body. The curves that led to her perfect arse, the soft swell of her beautiful breasts. Her arousal filled the air and he clenched his fists at his sides to keep himself from going to her, from taking her into his mouth right then.

"I've never touched myself in front of anyone before," Mouse whispered. She looked hesitant at first, and he was about to tell her she didn't have to when she dragged a hand up her abdomen to cup her breast. Her thumb grazed the tight nipple as she backed up, maneuvering around a display case, toward the red armchair. She sank down onto the cushion with hooded eyes. Her free hand wasted no time skimming between her thighs, finding its target.

Spreading her legs wide, Ferris got an unobstructed view of her gleaming core. His hands balled into fists in an effort not to reach out and touch her himself. She was so damn sexy. Every inch of her.

Mouse slid her fingers between her folds. Up and down, teasing herself. Then she pressed against her clit and arched into her own touch. Ferris groaned, moving toward her, desperately wanting his tongue everywhere she was touching. She circled the bundle of nerves with measured strokes before dipping the same digit inside. His cock throbbed and he stalked around the display case.

"Enough," Ferris growled.

He knelt in front of her, threw her legs over his shoulders, and stood. She gave that sexy squeak of hers, and her ankles locked around him, pressing between his shoulder blades, as her hips shifted toward his face. He walked them three steps to the wall and held her against it.

Gripping her thighs, he looked up at her. "I want to taste you so fucking badly."

"Then why aren't you?" Her fingers tangled with his hair,

guiding him to her and that was the only push he needed.

They both groaned when he ran his tongue along her slit. Her sweet flavor was better than any blood he'd ever tasted. He didn't know how he'd survived so long without feasting on her. Closing his lips over her, he sucked her clit into his mouth and swirled his tongue over it, drinking in her sweet flavor like it was fine wine. Again and again and again as she ground against his face. He fucking loved it, loved that this vampire could make him so wild with desire just from the sound of her gasping as he pleasured her. He wanted her for the rest of his fucking life.

His tongue slipped away from her clit and drifted downward. Her body quaked, and his name came out as a breath from her lips when her orgasm shattered. Ferris grinned against her core while she continued to writhe against his face, his fingers digging into her thighs.

When her grip on his hair relaxed, he gave one more lick, to taste the remainder of her arousal. Her legs relaxed and Ferris shifted away from Mouse to help her down. She brought her left leg over his shoulder at the same time he moved her right. Mouse slid sideways with a gasp, grabbing an elaborate picture frame to steady herself. Ferris pressed her against the wall again to stop her fall, the lengths of their bodies pressed together.

He chuckled into her neck. "Sorry about that, luv."

His own arousal met her wet center through his trousers and he moaned. But he didn't want to take from her. He *did*, but he also enjoyed giving with nothing in return. So he backed away, setting her gently on her feet.

"Am I still no fun?" he asked, his voice low.

Mouse smiled. "You're almost as fun as I can be."

She stepped toward him, eyes trained on the bulge in his trousers, when the picture she'd fallen into slipped from its hook. Ferris lunged for it, knocking it out of the way before it crashed into Mouse's head. It smashed into the nearest glass case and a small crack skated across the surface.

"Ferris?"

He looked up to see what had Mouse's voice sounding so curious. A large hole had been bashed through the wall. Jagged edges of stone and bricks hung around the opening where the ripped wallpaper frayed.

"Well, fuck me." Ferris squinted into the dark hole, seeing nothing but stone walls. "This place is full of surprises."

CHAPTER EIGHTEEN

MOUSE

Mouse's chest heaved as she stared at the peeled green and gold wallpaper, the opening in the center, not knowing where it would lead next. She drew on her clothing and Ferris helped her fasten the buttons of her dress. His fingers fumbled on one as exhaustion swirled in his gaze. He'd been through so much in a single day, *days*, long ones where he hadn't even slept as he fought to save her from behind the boulders.

"Thank you," Mouse said softly as he buttoned the last one. They smiled at one another and she stepped around him to peer inside the hole within the wall. Heavy darkness cloaked what looked to be another tunnel, and she let her eyes adjust to the dull black brick surrounding the space. The end seemed to curve, leading to the unknown. She had no idea how far it would go or if it would take them anywhere worthwhile.

"It's a tunnel," Mouse finally said, stepping back so Ferris could take a look. "How about we check it out first thing in the morning? You've had practically zero sleep in days and we

"

don't know where it will even take us." Besides that, she needed to recover for a moment, catch her breath, not only from everything she'd been through the past few days, the past few *years*, but from Ferris giving her the release she'd needed. She'd never thought she would be so bold as to touch herself in front of another. But she trusted Ferris, trusted him with her life.

He pressed his hands to the wallpaper and scanned the area. His rosewood scent enveloped Mouse as he inched closer to her, and her gaze naturally took in the hard muscles of his arms, the tight trousers hugging his buttocks.

Ferris furrowed his brow as he moved backward. "Are you sure? This might be the final place to search before we return to Ivory."

In reality, she wasn't certain if they should take a break to rest because the Jabberwocky had ventured to Ivory twice recently, yet they knew the beast still lingered in Red from when they'd rinsed themselves in the lake. She didn't know if the beast would go back any time soon or continue to terrorize the rogue werewolves here. But Ferris really needed to recover or he wouldn't be good to anyone.

"Yes, we will rest," Mouse started. "And I agree about us leaving after this. We've found a whole lot of nothing on the Jabberwocky so far, but we've also discovered other things." She closed the door to the room and locked it in case anything tried to come for them from the secret passage.

Ferris arched a brow, a smirk on his face. "The king's fingers in the bag? Is that our prize to take home?"

"I think Chess would be the most amused to learn that the queen saved his bones after feeding the rest of him to the Jabberwocky." Mouse grinned. She settled on the stone floor, resting her back against the wall, and patted the spot next to her. "Besides that, there are these treasures here that Ever and Maddie can examine to see if they might mean anything."

Ferris tossed his backpack beside her and used it as a

pillow while turning to face her. "Unless the dagger can be used to penetrate the Jabberwocky's flesh, then they're just some old relics." He placed a palm on her thigh and butterflies stormed in her stomach at his touch. Mouse thought about the way his tongue had trailed up her center, how he'd used it with such perfect precision as if he was drawing the night sky and all its constellations with it.

She ran her fingers through his hair while looking at the different items they'd rifled through. The belt, the key, the hourglass, the pearls, and much more. It was strange. They looked like nothing she'd ever seen in Wonderland or the mortal world. Most of these things seemed to have come from a storybook. Wonderland had swords and daggers, but nothing of this nature as if they held some sort of power.

"Perhaps the weapons can. We should take a few," Mouse said, staring at the dagger in the glass case, then at the collection of the others near a dusty iron sword on the wall. Even if they couldn't harm the Jabberwocky, she wanted to take them home to show Ever and Maddie. "Ferris?" She looked down at him when he didn't answer her, but his eyes were shut, his lips parted as he slept, his breaths even.

Mouse smiled softly, trailing her fingers from his hair down his face, to his plump lips, the curve of his neck, stopping as her digits brushed the metal chain. The necklace he never took off. She drew it from beneath his shirt and studied the ring that she now knew to be a promise to Ellie. Mouse wondered what she'd looked like, what Ferris would be doing now if she'd lived, if their baby had lived. Her chest tightened, not because she was envious of this ring, or his former love, but because of what it had meant. He would've been a wonderful father, would've had a different life. She could see him teaching his daughter how to play drums, teasing her, tossing her in the air then catching her as she giggled. But that life was gone, just as her old one was. And even though centuries had passed, she thought about what would've happened to her if Mr. Taylor had never ripped away her virginity. Would she have still discovered Maddie had been watching her? Would she have chosen to become a vampire? Leave the mortal world? There was no point in wondering because both of their lives had taken a different path, one where their worlds collided, her heart pulling toward his.

Tiredness no longer lingered within her, her mind spinning with too many thoughts. Perhaps because she'd slept for days.

Mouse tucked the ring back beneath Ferris's shirt, then stood and walked to the glass cases. She used her strength to break the seal on the first case and collected the dagger, along with the others resting on the shelf by the sword, then placed them inside her backpack except for one. A clear blade that looked as if it was made of glass, but it wasn't precisely that. It seemed to hum against her hand and she held it up to the light illuminating from the orbs. The glass reflected in a way she'd never seen before. A strange inscription in an unknown language was written on the handle.

"Where were you created?" she murmured.

Mouse looked toward the hole in the wall. Her thoughts turned to her sister, Ever, Des, Noah, and Chess. Even to Mock who had lost Didi. She wondered what they would do if they were here now, if they would explore the new tunnel or try to force themselves to rest. So far, nothing too dangerous was found in this hidden area, but Ferris wouldn't approve of her going alone. She glanced at him, watching his chest slowly rise and fall—she didn't want to disturb him.

Curiosity nagged at her and she chewed her lip as she weighed the choices. She would be quick. The door was locked, protecting Ferris, and if she heard anything she would run straight back to him. Mouse slid the dagger into the belt loop of her dress, then grabbed the gun from her bag. Ducking her head, she stepped through the splintered wood of the wall and entered the dark tunnel. A musty odor invaded her nostrils, heavier than in the previous room. Only a few cracks marred the faded stone of the walls.

The hallway led her down a curving path that turned into another room. Her heart pounded as she took in the circular area where six dark concrete coffins stood upright. Sets of three lined the walls across from each other, and if she were to step inside, they were tall enough to house two of her.

In the center of the wall between the two sets stood a door, this one looked to be heavy steel with multiple locks running up its length. The Red Queen and all her secret doors. But Mouse knew she was getting closer to something, a giddiness filling her.

When she'd been to the Red Palace last with Maddie and March for their tea party, she now wished they had thoroughly searched the palace. But even then, it was fate that had led her and Ferris to this secret place. Perhaps no one had believed the library would hide things of value since the jewels hadn't been kept there.

Tucking the gun at her waist, Mouse gripped the lid of a coffin and slid it to the side. The scraping sound echoed off the walls. She blinked at what rested inside, expecting to possibly find something useful. Instead, iron chains coiled within the empty space. One by one, she opened the five other coffins, discovering only chains and nothing useful, and a disappointed sigh escaped her.

Perhaps the Red Queen had brought vampires down there and placed them into the coffins, but why? From what she knew, the Red Queen would just murder them and hang their pieces in the forest. But maybe she had done what Rav and Imogen had done to her—punish them to get answers.

Mouse's heart thundered, pushing away memories of the Ruby Heart Palace attempting to surface. She focused her attention on the bolted-up door, her fingers itching to unlock it. Mouse pressed her ear to the cool steel, but nothing stirred from within. She started at the top, undoing each bolt with a grinding click. As soon as she released the last one, she leaned into the steel door with her shoulder and shoved it open, inch by inch. A new smell wafted out—decay, sickness. Nausea swirled in her stomach and she clutched it, hoping to not expel the contents from her last meal.

Mouse had come too far to stop now, and she took a tentative step into the room, then halted. Bones littered the floor, no two pieces still connected. Her gaze settled on part of a skull, the jaw ripped off and vampire fangs protruding. But then she found something else that made her suck in a sharp breath. These weren't normal vampires. *Wings* and claws curved from their fingers were scattered about. Thousands of scratch marks marred the black walls, along with deep gouges and small holes.

Bollocks, these were the *ancients*. Wonderland originally had six who'd wreaked havoc long, long ago. Well before Ever, Rav, and Imogen had ever stepped foot here. Older than even the Jabberwocky. It was believed they had vanished, but the Red Queen must've contained them here. For what purpose? But deep down, Mouse knew, it was to bend them to her will. The Red Queen had been one of the first to ever be turned and survive them.

The tales claimed that their blood ran black, their hearts of the same color, and that was why they had created other vampires, so they could feast on them whenever they chose. And it looked as though they had certainly had to feast on each other here.

But…

She held her breath, counting the skulls, and frowned. There were only five…

A rustling came from above and she didn't release her breath as she slowly glanced upward, her eyes widening. A single naked male form hung along an iron rafter from a domed ceiling. His alabaster skin was stark against the dark stone, his wings leather and obsidian. The vampire's bones jutted out, his stomach sunken, and his flesh tight against his frail form as if it could tear away at any moment. He stared down at her with golden eyes, deep crimson hair hanging in greasy clumps around his head. The vampire cocked his head and cracked his massive wings, hunger swirling in his gaze, his long black tongue licking his thin lips.

Mouse gasped, pulling herself from her staring spell. She bolted out the door, putting her weight against the steel to shut it. Her hands trembled, making her fingers fumble as she reached for the locks. Before she could slide the bolt in on the first one, the vampire rammed its body against the door, knocking her to the floor. The gun fell from her hand, skidding across the floor. And she cursed herself for not shooting at him inside the room.

She pushed up, lunging for her weapon, and snapped it up. But the vampire was already there, shoving her back to the floor. His claws dug into her flesh as he flipped her over, her fear spiking when he pinned her to the floor, trapping her. A reeking smell, like death and body odor, invaded her senses. "Ferris!" she screamed. "Run!"

The ancient vampire snarled, gnashing his sharp teeth at her. He then bent toward her neck, sniffing up her skin, speaking in an old language she didn't know. Her fangs dropped, her body writhing as she continued to scream to get this thing off of her.

Heavy footsteps pounded and the creature jerked back, hissing, giving Mouse enough time to pull the trigger at the ancient's heart. The loud shot pierced her ears, yet the ancient barely moved backward, the bullet unable to knock it out as it would any other vampire. He smacked the gun from her hand before barreling toward Ferris, but he ducked just before the vampire tore into his flesh.

The ancient moved too fast, caging Ferris in against the wall, sliding his fangs into his shoulder. Ferris growled, shoving against the vampire.

"No!" Mouse darted forward, a few centimeters away from thrusting her hand into the vampire's rib cage to retrieve his blackened heart.

But the vampire whirled around, releasing Ferris and grabbing her by the upper arms. He flapped his wings, the wind they created rustling her hair as he lifted her toward the ceiling.

Mouse jerked, drawing on all the strength she had, but he still overpowered her, holding her to him tightly, *squeezing*. The way Mr. Taylor had… Dread coursed through her and tears stormed down her face. She didn't want to be helpless again. But that was precisely what she was in that moment. And she screamed, screamed as loud as she damn well could, even though it didn't do a single thing.

The ancient didn't lessen his grip on her, only speaking words in that old language of his, then buried his fangs into her throat. The pain from his bite tore through her, not a single ounce of pleasure radiated within her—it was as if her skin was on fire, burning past muscle, blood, and deep into her bones. As he drank, ripping farther into her throat, she peered down at Ferris, who was shouting frantically, climbing on top of the coffins to try and get to her.

As the vampire planted her against a wall, his body pushing harder into hers, the dagger she'd taken dug into her hip. It was her only chance. Eyes fluttering, her fingers shook as she drew the blade out. She was unable to reach his heart to see if it would knock him out, so with all the strength she could muster, she thrust the dagger into his stomach, slicing to the side.

The vampire screeched, his hold on her releasing, and she fell, her body crashing to the floor, pain flaring, bones breaking, the room spinning.

Mouse took one last ragged breath, finding Ferris off the coffin and lunging toward her. "I love you. Now *run*," she rasped, her eyes falling shut.

CHAPTER NINETEEN

Ferris

*R*un? Fuck that. Ferris would sooner throw himself at the fucked-up vampire than let him touch another hair on Mouse's head. And that was exactly what he did.

Ferris barreled into the vampire as the male dove through the air for Mouse. The vampire looked ancient, emaciated, with bat-like wings and rows of sharp teeth. He snarled and snapped his jaw in Ferris's face. His body shook as he held the monster up, right arm pressed to the male's throat, left throwing punches. Each time his fist landed with a crack against ribs, the bones crunched. The vampire twisted and writhed, but he didn't deter the attack.

"Get out of here, Mouse," Ferris growled.

She let out a strangled, painful sob. *Fuck.* After that fall, she was probably too hurt to run. The vampire clawed at Ferris's chest and his arm buckled from the sharp, tearing pain. Fangs pricked Ferris's neck. He braced for the bite—for the fire it lit inside him—but it didn't come.

The weight of the vampire's body lifted from Ferris and he sprung to his feet. The clear dagger from the shelf protruded from the back of the vampire's head where Mouse had managed to find the strength to stab him. He released a wretched screech, flinging his head from side to side, as black sludge-like blood spilled from the wound.

Ferris swept Mouse off her feet and bolted down the darkened tunnel, his heart slamming in his chest. If they could make it back to the library, maybe they would have a chance of outrunning the motherfucker. Hunger churned within him, his body weak, weaker now that he had to heal from the vampire's bite. Even at full strength, he was still outmatched. The vampire had gone fucking mad and that was what fueled him now. If he had to, he would fight, but he couldn't do that if he was worried about Mouse, and she was clearly not going to leave him to save herself. Unless he could convince her…

"You need to leave me, Mouse," he told her, stopping just outside the room with the relics. The library shelves would never hold against this feral vampire and he needed to give her as much time as possible to escape. The male would likely kill him, though Ferris wouldn't make it easy. Hopefully it would give Mouse enough of a leeway to reach the portal on the edge of Ivory. Then, after he was dead, Wonderland would need to be ready. "Ever has to know what we found and prepare a way to neutralize the threat."

"No." Mouse pushed out of his arms to stand in the tunnel and stumbled into the wall. Her injuries would slow her down but she was brave—she could make it home. "We can do this together."

Ferris looked her up and down. The vampire had ravaged her throat. While it was healing, blood still covered her neck and chest, soaking into her dress. "Luv, please. You need to go. I'll slow him down."

Mouse's eyes widened, her hand going for a dagger but finding it gone from her hip, still lodged in the vampire's head.

"He's coming!"

Ferris whirled around, widening his stance, wishing he had a gun on him. It had barely made a difference when Mouse shot the ancient, but maybe if he took multiple shots… *Shit.* The wild look in the vampire's eyes told Ferris that he was too far gone to care about anything but feeding. The vampire ran toward them, hunched, claws out, fangs bared, nearly every bone on display beneath his skin. Mouse's dagger still protruded from his head.

"Fuck!" Ferris shouted. He needed to buy Mouse time to escape. Against all his training as a guard, he turned his back on the enemy, and shoved Mouse through the hole in the wall. She fell backward into the room with the strange relics. "Get out of here."

He couldn't lose her. If he died right now, the fucker would only go after Mouse next—he had to kill him. Ferris whirled around, baring his own fangs at the vampire. Eyes trained on the dagger in the bastard's skull, Ferris sprinted forward using his vampire speed.

If he could get the dagger, he could use it to—

The vampire punched Ferris in the side of the head. Stars burst in his vision and then the momentum of the blow sent him crashing into the wall before tumbling to the ground. His temple took the impact and then… darkness stole his vision. Mouse screamed and he stumbled toward the sound. He shook his head, pressing his eyes shut. The sound of shattering glass and splintering wood echoed through his skull. *Fuck!* Blinking rapidly, the stars finally broke through the blackness. A few more times and he could finally see. Mouse screamed again and he leapt to his feet.

Fucking motherfucker!

Ferris darted through the hole and into the hidden room. Gulping sounds greeted him first. His body froze, the world seeming to crack in half as he locked onto the horrific scene before him.

Mouse, splayed on the floor, surrounded by shattered glass. The vampire straddling her lifeless form. Head bent to her neck. Feasting. His vision faded around the edges, fear and anger blistering through him.

No!

Not Mouse.

Teeth bared, blood boiling in his veins, he dove for the vampire, everything moving in slow motion, and latched onto the dagger in the vampire's skull. Ripping the blade free, Ferris drove it straight down into the back of the fucker's neck, severing the spinal cord.

"Mouse?" He yanked the vampire's lifeless body off her and threw him to the side. "Mouse, are you okay?" Pausing, he waited for her reply, but it never came. "Luv, you need to wake up."

She was silent. Unmoving.

Ferris spared a moment to rip the vampire's head from his body, then to tear his heart out, not willing to risk another attack while he saved Mouse. He barely noticed himself doing it, even as black blood sprayed over his hands. Mouse's throat was torn to shreds, bright red pooling from the wound. Her chest still.

Bone was visible inside her neck. Tendons and muscle exposed. Her glassy eyes stared up at nothing. Ferris fell to his knees beside her. "You'll be okay," he promised her. "I'll save you."

Lifting her to lay her head in his lap, he really noticed just how deep the vampire had torn into her. There were only a few inches of skin still holding her head to her body, but the spine hadn't been severed. It wasn't too late…

It wasn't fucking too late.

He bit into his wrist and pressed his skin to her lips, allowing the blood to drizzle inside her. There was enough in him to save her, even if it drained him dry. All she had to do was drink. But his blood pooled into her mouth and spilled over the corner of her lips.

"Luv?" Tears blurred his vision. "Luv, you have to drink."

Still, her lips didn't move against his skin, not even a tiny twitch.

"Please!" he screamed, the sound reverberating off the walls. "Mouse. Don't do this to me. Don't you dare fucking die!"

His heart thundered painfully in his chest as he pressed his wrist harder against her mouth. The blood leaked down her chin, spilling into the open wound. She was *nearly* decapitated—that didn't count. He'd seen Rav bring back vampires in similar conditions. *Worse.* With their skin peeled back from their skulls, flesh scraped away from limbs until all that remained was bones. All she had to do was fucking drink.

"Please, luv." Hot tears flowed down his cheeks. He bent over her small frame and placed a kiss on her forehead. "Please. I love you. I'll do anything. *Please.*"

This wasn't fucking doing a damn thing. Ferris pulled his wrist away and laid her carefully onto the floor. Rav had used an IV. But Ferris didn't have any needles ... hadn't since he'd stopping using drugs. Pressing his ear to her chest, he heard a faint thump of her heart. Too quiet, too irregular. *Fuck!* She wasn't going to make it. He tore across the room, yanking books off the shelves, smashing the glass cases open. Rampaging like the vampire had.

Only one thing mattered.

Mouse.

In his entire miserable life, he'd never been able to hold onto anything good. Not his friends nor his family. Not Ellie. Their baby. Everything he touched turned to fucking shit. It withered and died. But not Mouse. She was immortal. Too full of life for it to be real.

Ferris stood amid his chaos and gasped for breath.

But she was gone. Her eyes ... they were just like Ellie's had been that day in the car. They were *dead* eyes. He collapsed beside Mouse, gently wiping the hair from her face, a crackling sob breaking in his chest.

There was no stopping the tears now. No mending the shatter of his heart.

Mouse was dying because he couldn't save her. He became a vampire for that very reason. She had given him his mortal life back the day she'd drank the drugs from his system, let him live on borrowed time. And all he wanted was to give her *forever*.

But he was a damned failure.

"I love you," he whispered, closing his eyes. There was nothing left for him now. Not without her. "I love you. Please, please, please…"

And all he could think about in that moment was how she would die just like Ellie had.

"It's raining." Ellie turned to face him and cradled a large baby bump. "Maybe we shouldn't go today."

Ferris chuckled. "I know you don't like going out in this type of weather, but it's Oliver's birthday party."

Ellie crossed her arms. She wore a blue and white striped jumper, her hair neatly curled. "I have a bad feeling today."

He paused, watching her chew her bottom lip, and pulled her closer. Her baby bump brushed against him. "If you really don't want to go, we don't have to. We can stream a movie or something."

"No, I'm being silly." She stretched up to give him a quick kiss. "We should go for Oliver, but afterward we can have a cozy night on the sofa."

Ferris bent down, speaking to Ellie's stomach. "How does that sound, Luna?"

"She says she likes the idea very much." Ellie giggled.

Ferris held an umbrella over Ellie and rushed her to the car so she wouldn't get soaked before hopping into the front seat. Rain was coming down hard as he drove them to Oliver's, pelting the windscreen, making it nearly impossible to see. He eased off the accelerator, slowing the car.

"We should pull over until it lets up," he said.

Ellie nodded in agreement. "I think there's a place around the curve that—"

The squeal of breaks stopped Ellie mid-sentence. Ferris's grip tightened on the wheel, drawing a sharp breath as he saw the inevitable too late, a car coming straight toward him. The other car slammed into theirs, jerking them sideways, the tires skidding over the side road. His head struck the side window, glass shattering. Then there was only silence, smoke, and the white of the airbag.

"Ellie," Ferris rasped.

No response. The smoke faded a little as he turned to face her and a strangled cry tore from him. Ellie's eyes were glazed with death, blood running down her forehead. More blood pooled between her legs. Their baby...

"Ellie!"

Fuck. No. No no no.

"You promised you'd never leave me!" he cried. "Ellie! Wake up!"

Wake up!

Wake up.

Wake.

Up.

"Ferris?" Mouse whispered.

CHAPTER TWENTY

MOUSE

"Ferris?" Mouse murmured, holding back a scream as pain roared through her. She tasted blood in her mouth, *Ferris's*, and panic coursed inside her chest. Every single one of her nerve endings felt as if they were engulfed in flames. Her gaze locked on Ferris—he was above her, holding her, *alive*, his eyes red-rimmed and puffy, but he didn't look hurt. "Where is that bastard at? I'm going to rip him apart," she seethed, choking on a cough that only made the aching throb once more. Mouse didn't know if she could stand, but it wasn't like the days beneath the rubble. She could move her body, but everything was heavy.

"Mouse?" Ferris said with a choked sob. "You're alive."

She remembered the ancient vampire storming into this room, cabinets breaking, glass shattering, him yanking her head to the side as his teeth tore into her flesh. Mouse knew he was furious after she'd stabbed him twice so he hadn't been gentle with her in the least.

"After everything I've been through, do you honestly think I would die so easily?" Mouse tried to smile but could only clench her teeth together as sharp aches radiated up her neck. "I'm sorry I went in there. I just couldn't sleep and didn't want to wake you to explore quickly, but then I came across the ancient."

"It's all right—I killed the fucker," Ferris growled, drawing her to his chest as if she would fade away unless he held her. "I decapitated him and ripped out his heart a few moments ago."

Mouse pushed up with her hands but she was too weak to hold her weight. Ferris's lovely scent caressed her nose and she reeled in the temptation to drink from him as her fangs dropped. But then another heavier, metallic smell made her eyes flutter. It wasn't the decaying scent of the ancient that called to her, but his *blood*.

"I'm famished and don't want to hurt you," she said. "Will you bring me a pouch from my bag?" There was a legend that blood from ancients contained fast healing properties amongst other things, but she didn't want to risk drinking from a dead vampire. Perhaps that was another reason the Red Queen had kept them, to use their blood to bathe in while drinking it until she grew bored with them and put up a wall to hide them. Even though she believed that was the truth, Mouse would never know the precise answer.

Ferris nodded and lowered her to the floor, careful to not jostle her. A rustling echoed as he fished out her canteen and the powdered blood from her bag. She held her breath to avoid inhaling Ferris's alluring scent, running her tongue over the back of a fang while she waited. He shook the mixture and she greedily snapped the canteen from his hand. She gulped it down, the flavor making her moan as it brushed her tongue and drifted to her stomach.

As soon as she finished, Ferris gave her the second

canteen. Her body was sewing itself back together, the blood working wonders even though she would've rather had a mortal's in that moment.

"Drink," Mouse rasped, forcing herself to stop but not wanting to.

"I wanted to make sure you didn't need another first."

"This is enough for now."

Ferris nodded and reached for his backpack, not taking his gaze away from her. He wasn't worried about himself, but *her*.

As her appetite sated, Mouse felt more like herself than she ever had in the past two years. Perhaps part of it had been due to the vampire bite the ancient had given her. Only a bit of exhaustion lingered, and she realized how close she'd been to death. If the ancient had only pulled a little harder on her head, shifted her body further in the opposite direction, he would've severed her spinal cord.

After Ferris finished his canteen, her eyes fluttered and she managed to get a few words out. "I need to rest a little. I don't think I can make it home right now."

"I'll find you a better room without a corpse." Ferris collected their bags, then scooped her into his arms, cradling her close to his chest. "You're not leaving this castle until your strength is up. I don't care if I sound like an arsehole or not."

"Mmm, I like when your alpha side slips out." Mouse's voice slurred as she smiled, and she could no longer hold her eyes open, yet she relished the way his muscles flexed against her body while he carried her through the tunnels.

"This will have to do," Ferris said and she became alert once more, finding they were already in a room.

The space was nicer than the other ones she'd seen thus far. Only a few layers of dust covered the area and besides a mirror, nothing else was broken. Other than the bed, a spinning wheel was propped in a corner and across from it rested a dresser and a vanity.

Ferris lay Mouse on the bed and slid off her boots. "Let me

help clean you up, then you can rest."

She nodded with a yawn and he helped her remove her clothing until she was bare before him. He took out a cloth from his bag and poured water from the canteen. With delicate motions, he cleaned the blood from her throat. She bit her lip, watching as he continued his tender movements.

"Thank you," Mouse whispered once he was finished. Tiredness washed over her and she couldn't focus on what he said, yet she felt him pull the covers over her while she drifted away again.

Mouse cracked open her eyes and looked around the room, now that she could focus clearly. There wasn't as much dust as when Ferris had brought her into the space. That was strange. Had he cleaned it for her?

Where was he? Mouse caught a glimpse of his brown hair outside the open door, finding him sitting in the hallway.

"Why are you out there?" Mouse called, drawing the blanket tighter around her naked form.

"You're awake." Ferris whirled around and shoved up from the floor. He smiled, but it didn't reach his eyes. "You didn't sleep long, only about an hour. We can spare a few more if you need it."

"I'm fine." Mouse couldn't fall back asleep even if she tried. She was too alert now. "What were you doing in the hallway?"

He ran a hand across his square jaw. "Thinking, but mostly I wanted to stand guard outside your room in case some other fucker decided to show up."

Her chest tightened. "I don't want you to worry about me. I don't mind being saved, but I don't want you to think I have to be protected all the time."

"Luv, I think you're stronger than me." When he smiled this time, it finally met his eyes.

"We'll have to arm wrestle on that sometime." She laughed.

"Are you strong enough to head back to Ivory?"

She was about to nod, but a thought crossed her mind and she mulled it over. While in Red, they'd faced werewolves, the Jabberwocky, an ancient vampire, her fear of libraries, them falling into a cavern, her attacking Ferris. It was as if she'd survived a lifetime of tragedies. Between the road home from Red to Ivory, Mouse didn't know what they would come across next. And frankly, she was sick of it. She wanted to put an end to the never-ending Shakespearian tragedies in her life and become something not so bleak. It didn't have to be perfect, only something where she and Ferris were happy.

"There's something I want to do before we return home," Mouse finally said, fidgeting with the blanket.

"What's that?"

Heart pounding in her chest, she leaned forward, her voice breathy. "Remove your boots and turn around."

Ferris arched a brow and smirked but did as was instructed. Taking a deep swallow, she drew back the blankets, her bare feet touching the cool floor.

With her body still bare, Mouse slowly walked toward him, her gaze never leaving his muscular form. Once she reached his warmth, she brushed her hands against his hips, then trailed her palms up Ferris's defined chest beneath his shirt.

"So, I take it we won't be leaving soon?" he said in a gruff voice.

"We have a few hours to spare, as you said." She grinned, grasping the hem of his shirt, and he helped her lift it over his head.

"Mmm, taking a few hours to ourselves after the shitstorm

we just faced sounds fucking amazing."

Mouse traced the lovely tattoo on his back, following each curve of ink, gliding across the gears, making him shiver at her touch. She shifted forward, pressing her breasts to his back, and skimmed her fingers over his abs to the front of his trousers. His breath caught as she unfastened the button and peeled the fabric down his legs.

"Do you want me to touch you?" she asked as she stood, her hands sliding up his thighs to just beneath his navel.

"All the fucking time," he groaned. "But how healed are you?"

"Completely." Mouse grasped his hard length, slowly pumping him, her finger circling the piercing at the tip that she loved so much. "You can turn around now."

She released him and he spun to face her. He didn't hesitate to hoist her up, eliciting a squeak from her as he backed her into the wall. Her legs circled his hips and his cock pressed against her core. Ferris's lips crashed to hers, the kiss rough, just the way she needed it. She nipped his lower lip before tangling her tongue with his, the taste of him sublime. Gripping his shoulders, she dug her fingernails into his flesh as he slid his delicious length up and down her slickened folds, his piercing adding a wonderful sensation.

"I love you," Mouse murmured in his ear, not ever wanting to hold back those words. She'd said them in the room with the ancient, she said them here, and she would keep saying them because he deserved to hear how she felt. "I love you so much it hurts."

"Fuck, I love you. If you were dying, I'd rip out my heart and place it inside your chest."

"Your words are a hundred times better than Romeo's." Mouse grinned.

"You woke something in me the day you saved me," he rasped, gripping her hips, grinding into her even harder. "It's been building and building and *building* for four years. I fucked Imogen to save you. The whole time I was in bed with her, I didn't think of anyone but you."

Jealousy didn't burn within her that he had to tumble Imogen, only sorrow and rage. But the queen was dead and Maddie had gifted her precisely what she'd deserved. Otherwise, Mouse would've faced her fears now and gone back to the palace to rip out the queen's throat for how she'd treated Ferris.

"Then it looks like we deserve to let that dam break." She threaded her fingers in his hair as she kissed below his jaw. "I want you to make love to me the way lightning strikes, the way thunder roars."

"Then let's make it fucking storm," Ferris growled. His cock slid down her core once more, then he thrust inside her, making her gasp in pleasure.

"Keep going," she moaned. "Don't take it easy on me."

In answer, he thrust again, hard, so bloody hard that when she was about to cry for more, he did it again. Blissfully again and *again*.

He carried her away from the wall and to the bed, bringing her into his lap. "Ride me," he ground out, his dark eyes fastened to hers.

Wildness rose within her, but she hadn't done this before. Yet, as his hands gripped her hips, urging her to move forward, her body naturally gave in to the motions. Slow at first, then her pace picked up, going harder and harder until she was the one fucking him. A pleasureful feeling thrummed at her center as his hand cupped her breast and his mouth captured hers once more.

They continued this delectable dance, and as she grew close, so close to frenzy, she pulled away from his mouth to whisper in his ear. "Take me from behind and we'll come together." Mouse's sexual exploration had been quiet for centuries and she wanted Ferris to wake everything within her. No longer was there fear or worry about someone stealing something from her they shouldn't.

He didn't hesitate, easily rolling them so she was on all fours. She only missed him inside her for a moment before he slid back into her, making them both groan in satisfaction. His hand trailed up her spine as he drove into her over and over, his piercing delightfully rubbing her inner walls, until their bodies were both slick with sweat. And then she felt a tempest brewing inside her, prepared to wipe out all of Wonderland. Her eyes fluttered as lightning struck, the earth splitting open. Thunder roared, rumbling fiercely, then the rain poured within her. Paradise rolled through her entire being, touching all the way to the tips of her fingertips and toes. With each quake that came, she whispered Ferris's name.

"Mouse." Her name fell from his lips in a low growl as he spilled himself inside her.

Ferris slowly kissed his way along her spine, to the back of her neck, his arms holding him up on either side of her. Their chests heaved in sync, his soft skin on hers, then he scooped her up, keeping her back against his chest as he brought them to their sides.

"That was perfect," she breathed. It had been worth it for her to wait centuries to find him.

"Fucking perfect," he murmured. "I love touching you. I love you touching me."

Heat spread through her at his words and she arched into him. "I think we have time for one more round before we head home, don't you think?"

Ferris grazed his hand to her breast, his thumb caressing her nipple as he hardened again. He drifted his fingers down her stomach to between her thighs and, as her heart screamed in anticipation, he buried his length deep inside of her once more.

CHAPTER TWENTY-ONE

FERRIS

"Do you feel okay, luv?" Ferris asked.

Mouse snuggled closer into his side beneath the blankets and wrapped an arm around his waist. Her breasts pressed against him, stirring his lust. But after worshipping her body three times last night, it was safe to say they were both too worn out for another round. Still, he trailed his fingertips up and down her bare back. Having her next to him like this made him feel like he would combust. Like he was free. He couldn't remember the last time he'd felt so … content.

"Mm-hmm," Mouse mumbled around a yawn.

"I hate to say this since it's so cozy in this bed," Ferris said as he kissed her forehead, "but we've both finally gotten the rest we needed, so we should head back to Ivory."

"We should." Mouse sat up slowly and stretched her arms over her head, giving him a view of her full breasts, nipples peaked. "I don't like going back empty-handed though. None of the things we found answer any questions about the Jabberwocky."

"Me either, but they'll worry if we don't come back soon." All they'd found in Red were fucking monsters. Rogue werewolves, the Jabberwocky, a rabid ancient. A few foreign relics and finger bones, for whatever those were worth. If there were answers, it would take longer than they had to locate them, especially with all the hidden rooms. And that wasn't even counting the rest of Red. The answers could be anywhere in the territory.

"That's certainly true." Mouse gave him a lingering kiss on the mouth, then shoved the blankets from her lower half and climbed out of bed. "Maddie is probably losing her mind by now."

Ferris chuckled and swung his legs off the bed, standing. Mouse's gaze raked him up and down, her lips tugging up at the edges. He smiled, turning around so she could admire his backside. That they were comfortable enough to look at each other naked with nothing unspoken between them put a smile on his face.

Ferris leaned over to get his trousers. Mouse followed suit, gathering her dress and shaking the wrinkles out. He grabbed her panties and held them out to her, dangling them from his fingertip. "Missing something?"

Mouse laughed and snatched them from him. "Are you sure you wouldn't prefer it if I left them off?"

"Of course I fucking would, but then I'd be distracted the whole way back to Ivory." He winked at her and they both finished dressing. Mouse fished out a dagger from her backpack, one from the relics room, and tucked it into her boot. With a quick peek inside their bags, he realized they only had six blood pouches left. That would be plenty enough to get them back home, but their canteens needed to be filled. "We should stop at the lake for more water before we head out."

"You read my mind." Mouse brushed a kiss against his

cheek. "Let's go."

Ferris followed her through the palace, throwing glances down at her to make sure she was all right while keeping an ear out for the Jabberwocky's boisterous screeching. His free hand lifted subconsciously to the ring hanging beneath his shirt. Circling the metal through the fabric, a sense of peace descended over him. Like he was finally ready to let them go. No—maybe that wasn't the right way to explain it. Ellie and their daughter would always be with him, but he was ready to let go of the guilt over the accident. To move on and allow himself to finally fucking *live* again. They would want him to be happy.

"I love you," he whispered to Mouse.

Though he'd said it before, her eyes lit up like she was hearing it for the first time. "I love you too," she murmured.

"Let me make sure the coast is clear," he said when they reached the broken front doors. Stepping out first, Ferris scanned the sky for the Jabberwocky. The horizon was lightening to a soft gray as morning rose, but there was no sign of a threat. "All right, luv. Come on."

Together they went back to the same lake they'd bathed in the day before and he listened again for the return of the Jabberwocky. Only silence greeted him as they reached the water's edge. Clouds reflected on the glassy surface and, as Ferris dipped his hand into the cool liquid, goosebumps prickled his skin. It was colder than last time—or maybe he hadn't noticed because he'd been too focused on Mouse. Still, he cupped the water in his palms and splashed it on his face. He'd give anything for a warm bath or shower after this journey.

Mouse handed him one of the empty canteens and they filled them in companionable silence. When they were finished, she tucked them in the backpack again. "I can't wait to be home," she said, digging through Ferris's bag for the other two canteens. "To feed Des a new leaf, to watch my sister work on a new hat, to hear Ever's viola. I still wish we had better news to bring."

"We'll figure it out," he assured her. "There's always more than one way to fix a problem."

"But if someone could've killed the Jabberwocky, why—" Mouse's body froze, her eyes growing wide before she shot to her feet and pointed across the lake toward the dead gardens. "Do you see that?"

Ferris sucked in a breath and stood, his heart pounding as he saw what she was staring at. Bright green light shimmered in the air. What looked to be an emerald rectangle expanding, glimmering wider, until it formed a doorway. It carried a light, earthy scent, like a field after it rained. And it … it seemed to be a portal. That was impossible though. Portals just existed where they were—they didn't appear out of nowhere like this.

"What the hell is that?" Ferris hissed, grabbing Mouse by the wrist and hauling her over the low stone wall that circled the lake, kneeling behind it. It was best to see their new potential foe before they were seen *by* it. Ferris could assess the probability of winning a fight or if they needed to haul arse out of there. Honestly, as much as he enjoyed taking down a rival, his body was a wreck. He'd healed from all the injuries he'd received over the last few days, but he needed a live mortal to feed on to truly regain his strength.

"Stay low," he whispered to Mouse. They both peered over the top of the wall, waiting to see what would happened next. He held his breath and reached in his bag to retrieve a weapon. Except—*shit*. Their bags were still by the lake. A few yards away. "Do you still have that dagger on you?"

"Yes." Mouse pulled the blade from her boot and handed it to him.

Just as he wrapped his fingers around the handle, a form stepped from the green doorway. A shadow at first, then a fully formed male. Dark silky hair hung down his back and he wore a loose white shirt, shoved up to his elbows like he'd just walked out of a renaissance faire, with a brown satchel slung over one shoulder. Another looming form appeared behind him. Taller. Carrying an axe. He had long silver hair, a blue tunic, and fucking green sparks shooting from his hand. They exchanged a few words, but Ferris was unable to hear from this side of the lake. Whatever they'd said had the dark-haired male rolling his eyes as a swirl of red smoke curled around his arm.

A quick flick of the silver male's hand and the doorway snapped shut with a crack. Whatever the fuck was going on— this was unnatural, even for Wonderland. Ferris stared at the space where the green light had just been, mouth parted. No one could create portals and make them vanish at will. They needed to get back to Ivory to tell Ever and Chess that there might be a more serious problem than the Jabberwocky. He couldn't risk fighting them, not if they were… What the fuck were they? Sorcerers? It sounded insane, but he would've said the same about vampires a little over four years ago.

The pair walked around the lake with slow, cautious steps and examined their surroundings. The silver male shifted his axe as he turned, walking backward for a few paces, while the dark-haired stranger carried no weapon. At least not in his hands. Which made him the more dangerous one, Ferris thought, because he certainly didn't look like a fool. This male would undoubtedly have another way to defend himself.

"What should we do?" Mouse whispered.

Ferris swallowed. "We need to get back to Ivory. *Now*."

"But how? They'll see us if we run."

He had no answer. They were trapped between the palace and the lake. Unless the fuckers turned their backs or wandered away from the lake, they were screwed. It would only take a second for Ferris and Mouse to get away with their speed. If these two would just look the hell away… But they seemed focused on the palace. To get there, they would pass right by Ferris and Mouse.

The two males were in no rush, studying the surface of the lake, the dead trees in the distance, the crumbling walls of the palace, with grim expressions. Their booted feet carried them closer and closer by the second.

Bloody hell! Ferris's mind screamed at him to attack—he and Mouse were strong enough to take down two males—but they were using *magic*. They didn't stand a chance.

"Looks abandoned." The silver male paused and lowered his axe a fraction. From this distance, Ferris could see his pointed ears. Was he a fucking *elf*? Ferris held his breath, letting the reality sink in. The newcomer turned his head, surveying the sky, and exposed the silver metal snaking over his left cheek. "Did you give me the right coordinates?"

"Do I *look* like an amateur?" the other male said. Their accents were strange, light and airy. "Of course I'm right."

"Tik-Tok, I swear to the fucking stars, if you don't stop being an ass, I will leave you here."

The dark-haired male—Tik-Tok—laughed, humor lighting his red irises. His right arm caught the faint moonlight. Ferris squinted at the limb, making out gold, mechanical joints. *What the fuck?* "And tell your daughter that you abandoned me in a world full of blood-thirsty vampires? Nice try, Tin. She'd have your head on a platter."

Tin grumbled as they rounded the edge of the lake, then stopped short. "Someone's here."

Shit, shit, shit. Ferris followed their line of sight to the bags they'd left beside the water. His pulse sped up and he shifted to balance on the balls of his feet. Fighting these two pointy-eared males was a bad fucking plan, but he would do what had to be done, if need be.

Tik-Tok stalked over to the bags and crouched. With his golden arm, he rifled through them. "Water, some clothes…" He pulled out one of their remaining blood pouches and held it up to show his companion. "Whatever the fuck this is."

"They have to be close. There's still water on the outside

of the canteens," Tin said. He stood tall as he scanned the area. Ferris yanked Mouse down beside him before they could be found peeking over the wall. They were boxed in, their backs to the lake and too much space to the palace. If they tried, they would be seen.

Tik-Tok sniffed loudly. "Mmhmm."

There was a long pause and Ferris reached out for Mouse's hand. They were both fast, but there was no telling if these males were faster. Still, they would need to risk it. With any luck, they could outpace the magic too. Run straight to the edge of Ivory and leap into the portal that had brought them there. Ever and Chess could send guards to figure this shit out.

But before Ferris could inform Mouse of his plan, Tin said, "Do your thing."

"My *thing*?" Tik-Tok scoffed.

"Yes, your fucking thing, jackass."

"Calm your tits, *Father*."

Tin growled. "I will never understand what my daughter sees in you."

"Aw, you love me. Don't deny it," Tik-Tok purred. "Stand back."

Fuck! Whatever this *thing* was, Ferris had no intention of sticking around to find out. "We have to go," he whispered in Mouse's ear.

She nodded, then let out a cry. "Ferris!"

Stone crept over her body, encasing her legs. Rising up her thighs to her torso. Panic sliced through him. How could he stop this? How could he save her? What the fuck was happening? Ferris tried to shift to better face her but his own legs were hardening, becoming heavy. Swallowed by stone. He glanced at Mouse and his wild fear reflected on her face. His fangs dropped, his lips pulled back into a snarl.

There wasn't time to scream, to beg, fight. One moment, the stone was creeping up their chests, the next it had turned them fully into statues. Ferris strained his muscles, trying to break free, but it was impossible. He was trapped. Made of stone, yet aware of his surroundings. Of the crunch of two pairs of boots on the ground. Of Tik-Tok's *hmm* of intrigue. And the two forms that now loomed over them.

"Interesting," Tik-Tok said. He leaned down in front of Mouse. "I expected them to be bigger."

"Didn't you say they were human once? They're appropriately sized." Tin dropped to his knees in front of Ferris and poked at his exposed fang.

Even made of stone, they were sharp enough to cut flesh. Evidence of which beaded on Tin's index finger. Ferris could still sense the blood, smell the strange, sickly-sweet notes it carried.

"Well, damn," Tin murmured. "Let's avoid getting bit while we're here."

Tik-Tok chuckled. "Lucky for you, axe man, they're easily killed by decapitation."

"Let's not rampage through this world if we can help it. Release only their heads so we can talk to them."

"If I had the ability to turn certain body parts to stone, I would've started with your mouth," Tik-Tok said, raising a brow as if challenging him.

"I dare you to try that shit on me again. Once was enough." Tin's gaze fell to the dagger still clutched in Ferris's hand. "They have fae weaponry."

"Good," Tik-Tok said, studying the blade with a smirk. "We're close then."

CHAPTER TWENTY-TWO

MOUSE

Mouse's flesh was now stone, and she tried to scream, yet nothing would escape her mouth. She couldn't shift her eyes, only focus on what was directly before her. Which looked to be two males who had come straight through a portal from *A Midsummer Night's Dream*. She wouldn't be the least bit surprised if Shakespeare had conjured up his play after seeing them. Their pointed ears, the light way their words flowed from their mouths, their elegant movements. Their *magic*. Magic that had turned her and Ferris into stone statues that could still see, hear, and smell. The unwanted guests had said the dagger was fae weaponry... Were they truly fae like in the stories?

"Now," Tik-Tok cooed, his red irises sparkling with mischief. "Which of these two should we unleash first?"

"Just fucking pick one," Tin seethed, his shoulders broad like Ferris's, his muscles bulging beneath his blue tunic. Silver hair hung down his back in a beautiful thick sheet.

Tik-Tok tapped his chest with his hand, one that appeared as if it was constructed of golden metal. And were those bolts she was seeing? "I'm only trying to protect us so we *both* return to our females in a safe fashion."

Tin's fingers tightened around his axe. This was no itty-bitty little weapon—either side of its sharp blades could easily slice cleanly through her throat. She would brush her fingers across her neck at the moment if she could.

Mouse's heart jolted in her chest as Tik-Tok crouched in front of her, cocking his head, studying her. A sandalwood scent drifted up to her, accompanied by a rush of metallic. His blood smelled of pure heaven, the way Tin's also did. She tried to burst from her stone prison, but not one inch of her budged at all. Only he could free her, if he chose to. Panic set in as she realized this was another prison, *trapping* her…

Tik-Tok moved his finger back and forth between her and Ferris before he finally spoke. "We'll go with the female since she's unarmed." He glanced up at Tin and chuckled. His attention focused on Mouse but, thankfully, he didn't try to touch her stone flesh. "Now, listen, and listen closely. I'm going to release you, but you will not attack either one of us. If you can accomplish that, then we won't have to remove your pretty little head. Do you understand? Tin here never misses with his axe. And if you die, I doubt your friend here will be of much help to us. I'd prefer us not to have to get our hands dirty." His grin spread across his face, lighting up his red irises before he turned to Tin once more. "I do love it when they have a partner that we can use to threaten them with. Do you remember the game I played with our good friend Jack when I first met him?"

"I would've rather come with him," Tin grunted.

"Too bad he doesn't have one of these." Tik-Tok smirked, flashing some type of golden ornament to Tin.

Mouse wanted to hurl herself at his throat, dig her teeth in and rip it to shreds, all while lapping up his otherworldly blood. But his words sank in, and as they did, it made some sense. They wouldn't hurt her … if she didn't hurt them. Even in the palace, Rav and Imogen had never given her that ultimatum. It was only hurt, hurt, *hurt*.

"I'm going to take your silence as a yes." Tik-Tok chuckled, straightening and popping his back as if he had all the time in the world.

"Do you always talk this much when you're threatening people?" Tin growled.

"I find it more effective than swinging a weapon around." Tik-Tok clucked his tongue.

Tin only narrowed his eyes and clenched his strong jaw. The silver scar was twisted like spiderwebs across his cheek, and his blue eyes mirrored pure ice, as though he was used to being feared. But for some reason, she didn't fear him, even though he held an axe.

"Remember what I said," Tik-Tok cooed at Mouse while lifting his hand, his fingers covered in thin silver rings with jewels of various colors.

Her body loosened as the stone gave way to her flesh. She fell forward, her fists catching on the grass while she took deep breaths. Ferris rested beside her, still stone, his fangs protruding, and her heart sank at seeing him this way. "Release him," Mouse rasped, her fangs still lowered, but she didn't leap forward, didn't attack, or even hiss. She had to control herself for Ferris's sake. "Please."

Tik-Tok tapped his canines. "Now, now, first tuck those little fangs of yours away. From the tales I've heard about vampires, I know you can. And as for this handsome fellow— your lover, I assume, since you both reek of each other's scents—that will come in due time. Depending on you, that is." He then reached into the pocket of his trousers and drew out a small black vial. "I need you to drink this so you won't feel the urge to attack us.

Mouse eyed the vial. "What is that?"

"Fae blood. One sip is strong enough to keep your appetite sated for days."

"So, you *are* fae," Mouse murmured. "Like Puck from a *Midsummer Night's Dream*."

"Sorry, can't say that I know a Puck. Unless he's dead." Tik-Tok's lips curled up at the corners. "But yes, I'm fae, directly from Oz. I'm Tik-Tok, Captain of *The Temptress*, and this grumpy male is Tin, a once-famed assassin." He motioned at the ground. "How about we sit down and you can tell me your name, then how your friend came across the fae dagger he's holding." Tik-Tok lowered himself beside her as if they were to be guests at one of Maddie's tea parties, then handed her the vial. "And drink up."

Mouse stared at the black glass, peering over at Ferris who was most likely yelling at her not to do it—but there was no other choice. Don't drink it and be turned to stone, possibly have her head cut off, or worse—Ferris remain as he was if she refused. She uncapped the vial, letting the sweet aroma caress her nostrils. With prayers that she would live after this, she tossed the contents back. A bright flavor burst along her tongue, delicious, divine, as it slid down her throat. She handed the container back to Tik-Tok, wishing there was more, but the hunger wasn't there—her appetite filled for the time being. Mouse couldn't deny that she liked the way it made her feel, that she didn't have to lose control.

Tin continued to stand, glaring daggers at Tik-Tok but remaining silent. However, his fingers didn't loosen on his axe as his gaze turned to her.

"I'm Mouse," she said softly to Tin. "I do indeed find your axe rather pretty."

"I suppose." Tin's voice came out gruff, his brow arched. Tik-Tok side-eyed him while smiling, appearing amused.

"Ferris and I were here in Red to learn how to deal with a threat in another part of Wonderland, where I'm from."

"Would this threat happen to be a flying vicious beast?"

Tik-Tok drawled.

Mouse gasped. "You know about the Jabberwocky?" How would he know? Was this not their first time in Wonderland? "Have you been here before?"

He shook his head. "No. There used to be a portal in the sea, but decades ago, it vanished. I only recently convinced Tin to open one on land for me. His portal magic can be quite handy when he bothers to use it."

She wondered if they ever went to the same mortal world. Never once had she seen a fae before … unless they used glamour like in the stories… "We can venture to the mortal world, but our portals have always been here."

Tik-Tok leaned back on his hands, drawing a knee to his chest, getting comfortable. "Let me tell you a story. I have a sea witch friend who has visions after a good fucking. A crew member of mine has been ravishing her for almost a century and we were told that two lone vampires would be here to assist us. That means *you*."

Mouse frowned, glancing at Ferris, wishing he was there to give his thoughts. "We found nothing on how to kill the Jabberwocky. Its body is like iron and nothing penetrates it."

"Damn, you're vicious. We don't want to *kill* him," Tik-Tok purred. "Centuries ago, a fae male was cursed by a nasty bitch named Locasta. She was one of the witch rulers in Oz, who was rather good at hiding her deceitfulness before she was slaughtered. I don't know Pipt's full backstory, but somehow this male was cursed as a beast and hidden in your world by her."

Mouse inhaled a sharp breath and mulled over what he'd just confessed, how she'd always wondered where the Jabberwocky had come from, why there had always only been one. The beast wasn't from Wonderland at all—it—*he*—was from Oz. A fae male cursed as a beast, one she didn't know anything about, but if she were to guess, perhaps in his true form he was never vicious at all. "So, do you know if he was ever meant to destroy our world? He's part of the reason this territory looks like this, and I believe he's going to end up doing the same to my home."

"I don't believe that was the intention," Tik-Tok started. "A trusted witch knew him and said he was a good male. A bit reckless but good. If he's destroying your world, he likely doesn't mean to or can't control himself anymore."

Mouse knew what it was like to not be in control of oneself. She may not have been under a curse, but when she'd slaughtered those mortals in the donor building, her hunger had felt like she was. "I'll help any way I can, but tell me how to cure him."

Tik-Tok rubbed his hands together. "This is the fun part. It's simple really. My compass will lead us to his location, then we will need to pour the potion the sea witch provided down his throat."

Mouse's lips parted, her eyes widening in horror. "You can't just waltz up to the Jabberwocky and pour something down his throat. He'll eat you whole! Are you mad?"

"Sometimes, perhaps." Tik-Tok's grin grew wide. "But I think I've traveled to other worlds that are more dangerous than this one. If we set a trap, it should be easy enough."

"If it were that easy, it would've been done already," Mouse huffed. The vampires in Red had tried relentlessly until they'd finally abandoned the territory. "You had centuries to claim him and you didn't. He's done so much damage here." Tears pricked her eyes as she looked at Ferris who could've been killed when the Jabberwocky had broken into the palace.

Tin gritted his teeth. "If you tell her the rest, you ass, she would understand more and we'll be finished here."

Tik-Tok flicked his hand in the air. "And you're the one to talk. You've been silent almost this whole damn time." His intense gaze locked on hers once more. "The fae didn't come sooner because no one knew what Locasta had done with him." He paused, flexing his fingers. "This would've been much easier if North was here. She's Tin's daughter, my North Star, but he's the only one who can open land portals. You see, she's with child, our first child, and she's been bedridden. The sea witch needs Pipt to return for her own purpose. If we bring him back to her, she'll give us a concoction to heal North." It was the first break in his cocky expression. He tightened his gold fist, his eyes glassy for a moment.

Mouse blinked, her chest tightening. They were both doing this for love. Tik-Tok's lover and Tin's daughter. She knew that feeling, would do anything for Ferris if circumstances arose. "We'll do everything we can."

"You still didn't answer how you came across a fae dagger," he said, his smirk returning.

"When we were searching the palace, we found a secret room with ancient relics. I suppose they are all from your world."

"Interesting." Tik-Tok rubbed at his chin. "We should have a look in there."

"Fuck that." Tin frowned. "We're here for one purpose."

"It is quite a bloody mess after we encountered an ancient there and most of the things are now broken anyway." She held up a finger. "But before I go any further with helping, you will break the spell on Ferris now."

"That's fair," Tik-Tok said. Just as he lifted his hand and the stone unfurled from Ferris's flesh, a boisterous screech broke out in the distance.

The Jabberwocky.

CHAPTER TWENTY-THREE

FERRIS

The Jabberwocky's cry shook the ground beneath Ferris the very moment his body was no longer stone. He gasped for a breath, finally able to fill his lungs, and leapt up to stand beside Mouse, pulling her close. He'd heard every word the fae had spoken and wasn't sure exactly how they were meant to help these two fuckers. A sea witch? Bullshit.

But he'd think on the conversation as soon as they figured out where the beast was. Not a beast—a cursed fae. Whatever the fuck he was, the Jabberwocky would eat each and every one of them if given the chance. The sky was still free of danger, even though the beast's screech had echoed from a distance.

"Ferris, I presume," Tik-Tok said, then held up a golden compass. The face looked normal enough with the usual north, south, east, and west, but it emitted a soft golden glow. And, instead of pointing north, the needle aimed in the same direction from where the Jabberwocky's sounds had come.

"And *that* would be Pipt."

"Yes, that's the Jabberwocky," Mouse confirmed.

"Here, take this." Tik-Tok tossed a black vial at Ferris without looking up from his compass.

Ferris caught it and rolled the glass between his fingers. Even though the fae's blood pumping in their veins had an intoxicating smell, he had no desire to lay a single fang in them. "I'm not going to bite you."

"Nevertheless," Tik-Tok quipped.

Bloody hell. Was he really going to ingest mystery blood just to humor this asshat? But Mouse had drank it, so that meant he would risk it. Only for her. Popping the top off with his thumb, he sniffed it. *Fruity. Tempting…* Ah, fuck it. He tipped the contents into his mouth and swallowed the thick liquid. Savory, alluring, and it sated his hunger completely.

Tin held out his hand to Ferris. "Dagger."

"What?" He wasn't giving up the dagger to this conceited looking fucker—especially not now. The fae claimed to want their help but Ferris wasn't about to lower his guard before he was sure of them. Not after having survived in the Ruby Heart Palace where trust didn't exist. "Fuck you."

"Fuck *you*," Tin retorted. "That's a fae blade and iron hurts like a bitch. I won't risk you using it on one of us."

"Well, now that I know it's extra effective against you…" Ferris tucked it into his belt and offered a smile, his fangs bared. He cast a glance at the axe over Tin's shoulder. "Besides, you already have a weapon."

"Play nice, you two." Tik-Tok pulled his satchel off and held it out to Mouse without looking away from his compass. "What we need is in here."

"And you want me to carry it?" she asked.

"Your paramour can, if you prefer it."

"No, it's fine." Mouse grabbed the leather bag and tilted her head at Ferris in confusion. When Tik-Tok released it, her arms dropped from the unexpected weight.

"It's spelled to carry more than its size and helps lighten the load," Tin explained, though no one questioned it.

"I've got it." Ferris took the bag from Mouse—not because she couldn't carry it but because it was the gentlemanly thing to do—and swung it over his shoulder. *Damn.* It had to weigh almost as much as he did—if this was *lightened*, what the fuck was in there? Lifting the flap, he peered inside to find a ludicrous amount of large, heavy-linked chains. He picked up a section to test its weight and his brows rose. "That's a good fucking spell," he mumbled to himself. Just one of the links had to be around nineteen kilos.

Tin released a sharp breath. "It's beginner magic."

Well, la-de-fucking-da. "So, what's the plan then? Because I hate to break it to you, but chains won't do shite against the Jabberwocky."

Tin's nostrils flared when he looked down at the chain in Ferris's hands. "Those are iron chains, dumbass."

"And they will do jack-shit," Ferris said again.

Tin tilted his head and tapped the metal trailing over his cheek, wincing. Twisting silver lines covered most of his right cheek. If iron hurt fae so much, why would this fae imbed it on his cheek? Unless it wasn't there by choice...

"It will do plenty against a fae," Tin said in a low voice.

"That's where you two come in," Tik-Tok interjected. "Tin and I will distract Pipt. You'll immobilize him with the chains, just long enough for me to turn him to stone." He snapped his fingers. "Then voila. Cured."

"Just like that?" Mouse asked in disbelief.

"I may have skipped a few minor details." He glanced at Tin, his red eyes alight with mischief. "Are we moving out or do you prefer to stand here all day?"

Tin hefted his double-sided axe back onto his shoulder. "The sooner we get this over with, the better."

Ferris couldn't agree more.

Mouse shifted closer to Ferris, eyeing the two fae as they

spoke a few lines in a soft, lyrical language full of rolling letters. "Are you okay with this?" she whispered.

Was he? There didn't seem to be much of a choice—Tik-Tok would easily turn them to stone again if they refused. But what other options did they have? If these two had a shot of ridding Wonderland of the beast, he and Mouse would be fucking insane not to give it a go. And then he thought of something they'd said that made his chest tighten. Helping Tik-Tok's wife and child in the process wasn't something he could deny either. He hadn't been able to save his girlfriend and daughter, but maybe he could help them.

"For now," he replied quietly.

She stuck close to his side as they followed the fae through Red and away from the castle. They passed the wreckage of a city with half crumbled walls, then meandered through a forest of rotting trees, and climbed a small, craggy hill. While Tik-Tok stared at his compass and Tin kept a sharp eye on their surroundings, Ferris watched *them.* They moved with a fluid grace, not completely unlike vampires, though they gave off otherworldly vibes. Different than both Wonderland and the mortal world. Cocky, mysterious bastards.

"Ferris, was it?" Tin asked when they'd been walking for a good while.

"Yeah," he replied warily, side-eyeing the fae. They entered a prairie with patches of brown crunchy grass and a dried-up stream.

"I'm curious." The silver-haired male slowed his steps until he walked beside Ferris instead of Tik-Tok. His axe rested casually on his shoulder. "How does one become … like you?"

Ferris scratched the side of his neck where Imogen had torn into him. It hadn't been a pleasant experience—feeding her, fucking her, drinking her blood. He'd hated every second of it, not knowing if Imogen would uncover his plan with Maddie through his memories. It was the painful ones of Ellie the Queen of Hearts had seen though. But Mouse was worth it. If it had been someone else… If it had been *Mouse* who'd turned him, Ferris was sure it would've been a vastly different experience. "Why? Are you interested?"

"In drinking blood? Fuck no. You're immortal, I hear, yet your kind can't walk in the sun. It sounds even more pathetic than having iron imbedded on your face." He switched his axe to his other shoulder and stared out over the emptiness that was Red. "I don't understand why anyone would choose to live eternally in a shit place like this."

"All of Wonderland isn't like Red," Mouse drawled, motioning at the bare trees. "Ivory is beautiful and thousands live in Scarlet."

"Not everyone chooses this life," Ferris added. Maddie certainly hadn't. Imogen and Rav had never asked anyone's opinion on the matter. Noah's sister, Alice, flashed through his mind. The journey Noah and Maddie took to save her life after Imogen turned her was nothing short of perilous. "The Queen of Ivory and the King of Scarlet are working together to make sure no one is forced anymore."

Tin's brows furrowed, then smoothed out as he shrugged. "Tik-Tok once turned me to stone."

"Fucking brutal." The sense of suffocating, of being unable to move, but being fully aware of everything was torturous.

"He does it to everyone who might attack. Cowardly, if you ask me," Tin grumbled. "He kidnapped North right in front of me and her mother. There wasn't a damn thing we could've done about it because he'd turned the entire ballroom into statues."

Mouse gasped. "Kidnapped her? I thought—"

"Yes," he said in a hard voice. "They're together now. Going on almost a century at this point, so I've given up trying to get rid of the bastard."

A screech blasted through the air and pebbles shook

against the parched ground. Ferris threw a protective arm around Mouse, looking toward the sky, catching sight of the Jabberwocky's silhouette following above them. "He's too close."

"On the contrary." Tik-Tok threw a smirk over his shoulder. "We're not close enough."

"I don't think you fully understand what the Jabberwocky is," Ferris mumbled. They were in the middle of a damn *prairie*. Nowhere to hide. Nowhere to run.

"Pipt doesn't breathe fire, does he?" Tin asked the vampires. "Or have any long-range attacks?"

"Not that we've seen," Mouse said. "He's a relatively new risk to those outside of Red, but no one has ever reported him breathing fire."

Tik-Tok tucked the compass away in his back pocket. "If I need to turn him into stone to knock him out of the sky, we'll just have to hope no limbs break off when he lands. Celyna never said anything about bringing him back in one piece."

"Who?" Mouse asked.

"The sea witch." Tik-Tok shrugged. Ferris's eyes lifted to the sky just as the Jabberwocky's shadow fell over their group, his wings giving a deafening clap. The shadow moved swiftly, swallowing them and spitting them out just as fast. "Show time."

"Take out the chains," Tik-Tok ordered Ferris. "We'll lure the dreadful creature down. As soon as you've got him tangled, I'll handle the rest."

With that, the fae sprinted ahead, leaving Ferris and Mouse to stare after them. Their feet barely seemed to hit the ground. Red magic sparked off the tips of Tik-Tok's golden fingers and Tin lowered his axe to hold with two hands.

"They're giving us a lot of trust here." Ferris turned his eyes up to the gray sky. A tip of a taloned foot dipped below the clouds, then the giant beast came into view, throwing his head back to release a rumbling roar. *Fuck.* "Either that, or they're using us as the perfect appetizer to distract him."

"The chains," Mouse hissed.

"Shit." Ferris reached into the bag and handed one end to Mouse. She took two steps back, helping pull the links out, until there was a massive coil between them. Finally reaching the other end, he wound it around his fist once for a better grip.

The two fae spoke loud enough to draw the Jabberwocky's attention from where it circled above them. Scuffing their feet on the dry earth, they kept their gaze trained upward. Waiting for him to attack.

But the beast cracked his wings, lifting higher into the thick clouds, and disappeared. He didn't reemerge—not a single sound came from the Jabberwocky as though he was *toying* with them, his prey. *Oh shit*. Ferris held his breath. This couldn't be good.

His gaze scoured overhead for any sign of the Jabberwocky. A shadow, the dip of his tail. But there was no hint of the sneaky fucker. Not before he tore from behind a cloud, teeth bared, wings pressed against his body, diving down from the sky—straight toward him and Mouse. *Bloody hell!* This wasn't the plan. The fae were the bait. Ferris lunged for Mouse, knocking her down and rolling them both out of the way just as the Jabberwocky crashed to where they'd been standing. The ground shook, trees rustling, chain clanking. A roar vibrated the air around them and the fae shouted. Ferris leapt up, dragging Mouse to her feet beside him.

The Jabberwocky's cry turned to a whine. Ferris tightened his grip on the chain and turned to find gray stone slipping over the beast's body. It oozed down the quills, sliding over dark fur, around his abdomen and neck. He stomped his taloned feet, but then the stone was there, too, holding him in place. And, finally, silence, as the last of his snout hardened.

"Damn it," Tin muttered. "How are you going to get him chained up now, fucker?"

"Oh, I'm sorry. Did you want *them* to become a snack?"

Tik-Tok adjusted his rolled sleeves, exposing more of his golden arm, and peered around the Jabberwocky to smile at Ferris and Mouse. "You're welcome."

"Cut the shit, pirate. The cure takes time to work. Unless he's flesh and bone, he can't ingest anything and if he's not tied down, he's going to use our bones as toothpicks." Tin let the head of his axe thud to the ground and squeezed his eyes shut.

"It's fine. This might work better than expected. Fangs"—Tik-Tok pointed at Ferris—"wrap him up nice and tight."

Mouse snorted in disbelief, scanning the fae up and down.

"I wonder how much we could sell their blood for if we bottled it," Ferris said. "With the Jabberwocky turned to stone like this, they can't release him so our problem seems to be solved."

"Oh, feisty! I like it." Tik-Tok laughed, seeming to be completely unfazed by the threat. "Unfortunately, if I get too far away, he'll turn back into a beastie. So, get wrapping."

Ferris rolled his eyes. He'd like to wrap the chain around Tik-Tok's throat instead. "Let's just get this over with."

Dragging the chain between them, Ferris approached the stone Jabberwocky. The beast remained crouched like he was still about to attack, lips pulled back slightly, exposing the tips of his sharp teeth. But there was something else in his expression. Shock, fear. His furry brows were slightly lifted in surprise. If this worked, he would be able to go home after all this time.

"Hopefully he still remembers how to speak." Tik-Tok rapped his fingers against his golden arm. "If he's not rational after the cure, you can knock him out."

"May I?" Tin drawled.

"Just don't hit him too hard and kill the poor male." His red gaze landed on Mouse. "Chop, chop, my pink little confection."

A low snarl left Ferris. He would love to attack Tik-Tok

just once if it weren't for the unknown magic shit he'd retaliate with—somehow, he doubted Tin would help until the very last moment too. But there were more important things at play, so he wrapped a loop of chain around the Jabberwocky's left leg, ensuring it was nice and tight, before dragging more toward his back one.

Mouse mirrored his movements, throwing the chain to each other over the beast's back and beneath his stomach, until they were out of links. Tangled as he was, it would take forever for him to escape and, given that the chain was made of iron, Ferris was confident they would have enough time to cure the cursed fae.

Or get the fuck out of there if Tik-Tok's concoction failed.

"Now what?" Ferris asked, wiping his sweaty palms on his trousers.

Tin reached into his tunic and produced a gold vial. "We get him to drink this."

Mouse blinked, her lips set in a thin line. "I suppose we'll find out if this final act becomes a tragedy."

There was no way they were going to get close enough to the Jabberwocky's mouth to feed it jack-shit. Not unless they were also determined to lose a hand in the process. But, hey, as long as the Jabberwocky got the cure, it made no difference to him if one of the fae lost a limb. Maybe Tik-Tok wanted a matching set.

Tin turned to the cocky fae and grabbed him by the shirt. "If you fuck this up and I get eaten, remember that you have to face my very expectant, bed-ridden daughter."

"If you get eaten, I won't be facing another fae for a *very* long time, will I?" Tik-Tok brushed him off. "You're my ticket home, so fear not."

Tin let out a string of low curses as he approached the Jabberwocky and popped open the vial. "Stand back," he told Ferris and Mouse. Then he took a deep breath. "Fucking do it."

The magic faded from the Jabberwocky, lightening dark stone to his gray hide. His growl rumbled lower than before, his lips pulling back into a sneer, and his eyes narrowed as he waited for the moment he could move again. Attack. Devour.

But then the iron links touched his hide instead of stone and his jaw fell open on a high-pitched whine. Tin shoved his hand into the beast's mouth, pouring bright purple liquid onto his red tongue, before flinging himself backward just before the Jabberwocky snapped his mouth shut and released a blood-curdling howl.

Mouse grabbed Ferris's wrist and drew him out of the Jabberwocky's range of attack. If this failed, they'd just royally pissed off the most dangerous creature in Wonderland.

"Is it working?" Ferris shouted over the wail.

"Fuck if I know," Tin grunted.

CHAPTER TWENTY-FOUR

MOUSE

The Jabberwocky's body shook, the quills along his head vibrated, then his wild orange gaze found them. Mouse was about to use her vampire speed to drag Ferris and get out of this horrid situation, when a mixture of emotions in the beast's stare gave her pause. Suffering, regret, sadness.

Compassion stirred within Mouse. He was a cursed fae male who hadn't chosen to become this, just as she hadn't chosen for her hunger to become monstrous. They'd both been hurt and altered in different ways and no pain rivaled another—pain was pain.

The Jabberwocky's legs buckled beneath him and he collapsed onto the dirt, releasing a low wail as he tried to push himself up before falling once more. He writhed within the chains, his eyes rolling back in his head. And then his body stilled, his breaths decreasing.

"Bollocks, I think he's dying," she said, racing to his side. He didn't appear strong enough to fly or escape as his body continued to tremble.

"He better not fucking die," Tin growled. "We need him." Even though the fae's face was icy, his gaze held worry, most likely for his daughter.

Mouse pressed her hand to the beast's stomach while it rose and fell from his ragged breaths. Ferris stood beside her, not as inclined to comfort the Jabberwocky, but he didn't ask her to move away.

"Just wait," Tik-Tok cooed.

Wait for what? And then in answer, small whines escaped the Jabberwocky. But that wasn't what he was referring to— the beast's body shook once more, only this time it was more of a convulsion, bright white foam spilling from his mouth.

"It's all right," she whispered in a soothing voice. But she honestly didn't know if it was at all. The dark fur sank beneath his flesh and the skin turned golden, then became lighter until it looked as if his outer layer had been kissed by the sun. Sun she hadn't seen in so long, and frankly, never truly missed. Deep green, almost black strands of hair sprouted from his head, growing longer, his body shrinking, until he was no longer a beast. Mouse stripped away the chains that were too big for him now, then dropped to her knees beside the fae male, his face ethereal and beautiful like Tin's and Tik-Tok's. His ears came to sharp points and his cheekbones were high.

Pipt's orange eyes met hers. "Water," he croaked.

Ferris was already unzipping his pack, fishing out a canteen for him. Pipt's hand trembled as he took it, then guzzled the liquid down.

"I would give you clothing, but I'm fresh out, mate," Ferris said, rifling through his pack again.

"Just give him the shirt you're wearing," Mouse said, staring at the fae's lithe and toned form. "He can cover himself with it."

Ferris lifted his shirt over his head and ripped it down the front for Pipt to wear around his waist like a towel.

"I remember you," Pipt said, pushing himself to sit, not doing anything to cover himself with the shirt while exchanging a glance between Ferris and Mouse. "In the tunnels. I couldn't control myself, even though I'd wanted to." His gaze shifted to Tin and Tik-Tok. "Who are you?" He squinted, seeming to try to recall if perhaps he knew them from Oz.

"Your rescuers, of course," Tik-Tok cooed. "We're from Oz."

Pipt's lip trembled and tears beaded his lashes. "Locasta, she—"

"That bitch is dead," Tin grunted. "Reva and Crow killed her. If you remember them. They sure as fuck remember you and your reckless magic."

"What about Glinda? She was helping me master my magic, but then I made a grave mistake and went to Locasta, not knowing she was truly an evil witch in disguise."

"Sadly, Glinda is gone." Tik-Tok sighed. "You'll discover a lot has changed when we return. And dare I say, for the better."

Pipt peered down at his hand where black vines were tattooed on his ring finger. His eyes cleared, and he pushed himself to stand, wrapping Ferris's shirt around his waist. "My wife!"

"Is still marble," Tin said. "Reva knew you would ask about her and she's safe."

"I did this." He sobbed, his head falling into his hands. "It was an accident with the Liquid of Petrification."

Tik-Tok tapped a golden finger against his chin. "Yes, reckless magic you shouldn't have been toying with. I'll help return her to you, but you must first meet with the sea witch."

"Celyna?"

"So, you *know* her." Tik-Tok smirked.

Pipt ignored him and surveyed Red's bare trees, the dead bushes, the dust in the air. "I didn't mean to do this to your world. I didn't mean to do any of this."

"Wonderland is safe now," Mouse whispered, grasping his hand and giving it a gentle squeeze. "*You're* safe."

"We're wasting time," Tin grumbled. He lifted his free hand and chanted words in that lyrical language of his while drawing a small rectangle in the air with his fingertip. A green outline formed in the same shape, only taller, wider. A portal like the one she'd seen earlier by the lake.

Tik-Tok removed a jeweled ring from his golden finger. "I'll owe you one favor, if you ever need it. Put this on and I'll know you're ready to call it in. It will only work once though, so don't be hasty." He handed her the ring and it glowed a light red, tingling against her fingers. She unzipped the front of her pack and slipped it inside, hoping she would never have to use it.

Tin stepped forward, his axe relaxed at his side, his gaze shifting between Mouse and Ferris. "You did well today."

"I hope your daughter feels better," Mouse murmured.

Tin gave a small nod, lifting his weapon over his shoulder while stepping toward the portal.

Pipt ran a hand across the back of his neck. "It was a curse I never believed I would be free from. Centuries like this. Thank you all for freeing me."

Mouse felt as though she didn't do much, only threw chains across the Jabberwocky to hold him in place, but the four of them had done it together.

The trio of fae then walked through the portal and the green light flickered before vanishing. Mouse pressed her hand into the space where the portal had been and she felt nothing, not a single buzz of magic.

"This was an unexpected ending," she said, dropping her hand back to her side.

"Or a fucking miracle." Ferris sighed, drawing her into his side as she wrapped her arms around him.

"*Now*, we finally go back to Ivory." If this wasn't all a

wonderful dream, then that meant the Jabberwocky would no longer terrorize Red, wouldn't attempt to do the same to Ivory. Rav and Imogen were gone. And now the Jabberwocky was gone. Wonderland could become better. The seductive touch of a vampire, their dark habits, and ravenous appetites would still rule the nights, yet no one would have to worry about getting eaten by a vicious beast.

Mouse and Ferris journeyed back through the forest, finding no sign of any rogue werewolves, only bones scattered or in piles across the ground. After a bit, they reached the edge of Ivory, then crossed into the mortal world since it was still nighttime.

"Are we sure we want to use this portal, luv?" Ferris asked. "I think I know what's going to happen when we pass through since we had to leap off the bridge to get to it."

"Why, Ferris, have you never gotten a little wet before?" she drawled, then leapt into the portal with a laugh as he cursed behind her.

"I'm never going through that portal again," Ferris said once Mouse grabbed his hand, helping him up from the Thames.

"The Knave who is always up for anything, even risking his life to break me out from a palace, is afraid of a little water?" she teased.

He traced a finger across her lips, sending a delicious shiver through her. "Tonight, you'll pay for making me go through it twice." A grin spread across his face. "With my tongue between your thighs."

Mouse blinked, heat creeping up her neck and into her cheeks as he turned and walked away from her. "You can't go teasing me like *that*," she shouted, catching up with him.

"Oh, well I just did." He chuckled.

"See you at the palace then." She smiled and took off with her enhanced speed toward the portal in the cemetery. It didn't take them long before they crossed back into Wonderland, the alabaster gothic-like palace resting before them.

Noah stood in his Ivory uniform, guarding the front of the castle. "You're back. It's about damn time," he said, pulling open the door for them. "Ever already put a search party together and they were going to leave in two days."

"Suppose she'll have to cancel that then, yeah?" Ferris asked.

Noah cocked his head. "Cancel?"

"You'll find out soon enough."

Mouse patted Noah's shoulder. "Let's just say we don't have to worry about the beast any longer."

Noah's brows shot up as they stepped inside the palace. Mock lingered on guard near the stairs and his lips parted in surprise. "I knew you two would come back."

"I'm glad you were so confident," Mouse whispered with a smile. "Can you tell us where Ever is?"

"She's in the study." Mock studied her, his lips curling upward. "I like this talking side of you. Don't go back to being quiet around me."

"I'll try." Mouse left Mock to continue guarding and walked beside Ferris to the study, where the deep sounds of Ever's viola spilled into the hallway. Mouse could tell by the faster sounds that the queen was stressed, nervous, and she had more than an inkling of why. Not only because they hadn't returned but because her territory had been at risk.

Ever stood in the middle of the room near a plush white chaise while Chess watched her from behind the desk. He held a stack of papers in his hand, but he wasn't focused on them—all his attention was on Ever. Chess was the first to notice them, rising from his seat. "Well, well, look what the cat dragged in." He gave them both a once over before cocking a brow at Ferris. "Do you own a shirt?"

Ever's hands stilled, the music coming to a screeching halt as she whirled around. "You're here!" She rushed to Mouse, wrapping her into a tight hug as if she thought she'd never return. "Maddie is already packed and prepared to hunt the Jabberwocky with a party of guards."

"No one has to go," Mouse said, stepping back from Ever.

"The Jabberwocky isn't in Red anymore," Ferris added.

"Then where the fuck is it?" Chess arched a brow. "The beastie hasn't played in any of the other territories since it was here last."

"Have you ever heard stories of the fae?" Mouse asked, running her fingers over the end of her plait.

"I don't think we need a bedtime story." Chess scowled.

Mouse rolled her eyes and continued, "The Jabberwocky isn't what we thought he was. He's from another world known as Oz and was cursed as a beast before being banished here. Two fae came through a self-made portal, then we helped them break the curse. They're all now back in Oz so we're safe."

Ever held up a hand, a frown on her face. She wasn't as relieved as Mouse thought she would be. "Should we be worried about an attack? Two fae came here from another world, who can just return at any time they would like without our knowledge? What if something worse comes?"

Mouse hadn't thought about that, and perhaps that was one of the reasons she wasn't and would never be a queen. "I know it's foolish, but I trust them. They won't come back, only if I ask them to. The portal doesn't remain open as ours does with the mortal world. There's a lot to discuss."

"Do go on then." Chess sat on the edge of Ever's desk, leaning back on his hands. "We have plenty of time."

Ferris clasped Mouse's hand, seeming to know what she needed. "I'll fill them in. Go to Maddie."

Mouse nodded and before she left the room, she heard Chess purr, "It appears the two of you discovered *other* things while in Red."

She bit the inside of her cheek to stop from smiling about the pleasureful things she and Ferris had done together as she ventured back into the sitting room to find Mock. "Do you know where Maddie is?"

"She's in the drawing room," he said.

Even though his eyes weren't puffy like they'd been when she left, she knew he wouldn't ever forget about Didi. He was going on, day by day.

"Thank you, Mock," she whispered, then hurried down the halls to the drawing room.

Maddie's legs hung over the chair arm and Mouse quietly padded in, watching as her sister's fingers thoroughly pushed her threaded needle in and out of a violet and cerulean checkered top hat.

"I've returned," Mouse whispered.

Maddie's hands froze, her head jerking up. "Mouse!" She leapt from the chair and threw her arms around her. "I've been going positively mad here, making hundreds of hats."

"Hundreds?" Mouse laughed. "That seems like a record number."

"You're laughing," Maddie said slowly, studying her as if she had twenty eyes on her face. "Like you used to."

"I should hope that's a good thing."

"It is." Maddie grinned, hugging her again.

"I have an interesting story to tell you." Mouse didn't wait for Maddie to respond before discussing the journey, starting with the rogue werewolves, the queen and her husband, the ancient, the relics, the fae, and their magical portal. A beast who wasn't one at all, but an ethereal male who had matters of his own to sort when he returned home. Like they all had to do.

"Well, that"—Maddie tapped her chin and smiled wider—"is quite the tale. But you're leaving out parts, aren't you?"

Mouse had… She'd left out the parts where she'd almost

died, where things had gone too far with the ancient because those parts didn't matter now.

Before she could speak, Maddie waved a hand in the air. "I know what it is. You and Ferris *fucked*."

Mouse gasped. *Oh, bollocks, it isn't what I had thought at all.*

"It's all right. I know it's hard for you to discuss these things, but I'm happy for you." The smile slipped from Maddie's face as she peered at her hands. "However, I do have news to give you about Des."

"She *died*?" Mouse shrieked.

"What? No!" Maddie grasped her by the arm and turned her to where the chess set rested on top of the table. Only, beside the set was something blue, an odd almost oval shape.

And then Mouse's eyebrows shot up as she glanced back at her sister. "It's a cocoon! *How*?" Caterpillars in Wonderland never formed cocoons, never became a butterfly or a moth.

"Species evolving? Maybe she's special? Perhaps her sadness did it. She had remained blue for a while, her yellow coloring gone." Maddie shrugged. "But she's been like this since the day you left."

"This is my fault." Her heart sped up and she blinked away tears.

Maddie wrapped her arm around Mouse, drawing her close. "We'll wait and see what happens when she emerges from it. She'll be fine, I promise."

Mouse didn't know what to think, but she would try to be positive the way Maddie always was. She hugged her sister, then sat in the chair across from Des. "Thank you for watching over her."

"Of course." Maddie took a seat opposite her. "How about you tell Des everything that happened while we play a game of chess? I'm certain she'll be able to hear you." She paused, scanning her over. "Unless you would rather bathe or nap first?"

"No, I'm not tired and I can have a proper bath later. I want to spend time with the two of you for now." Time that she should've been spending with them before instead of moping about.

Maddie inched a white chess piece forward. "Now tell me, what precisely led you and Ferris to fuck in Red?"

"Maddie!" Mouse laughed while moving a black pawn forward. She then turned to Des's cocoon and murmured, "Ignore my sister, she's too nosy for her own good."

CHAPER TWENTY-FIVE

FERRIS

Ferris paused outside of the drawing room after talking to the royals, listening to Mouse and Maddie laughing together. A smile tugged at the corners of his lips. This was how it used to be with them—how it *should* be. They had laughed together all the time before Mouse was taken by Rav and the Queen of Hearts, spent hours joking. Ferris hadn't always known what it was they'd found funny, but the sound was so contagious that he had nearly always laughed along with them.

Mouse and Maddie needed this time together. Ferris wasn't one to eavesdrop, so he stuffed his hands in his pockets and made his way through the hallways, up the stairs, until he reached the bathroom a few doors down from his bedroom. After turning on the water as hot as he could stand it, he peeled off his clothes. Usually he would take a shower, but he needed to soak the ache from his muscles.

Stepping into the massive granite bath, he released a low groan and sank down into the water with his eyes closed. The warmth was an instant relief to his body after the journey in Red. But, as frustrating as their trip had been before the fae arrived, Ferris would do it all over again if it meant he and Mouse could be together.

Ever and Chess had found the information about fae troubling, not that Ferris could blame them. Magical beings who could create a portal anywhere they wanted could be a problem. What was to stop them from portaling into a throne room and vanishing with a royal? But Tin and Tik-Tok had seemed eager to leave Wonderland. They might be back one day if Mouse ever decided to put on the ring Tik-Tok had given her, but until then he wasn't overly concerned.

Surfacing from the water, he dragged in a breath and found a bar of soap. The lake had done well to wash off the blood and dirt in Red, but by the time he finished scrubbing himself, Ferris felt refreshed. After sparing another moment to wash his hair, he drained the bathtub, dried himself, and wrapped the towel around his waist.

He padded toward Mouse's room, but the door was wide open, the bed perfectly made, the lights off. A small twinge of disappointment pinched his chest. He wanted to see her, to touch her just to reassure himself she was real. That she was safe and here, with him, but he knew she would find him when she was ready.

Returning to his bedroom, he passed by his drum set and ran a finger over his cymbal. It gave a low chime when he flicked it. He smirked and grabbed one of the sticks from where it sat on his snare. "Hello, beauty," he whispered to the instrument, twirling the stick between his fingers. "Did you miss me?"

Soon he would play them again, but there was no music drumming in his mind right now. He set the stick back down and stretched his arms over his head, yawning. Now that they were home, he had no doubt that he could sleep for days. He stood between his bed and the dresser. Ever had told him to go rest, so he likely wouldn't be bothered again tonight. There was no need to get dressed. *Not even for Mouse,* he thought with a grin. He pulled the towel from his hips and walked to the chair, draping it over the back to dry.

The only thing he wore now was his necklace with Ellie's ring. It felt heavy around his neck now, uncomfortably so. He lifted the jewelry from where it laid against his chest and stared at the white gold band. The small solitaire diamond. He'd worn it every day since the coroner returned it to her family, who then returned it to him, to remind him of Ellie and their daughter. To carry them with him as he struggled through life, knowing they were gone.

But he wasn't struggling now. He missed them and would always miss them, but he had finally accepted the hard truth of it. Ellie and Luna lived in his heart and always would. This ring though… Ferris hadn't been carrying their memory around his neck. He had been carrying his guilt.

Biting his lip, Ferris carefully lifted the chain over his head and ran his thumb over the ring's stone. It was time to let go of the bad and remember only the good. To stop wondering *what if* and start living again. Truly living. He opened the top drawer of the dresser and set the chain inside, closing his self-blame away.

Ferris loosened a breath and perched on the edge of the bed, feeling lighter than before. So light, in fact, that he was no longer tired. His hand itched to draw. To bring beauty to life on page. He smiled to himself as he took his sketch pad and pencil from the bedside table.

Flipping past sketches of looming castles on cliffs, glass-like portals, of Ellie, Mouse, and Maddie, Ferris put the tip of the pencil to the page and began drawing.

"Ferris." A soft voice broke into his sleep. "Ferris, wake up."

"Hmm?" He cracked one eye open to see Mouse leaning over him. *Oh, shit.* He hadn't meant to fall asleep. One minute, he was sketching his third image of Mouse, then the next, she was waking him. Sitting up, he blinked the sleepiness from his eyes. "What's wrong?"

"Des somehow formed a cocoon. Maddie wanted to watch over her for one more night so I'm letting her." She gave him a soft smile. "I wanted to climb in next to you, but you're hogging the whole bed."

He rolled off his stomach and onto his side to give her room, not thinking that he was giving her a view of his dick. Pink rose in her cheeks but she didn't hesitate to lay beside him. She propped her head up on her hand. His gaze traveled down from her damp, loose hair to the large black T-shirt she wore. *His* T-shirt. And from the looks of it, nothing else.

"What are you drawing?" she asked, interrupting his lazy perusal.

Ferris glanced at the lines of what would've been Mouse's sleeping face had he finished and closed it. "Nothing."

"Liar." She reached for the book. "You always let me see."

He clutched the spiral spine a little harder, unsure how she would feel about the other two drawings he'd created before falling asleep. "I might have to rethink that policy."

"Oh?" Mouse's brows rose playfully. "And why is that?"

"Subject matter may no longer be suitable for all ages." He flashed a sheepish smile. "I might have drawn a couple things that, in retrospect, I should've asked permission for."

"Well, now I'm twice as curious," Mouse drawled. "Since I'm much older than you, it really shouldn't be a problem." She slowly pulled the sketchbook from his hand and he let her, giving silent permission. Flipping through to the end, she paused at the unfinished page. "What will this one be?"

"You," he said. *Fuck.* He really should've asked her if she minded being the subject of sexually charged drawings before he did them. It wasn't too late to burn the whole damn book… If she was uncomfortable, he would destroy the images and never do anything like it again. "You look peaceful when you sleep, so I was trying to capture that."

She beamed, then turned the page. The smile faded. "Ferris…"

"I'm sorry."

"What? No." She looked up at him. "Don't be sorry. It's just … is that how you see me?"

Ferris glanced down at the image of Mouse. It was the view he'd had when she was pressed against the wall as he licked her to orgasm. Her arched back, peaked nipples, eyes hooded with pleasure. His cock stirred at the reminder of how sweet she'd tasted on his tongue. "I'm not the best artist in the world so I couldn't capture your perfection. Do you not like it?"

"I just look so… I don't know." She let out a small, disbelieving laugh. "I've always been seen as quiet, reserved, which I can be, but you see more than that. You see all of me."

"So, you don't mind? That I drew you like this?" Ferris asked nervously. He really hoped not—he loved drawing her this way.

"No. As long as you don't show anyone."

He inched closer to her on the bed and used his index finger to tilt her chin up. "No one else will ever see that expression on your face. Not on paper and certainly not in real life."

"Only ever you." She gave him a small smile as she turned the page again to reveal a drawing of her on her knees, fingers wrapped around his pierced cock, mouth parted. She slammed the book shut and slid it back toward him, laughing. "That's quite enough of that. Perhaps I'm not brave enough to see my face in such a sexy way. But do go on and continue drawing whatever you wish of me."

Ferris chuckled and pulled her body flush with his, the warmth of her legs against his made him only want to feel more of her skin. In answer, she slid over his hip, giving him a definitive answer to his earlier wonderings. She did *not* have anything else on under his T-shirt. Her slick heat brushed against his semi-hard cock. Instantly, there was no longer anything *semi* about his hard-on.

"Would you like to fuel my imagination a little more?" Ferris asked, brushing his nose against hers, his hand trailing down to cup her arse.

"Hmm. I'm not sure," she replied, teasing, and rolled her hips once. "Do I get to benefit from *your* imagination too?"

Ferris grinned. "Are you asking if I have a new bedroom trick to share with you?"

"I'm asking if you have *multiple* tricks." She nipped gently at his bottom lip. "Though, if you don't, I'm not opposed to helping you figure out some."

"Oh, luv, I have *many* things I'd like to do with you, but not without talking them out first. And we'll need to take a trip to the sex shop. For now, though—" He rolled her onto her back and knelt between her thighs. The motion made the shirt slide up around her waist, giving him a view of her, wet and eager. His cock throbbed with the need to be inside her. "For now," he said again, his voice gruff. "This will have to do."

"What will?"

Ferris reached behind him and grabbed one of the pillows. "Pick up your hips for me." She bit her bottom lip and lifted them from the mattress. Sliding the pillow beneath her arse, he groaned at the sight of her slick folds. "Is that comfortable for you?"

Mouse relaxed into the pillow and nodded.

"Good." Ferris skimmed his hands down the outside of her bare legs, across her knees, and back up her inner thighs to her wet center. He leaned down and pressed his lips to hers. In response, she dug her fingers into his hair. He took ownership of her mouth, his tongue stroking across hers, as Ferris found her clit with his thumb, rubbing gentle circles.

"Faster," she breathed.

"So bossy," he said with a smirk against her mouth. And he fucking loved it. Loved that she was comfortable enough with him to tell him *exactly* what she wanted. He would give her anything she asked for and more. While his thumb moved faster, Ferris's middle finger slid inside, pumping. She squirmed beneath him, panting, and a pearl of cum beaded on the end of his cock. *Fuck.* He wanted to please her, bring her to oblivion numerous times, but he needed to feel her clench around him.

"Would you like to see the trick now?" he asked. "Or should I use my mouth again first?"

"The trick," Mouse panted.

Thank fuck. Ferris kissed her again and removed his hand to line his cock up with her core. She sucked in a breath when it passed over her folds. Ferris grinned and slid the pierced tip through again, before burying himself deep inside her with one thrust.

"Oh!" Mouse cried.

Ferris stilled inside her. The pillow made for deeper penetration, but was it *too* deep for her? "Do I need to stop?"

"No." She grabbed at his arse, pulling him forward, urging him to move, while widening her legs. "More."

Ferris groaned. Were those words ever sexier than when coming from her mouth? He pulled nearly all the way out, then pressed back in, slow, but firm. Unable to take his eyes off hers. When he'd first seen Mouse, he believed her to be an angel. While she might not be from Heaven, she had still saved him. In more ways than one. He loved her so fucking much and with each roll of his hips, he showed her. Again and a-fucking-gain. Until she dug her nails into his back so deep she drew blood, making Ferris growl in pleasure. His thrusts increased. Faster. Harder. With no real rhythm, only him and her making their own drumming beats.

Mouse tilted her head, exposing her neck. Her mouth brushed against his wrist. "Ferris." She flicked her tongue against his pulse point. "I'm so close."

Oh fuck. His balls tightened, his own release nearing. "Bite me," he rasped, fangs dropping.

Mouse extended her neck a bit more. "Together."

He lowered his head to her throat and ran his tongue up the vein, tasting the salt of her skin, then placed a lingering kiss there. When her fangs grazed his wrist, his thrusts became fast and erratic. "Damn, luv," he murmured, and sank his teeth into her flesh. Pleasure stormed through him, starting at his wrist where her fangs pierced. He drove his cock into her as her blood flowed over his tongue, her flavor driving him toward oblivion. Once. Twice.

"Ferris!" she whisper-shouted, pulling herself from his wrist to arch into him. Her walls fluttered around his cock in orgasm. The sounds she made tipped him over the edge and he roared out her name as he came inside her.

They stayed like that, his gaze locked onto hers as they panted. This moment right here, between him and her, was everything he'd ached for over the last few years. The way she looked at him… He knew it was mirrored on his face. And he wanted that expression on paper, to draw her just like this. *His* Mouse. Even though he didn't want to, Ferris found the strength to roll off her. Placing a kiss on her temple, he whispered, "I'm never going to get enough of you."

"I should hope not." She turned to him and smiled. "You have a lot of paper left in that sketchpad to fill."

Ferris chuckled. "I'll need to buy out the art shop."

"Oh?" She laughed softly, shifting the pillow out from beneath her hips and climbed toward the head of the bed. She snuggled beneath the covers then motioned for Ferris to join her. "I suppose on the way we can stop by the sex shop you mentioned."

Ferris grinned as he slipped under the blankets and wrapped an arm around Mouse's waist. "If you insist."

"I do." She closed her eyes and sighed, content.

"Let's rest," he said. "We deserve it after all that shit in Red."

"I already told Maddie I wasn't getting out of this bed for at least a day." She pressed closer into his embrace and yawned. "I love you."

Love didn't feel like a strong enough word for the emotions burning within him for Mouse. They'd saved each other's lives, sacrificed and suffered. She was his eternity and he would continue to protect her with his life. He drew her close and kissed the top of her head. "And I love you. More than I can say."

EPILOGUE

MOUSE

According to Maddie's estimate, from the time Des had first hidden herself away in a silk cocoon, twenty-two days had passed. Ferris had brought Mouse a book from a mortal library that read how it generally took five to twenty-one days on average for a butterfly or moth to emerge from their protective casing. Yet, some could be tucked away for as long as *three* years.

With Des resting beside her on Ferris's bed, Mouse thumbed through a book with more thorough butterfly and moth details, along with a collection of pictures of different species. She tapped her foot against the mattress to the beats coming from Ferris's drums. Every so often she would glance up to watch the way he bit his lip, how his muscles flexed while hitting a cymbal or a snare, and how the perspiration slowly slid down his chest and taut abs. The song was chaotic and beautiful and she hoped Des heard every glorious sound within her silk. Ever since they first moved into the Ivory

Palace, the caterpillar had loved hearing Ferris play, standing on her hind legs as the top half of her body would sway to the music.

Mouse peered beneath her lashes at Ferris once more, recalling all the new activities they'd experienced together. Emotionally and physically. Heart-to-heart chats, making love, him showing her what it was like to be truly sexually liberated. Although Mouse hadn't snuck another peek at the additions Ferris had drawn inside his notebook, she was tempted. Perhaps at some point, she would. The drawings had made her blush, and it was different seeing her face that way, happy and blissful. Something she hadn't been in a long, long time.

Soon, Ever and Chess's castle would be finished, and Mouse was excited for this new chapter, to truly unite Wonderland, start something fresh. It was what the vampires in Ivory and Scarlet both needed.

Mouse's stomach still felt heavy from her earlier meal. She continued to struggle with her hunger at times, but on those days, she would ask Ferris or Maddie to go with her to feed, to make sure she didn't become a ravenous monster. Unless she chose to be, when she would still hunt those who'd hurt others.

Movement beside Mouse's hand caught her attention, and she averted her gaze from Ferris. She blinked as the blue silk casing wiggled. For a moment, she thought it was from the vibration of the drums or her foot tapping. But then Des wiggled again.

Her heart slammed in her chest, and she shouted, "Ferris!"

He halted his movements, the drumsticks clenched in his fists, and looked at the cocoon now resting in her hands. It wiggled a little harder.

"Come on!" Mouse didn't wait for his answer as she left his room, skipping over steps while descending the staircase. She flew past Mock, his eyebrows raised to his hairline when he glanced her way.

"I'm fine," she called to the guard.

Before heading out the door, she looked back, and Ferris was nowhere in sight. She didn't wait as she hurried past the blossoming trees and toward the garden near the sparkling lake. White zinnias were in full bloom and vines weaved through the backs of the iron benches. Mouse halted in front of one of the benches but didn't take a seat, only continued to cradle Des in her palm.

The sky was dark and a swarm of crimson ravens flew overhead beneath the silvery moon and bright stars. Ferris's footsteps finally crunched across the pebbles of the garden pathway and Mouse whirled around. "Took you long enough," she teased, her gaze pinned to his captivating dark eyes.

"I had to grab something really quick." He shrugged, a smirk crossing his face.

She arched a brow, finding nothing in his hands. "Well, good thing you haven't missed Des's big return to Wonderland."

"I think Des would've waited for me."

Mouse rolled her eyes, then focused back on the blue silk. It shook a few more times, then remained still. They waited with bated breath, whispering encouraging words to Des as she worked to break out. She would stop, then go again, then stop. If it was a stressful endeavor for Mouse, she couldn't imagine what it must be like for Des. The sky slowly lightened in the garden until the morning's gray tones crept in, the stars and moon hiding away for the day. It had been a long while since Des's last movement.

"Maybe it was a false alarm. We should head back inside," Ferris said. "We've been standing out here for almost an hour."

"You can take a break, but I want to wait. I want her to be out in the open, free, when she hatches. Not cooped up in the palace after being in this cocoon for weeks."

"Even if it takes as long as it said in that book of yours?"

"Yes," she deadpanned and pointed at a comfortable spot near the flowers. "I'll sleep right there."

"I believe you would too." Ferris chuckled. "I guess I'll have to grab us camping supplies for *three* years."

"It won't take *that* long!" At least she hoped it wouldn't. In answer, the silk shell twitched, the soft casing on the left side tearing open. "Ferris, look." Mouse beamed, her eyes wide.

"I see it, luv." Ferris's arm slipped around her waist as they watched together.

A blue wing with obsidian edges slipped out, followed by a thin leg. It was one of the most beautiful things she'd ever encountered. Not once had she ever seen an insect come out of a cocoon in the mortal world. And then the rest of Des emerged—one of the most gorgeous butterflies in existence. She might be biased though since it was Des, but it was true. The assortment of blues and blacks shimmered, her antenna a glittering cerulean. Unlike the butterflies she'd seen in the book that came out wet and wrinkled, her friend was dry, her wings prepared to fly if she wished.

"Des," Mouse said softly.

The butterfly stood, her head lifting so her pale blue eyes, no longer black, could meet Mouse's.

"You're the first butterfly in Wonderland," Mouse murmured, tears beading her lashes. "I do hope you're not angry with me for leaving you here while I went to Red, but I couldn't put you in danger. Not after you risked your life by staying with me in the palace and helped me through my whirling emotions."

Des crawled up Mouse's palm and nuzzled her finger as she always did. She batted a wing at Ferris, and he brushed a finger across one. "You're the prettiest butterfly in Wonderland," he said.

"She's the only butterfly in Wonderland." Mouse grinned, then watched Des for a long while, knowing her friend needed a journey of her own. "You've been trapped in places long enough. How about you fly for a while. Experience the outdoors, *the world*." She held her hand toward the sky. "Return whenever you wish."

Des looked back at Mouse, and she gave her an encouraging nod with a smile. Somehow, Mouse knew she was smiling too. Then the butterfly fluttered her wings, lifting into the air, then took off toward the forest.

"I hope she'll be all right," Mouse said, watching her friend drift farther and farther away.

"I'm sure she'll be fine." He took his hand from her waist.

Mouse stared after Des long after she disappeared, hoping to catch another glimpse of her. But all she could see was the rustle of trees from the wind and a content smile crossed her face. Des was free. They both were.

"I wonder if there will be more butterflies in Wonderland now." Ferris didn't answer and she turned around to find him knelt before her. She cocked her head and studied him. "What are you doing down there?"

Ferris smirked, fishing out a silver ring from his pocket. Black and white diamonds embedded in the band glimmered. "I told you I had to grab something before coming out here, didn't I? I've been waiting weeks for this moment and was praying it wouldn't be three fucking years. And, just so you know, I even whispered to Des what I was planning."

Mouse took a deep swallow as she stared down at the loveliest ring she'd ever seen in the fingertips of the loveliest male she'd ever seen.

Ferris took her shaking hand in his, his thumb rubbing gently against her skin. "Will you marry me, luv? Not to entice you to say yes, but I'll even dress up as a Shakespeare character at the wedding." His grin grew wide, lighting all the way up to his dark irises.

"Yes!" she screamed, throwing her arms around him and pushing him to the ground. "Even without the Shakespeare, it would've been yes!"

"You knocked the ring from me." He chuckled, his hands trailing to her waist, his digits pressing in just right.

"We'll find it in a moment." She brushed her lips across his as he drew her even closer. Her tongue parted his lips as she rolled her hips against his.

"What is all the screaming?" Maddie shouted, rushing toward them, the purple feathers atop her black hat bobbing. She came to an abrupt stop farther back by the trees, staring at them. "Oh, are you two…?"

"We're getting married!" Mouse shrieked to her sister, her voice echoing through the gardens.

Maddie laughed, waving a hand in the air. "Finally, Ferris! Now we'll have the tea party to celebrate."

"We will"—Mouse grabbed a grinning Ferris by the hand—"but first we're finding the ring."

Did you enjoy Knave?

Authors always appreciate reviews, whether long or short.

If you haven't read the Vampires in Wonderland short story prequel, Rav, it is available now!

You think you know Wonderland. But you don't.

Imogen, the Queen of Hearts, is known for taking the hearts of those who betray her, including her servants. Her king, Rav, ventures to the mortal world to lure in new prey to replace their dwindling help. One bite, one simple exchange of her blood is all it will take for a mortal to become one of them. And this time, Rav chooses a girl named Alice.

Want to enter a sexy fae world? You may want to check out Faeries of Oz, beginning with the short story prequel, Lion.

Langwidere has an obsessive habit—collecting heads. She wears a new one each day, changing them out like she does her ivory dresses. But Langwidere doesn't have the one thing she truly wants: complete power over the territories in Oz.
When Lion—the once cowardly fae—shows up at her doorstep, he offers her an opportunity to achieve her desires. Will he use the courage the Wizard gave him to help her succeed, or will he betray her in the process?

Turn the page for Rav's prequel to the Vampires in Wonderland series.

RAV

CHAPTER ONE

RAV

The mortal world was a vampire's amusement park. There were rides to suit everyone's tastes—bars, seaside towns, sporting events. Rav preferred the adrenaline rush of night clubs. The bigger, the better. All those pitiful humans with racing heartbeats and building sexual desire as they ground against each other on the dance floor. The scent never failed to make his cock as hard as a rock. Just thinking about it made him crave the satisfaction of sinking into a warm body … in more ways than one.

Tonight, Rav had very particular plans, however. He made his way through the underground tunnel that led from Wonderland to the mortal realm. The white flames burning on wall torches reflected against the black slate walls and, before him, the portal gleamed. A shimmery red and black vortex that would spit him out into a wretched dirt hole in the ground of the mortal world. Once, centuries ago when he was first turned, Rav mused to the queen when he met her how the *rabbit hole* worked in Ivory compared to Scarlet, and she'd called him *Rabbit* ever since. His pet name from her, and he allowed it. She was too good a fuck not to.

With the task of bringing back a human—to turn immortal—hanging over his head, Rav pictured the outskirts of London in his mind and stepped through the portal. The trip was slightly less fun with a job to do, but only *slightly*. He and the Queen of Hearts were running low on servants—not surprising as they killed them nearly as quickly as they became vampires—and they needed to replenish their stock. At least he got to play for the night before returning, and he knew just where to do it. The man-turned-vampire who he brought back last week had piqued his curiosity with tales of a vampire club in London.

It took some convincing to get Rav to believe the place existed—apparently many did all around the mortal world— but it was such a far cry from the mobs with pitchforks from centuries ago. Back then, leave one villager drained of blood and the whole town was up in arms. He simply *had* to see this club with his own eyes.

Dressed in a sheer black shirt with metal rings running down the sleeves, his abs were clearly visible. His black jeans were slung low and the boots he wore were heavier than he was used to, but he wanted to blend in. The now-vampire who had told Rav of the club assured him this clothing would do the trick.

Rav brushed his white hair over his shoulder, the blood-red tips dancing in the cool London breeze, and approached a brick building with *Bloody Hell* in neon lights. He chuckled to himself at the name. Many new vampires compared Wonderland to Hell when they first arrived, and it certainly *was* bloody. But he doubted the club would live up to the name.

The bouncer—a broad, tattooed man with a safety pin shoved through his brow—opened the door without a second glance, allowing him entrance. Hard rock music raged with a furious strum of the guitar and chaotic drumbeats, while a fog machine coated the floor in a low cloud. Red brocade wallpaper clung to the walls. Velvet chairs and matching sofas were arranged on one side of the club, a dance floor with red lights and flashing strobes on the other, and the bar in between.

The energy nipped along Rav's skin. He smiled, his fangs on full display, and sauntered to the bar. With a quick glance at the list of drinks hanging on the wall, he flagged down the bartender. Her tight red corset lifted her breasts in a way that made his mouth water. Blue veins snaked beneath her skin just *asking* for someone to take a bite, but he was better off with someone else. She would have to wait until she was finished with her shift to follow him, and he didn't want the hassle.

"Type AB," he ordered. There was no way they served real blood, was there? He couldn't smell any of the metallic delicacy, but he was going to find out.

Someone with the rich, intoxicating scent of lavender brushed up against him. Rav glanced down to find a girl no more than twenty leaning over the bar. Wavy black hair reached her waist, but he noticed it wasn't her natural color as blonde roots were beginning to show. Dark makeup swept upward from the corners of her eyes and her lips were stained black. A silver bar pierced through the bridge of her nose and two more piercings dotted her cheeks like dimples.

"Like what you see?" she asked, looking up at Rav.

He lifted a brow. "Pardon?"

"You're staring." She turned to face him and propped an elbow on the bar.

Fingerless black lace gloves ran up to her elbows, but that was where she stopped fitting in with the sea of black and red. The dress she wore was pure white with straps and buckles around the waist. Tulle peeked out from the skirt, hitting just above her knees. She looked positively *delicious*.

"Can you blame me?" he asked with a smirk.

Her eyes flicked down to his mouth. "Nice fangs. Where

did you get them done?"

He swiped his tongue over a pointed tip. Why had no one told him about these clubs before? This was almost too fucking easy. "Wonderland," he told her.

The bartender returned with a thick red drink and Rav sniffed it. *Definitely not blood.* He frowned into the glass and stirred the little stick, making the ice clink. *Should've known.* It was better straight from the source anyway.

"Is that here in London?" she asked.

"Hmm?"

"Wonderland," she clarified. "Is it in London? I've been looking for a place to get my fangs done, but no dentist wants to file them for me."

Rav pushed the glass away and scanned the room once more. He could stay and play, grab a bite to eat, and take his chances luring another vampire wannabe to Wonderland. It didn't seem like it would be difficult. But would they be bearable? Rav lived in the Queen of Heart's castle and relied on the servants as much as anyone there.

And this girl had a bit of flare. A spark.

"I can take you there. It's not far," he said. "Get you an appointment."

Her smile faded, replaced with uncertainty. Rav caught the slight uptick in her pulse. "Oh… I don't think that—"

"They only accept new patients by referral," he interrupted. "And they close soon, so if you want in, we should go now."

The girl chewed her bottom lip. "I don't even know your name."

"I'm Rav."

She hesitated before holding her hand out to shake. "Alice."

"Alice," he purred, gripping her hand. "You would look divine with a set of fangs."

She smiled again and glanced around the club, hesitating.

Then she rolled her eyes. "Okay, fine. I've been desperate to do it. Hell, I'll be a rebel for the night. Let's go."

Rav beamed down at her before motioning toward the door. "After you."

CHAPTER TWO

IMOGEN

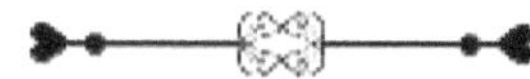

Under a vampire's touch, anyone's heart could be crushed.

Imogen adjusted herself in the red, velvet high-backed chair and crossed her legs, allowing the long slit of her gown to show off her pale flesh to Ferris, her Knave.

She'd brought the tall and muscular male through the portal to her palace several years ago to be her servant. The newly-turned servants came and went when she grew enraged, or the Rabbit—Rav—became bored. Ferris had been too willing to fuck when she'd met him at a club, desperate even. Before making him her servant, she gave in to the desire. With his lean muscles, dark hair and eyes, it was a worthy distraction. The temporary rush of euphoria along with the taste of crimson ecstasy was the itch that she'd needed scratched. But once a human became an immortal servant, that was all they were.

For the past two years, she could tell by the way Ferris watched her that he was aching for another fuck, but she was finished with him. Just as she'd been with her first husband, that pathetic male who had believed himself to be an actual king, who she and Rav had murdered together. Imogen had ripped his heart out—a signature death that made her known as the Queen of Hearts—and Rav became her permanent lover. Even though they relished in other's pleasures, no one could satisfy them completely except for each other.

Imogen felt eyes on her once more. "You're looking again," she cooed at Ferris.

"I'm only doing as you asked," he said softly. "Straightening your paintings."

Imogen stood from the chair, swaying her hips as she sauntered toward him. Her red gown dragged across the onyx floor as she stopped in front of him, her feathered collar swaying. The sitting room was scarlet and white with ivory anatomical hearts painted along each bricked wall. Several portraits of game cards hung around the area.

Ferris's hands nervously twitched as she reached inside her dress, feeling for the solid textures of her prized possession.

"Ah, don't be frightened, precious Knave." She fished out the deck of cards that she always carried with her. "I know you like games." With a smile, she patted the end of his nose.

His eyes widened as she shuffled the cards, her long, pointed scarlet and black nails tapping the top of the deck. Slowly, she spread them out before him, fanning herself. "Pick a card," she whispered. "Only one."

Ferris pursed his lips but knew not to deny her. If so, she would cut out his heart. He blinked rapidly as he tugged out a card. Flipping it over, he released a relieved breath. She fought back a smirk for causing him stress.

"Diamond," he murmured, his dark eyes catching hers.

"Looks like you won't have to watch me and Rav fuck tonight then, will you?" She ran a finger down his lips, catching on the bottom one. "I know you desperately want to get between my legs again, but you're weak, and your cock is nothing like his." Turning away from him, she laughed as she headed toward the door. She glanced back one more time before leaving and purred, "Oh, and don't forget to finish dusting the whole room … with your tongue."

Rine, one of her female servants, walked up to Imogen as she exited the room. "You have a guest waiting downstairs."

Imogen wasn't a bitch to all her surviving servants, more so to Ferris because it was fun toying with him. "Who is it?"

"The hat maker." Rine rolled her eyes.

"Ah, that crazy fool finally showed up. Can you make sure the Knave is cleaning up the dust with his tongue?"

"Only if I can play with him too?" Rine smiled wickedly.

"Do as you wish." Imogen brushed past her and descended the checkered steps to where she found the hat maker—Maddie—sitting in the middle of the black settee, tapping her feet in a mad rush. She wore bright purple arm sleeves, and her hair fell to her chin in spiraled curls that matched in color. Lace crisscrossed up the front of her tight black dress. Her skirt flared out to mid-thigh, and violet hues peeked through the black.

She wasn't beautiful in the slightest. But if Maddie wasn't so fucking crazy, Imogen would still have invited the hat maker to her bed, but she didn't do *mad*.

Maddie was always so antsy that Imogen only wanted to collect her commissioned hats, then quickly send the nuisance on her way. Imogen could just find another hat maker, but there wasn't anyone in Wonderland who made them the way Maddie did.

"Where is it?" Imogen snapped as she stood in front of her guest.

"Payment first," Maddie sang.

Imogen clenched her teeth. "You know very well that your payment is me not killing you after you allowed the White Queen to disappear. So quit fucking with me."

"I've told you I don't know where she is."

Imogen was certain Maddie *did* know—the Hatter was

such good friends with the traitor, after all—which was precisely why she was still alive. One day, Maddie would lead Imogen to her enemy, whether by slipping up or giving in. The White Queen—Ever—wanted to put an end to snatching unwilling humans from the mortal world. That wouldn't happen. Even Rav wanted Ever dead and she was his sister.

"You will give me one more hat in a month's time and then we'll come up with a new arrangement." Imogen lifted Maddie's chin harshly. "Understand?"

"Yes, Your Majesty." Maddie moved out from the queen's touch and stood from the settee. "Can I see Mouse before I leave?"

"No." Maddie's sister was still serving in the palace and, until Ever was found, would continue doing so.

Imogen didn't miss the flex of the hat maker's fingers before her shoulders sagged and she scampered out the door.

The Queen of Hearts smirked. Even if Maddie grew a backbone, what could she do? Try and stab Imogen through the heart with a hatpin? If the female attempted anything, she would be dead on her back before laying a finger on Imogen.

Forgetting about the Mad Hatter, Imogen lifted the purple box to inspect it as she headed into the throne room. She removed the lid and drew out the hat. It was perfect, delicate and oval with a fishnet veil. She placed it on top of her red waves and clipped the hat into her locks.

"I have a gift for you," a deep voice said from behind her.

Imogen whirled around, catching a lilac scent before seeing the human's face. Beside the new guest stood Rav, his white, scarlet-tipped hair pushed back over the shoulders of his sheer black shirt that displayed his taut chest and abs. She could lick him right here. But the human's scent made her pulse race.

Without blood, a vampire's heart would quit beating, and she would make sure hers never stopped.

"This is where you went to get your fangs done?" The

girl's bright blue eyes were as wide as saucers as she glanced at Rav. Thick black hair with blonde roots fell to her waist, and the belted dress she wore was hideous. She appeared to be somewhere in her early twenties—a good age for the change.

"Yes, right here in Wonderland." Rav stroked the tip of one fang with his tongue as he smirked, his brown eyes blazing. "Hundreds of years ago."

"I don't know what's happening." The girl's chest heaved, her body trembling. "But I want to go back home."

"That's funny." Imogen crept close to the girl, backing her up into the wall so she had nowhere to escape to. Leaning forward, she brushed her nose against the fluttering vein at the girl's throat. "Because you *are* home."

CHAPTER THREE

RAV

One brush of power and Rav had Alice following silently at his heels. He didn't always bother compelling the mortals before leading them through the portal to Wonderland, but it really depended on the person. Some ignored their fight-or-flight response right up until he told them to hop into a hole in the ground. A good chase could be entertaining, but he wasn't in the mood for running tonight. Alice had followed him from the club willingly enough. Leading her into a wooded park at night seemed like a stretch though—she was too self-aware. So a compelled human it was. That way, he could do whatever the fuck he wanted. Even if he were to drain every ounce of a human's blood, the mortal wouldn't bat an eyelash.

"After you," Rav said with a flourish.

He took Alice's warm hand and helped her leap into the hole at the base of a giant, ancient tree. Moss concealed the entrance while Wonderland magic deterred everyone who ventured close enough. Well—not *everyone*. Some people still hopped into the perfectly circular dirt hole and bravely went through the portal, finding themselves lost in a world of vampires. Just like Rav and his sister had all those centuries ago through the one in Ivory.

Rav jumped into the hole after Alice. Six feet from the bottom of the hole was the gleaming portal that led straight into the lower levels of his castle.

Because of his compulsion, Alice had landed on her feet without stumbling. He slipped down beside her. Alice's body shook with nerves as he pressed a hand to her lower back and escorted them both into Wonderland. It was a testament to how strong-willed she was—that she could still retain enough consciousness to feel fear. Rav smirked. Her blood would be all the more delicious for it. He loved the extra tang that terror added to the flavor.

"You're going to meet with the Queen of Hearts," he said conversationally. Her footsteps echoed throughout the gleaming slate tunnel while Rav's were completely silent. "And live in her Ruby Heart Palace."

A whimper escaped Alice's throat, sending a jolt straight to Rav's cock. *Fuck.* He pressed a hand to her lower back again and forced her to walk faster. The queen was waiting for him in the throne room and the sooner she turned the girl into an immortal servant, the sooner he could sink into Imogen's wet heat.

The palace blurred out of focus as his attention zeroed in on the fastest path to their destination. White marble hallways decorated with blood-red tapestries and paintings, low-hung chandeliers with glowing candles, and a crimson carpet stitched with anatomical hearts running down the center of the corridors. The glamour had faded for Rav centuries ago, but the pleasure he was about to partake in was another story.

Bursting through the tall doors, Rav led Alice straight toward his immortal queen. Imogen stood in front of the arched windows behind the throne. The city of Scarlet stretched out below the castle with a million lights burning through the constant dark of Wonderland. That, too, had lost its wonder for Rav, but Imogen still reveled in the power they held over so many. But Rav wanted more. He'd held authority in the palm of his hand since the day he became immortal. If he knew then what he knew now about his twin sister, the White Queen, he would've driven a stake through her heart and taken the Ivory kingdom the moment the late rulers made her their heir.

Then there'd been Imogen. He'd wanted her. And he *had* her.

Seeing Imogen in his favorite red gown, the train skimming over the black floor, the feathered collar caressing her neck, had him ready to take her before dealing with the mortal. But the queen didn't appreciate rash behavior. It's what kept the kingdom of Scarlet and their subjects in line.

"Imogen," he purred. "I have a gift for you."

She pivoted around slowly, her red lips curling into a smile.

Alice turned to face Rav with wide blue eyes. "This is where you went to get your fangs done?"

Rav cursed himself for letting his control of her slip. He couldn't help it though—Imogen made him irrational in every way. "Yes," he told her, flashing his fangs. "Right here in Wonderland. Hundreds of years ago."

Alice looked back and forth between him and the queen, and her body began to shake. "I don't know what's happening, but I want to go back home."

Rav tightened his compulsion over her to avoid the stage where she begged for her life. She would still have a life when they were finished—she just wouldn't be mortal.

"That's funny." Imogen backed her up into the wall so Alice had nowhere to move. Leaning forward, she brushed her nose against the girl's neck. "Because you are home."

Rav stepped closer to them and trailed a hand down the girl's throat. "I found her at one of those *vampire clubs*." His voice was coated with amusement. It was rare that something surprised him, but the existence of such places was a splendid novelty. "She was admiring my fangs."

Imogen's yellow eyes sparkled with cold humor. "You do have impressive fangs, Rabbit."

He grinned, exposing the sharp canines. As soon as she fed from the girl, he would sink them into the queen's wrist. Taste her blood. Then he would taste between her legs.

"Would you like a pair of your own?" Imogen asked Alice. When she didn't answer, her eyes glazed, the queen spared Rav a disappointed look. "You compelled her?"

"I was eager to get back."

Her gaze trailed down his body, pausing at the large bulge in his trousers. She rubbed a hand over her chest and grinned. "You always come back to me *eager*."

Rav's lust built at the sight of his queen's chest rising and falling faster than before. Paired with the quickening of Alice's pulse, he wasn't sure he could wait long enough for the business with the mortal to be finished.

"Hurry with this one and I'll *show* you eager," he vowed.

Imogen leaned down to lick Alice's neck and glanced up at Rav from beneath her lashes. "Let her scream. You know how much I like it."

Rav suppressed a moan and lifted the compulsion just enough for Alice to have her voice. The ear-piercing scream that followed was enough to rattle the crystal goblets sitting beside the throne.

Imogen gripped Alice's shoulders, her nails biting into the skin and staining the white dress with tiny drops of blood. The scent instantly filled the room and the queen inhaled deeply. Rav unbuckled his belt in anticipation of fucking Imogen when she was finished.

Then Imogen opened her mouth and bit into the girl's creamy flesh.

Drinking.

Drinking.

Drinking.

Fuck, Rav thought as he struggled to control himself. Blood-lust raged alongside his carnal desire, and his cock swelled eagerly.

Finally, Imogen lifted her head from Alice's neck. Twin puncture wounds marked the mortal who now slumped in the queen's hold. Imogen licked her lips and held out one hand to Rav. "Hurry," she rasped.

Rav wasted no time. He lifted Imogen's wrist and bit the tender flesh below her palm. Warm blood oozed into his mouth, but it wasn't meant for him so he pulled back. Imogen pressed her bleeding wrist to Alice's lips and held it there. Thick ruby liquid smeared the girl's mouth, a small line racing down her chin.

Seconds ticked by as Rav undressed the queen with his eyes. *For fuck's sake!* He was going to come in his trousers if she didn't speed the process along. The rich, spicy scent of Alice's blood clung to the air and soon he would get to taste it straight from his lover's lips.

"Ferris!" Imogen shouted, calling for the Knave. A series of heavy footsteps pounded against nearby stairs. When the side door swung open, the queen let Alice slide down the wall and collapse on the floor. "Lock her in the dungeons while she turns."

Ferris eyed Rav with fire in his gaze. The Knave wanted his queen … but she didn't give two shits about him. Rav rubbed himself over his trousers with a smug smirk as Ferris lifted Alice into his arms.

"Enough teasing him," Imogen whispered in Rav's ear. "I want you to tease *me* now."

"No." Rav prowled around Imogen. "You don't want to be teased. You want to be fucked."

CHAPTER FOUR

IMOGEN

Alice's blood was one of the sweetest Imogen had ever tasted. So lush, so perfect. The girl may not have appeared innocent by her various piercings, the clothing she wore, but Imogen had seen everything in the girl's blood. How Alice's family had wanted her to be more outgoing like her brother, not so reclusive. She'd never had many friends, never even had a boyfriend—she'd always been too focused on school, her grades. So Alice had decided to change, but not in the way her family had wanted. She'd started taking a liking to the vampire culture after researching mythology online, then attempted to alter herself, but there was no masking the innocence still hiding there.

"You have a little something on your lips," Rav whispered, his voice low, so delicious that she could almost taste his desire.

Before Imogen could lick the lingering drops of blood clean, Rav's tongue trailed slowly along the edge of her lips. A rush of heat went straight to her core, lighting her on fire.

"There," he murmured in her ear. "Got it."

Imogen pulled closer to him, draping her arms over his strong shoulders before wrapping her legs around his narrow hips. "Take me upstairs. To Ferris's bed."

He growled in approval and held her tight, his nose nuzzled into her hair.

Rav led them out of the throne room and walked them up each step, not once stumbling as his lips found hers again, their tongues entwining. Their kisses became frantic when he reached the top of the stairs. He threw open the first door at the start of the hallway—Ferris's room—and took her inside. Ferris shouldn't have given Rav that fiery look earlier, which was why the Knave needed to be disciplined. Rav was his king, and Ferris needed to treat him as such. The scent of their fucking would remain in his bed long after they finished, and the thought pleased her.

"Unbutton me," Imogen demanded as she stepped to the floor, gliding her breasts down his muscular chest.

Rav spun her around, his fangs grazing her neck as he slowly unbuttoned the back of her dress, inch by agonizing inch. He pushed the fabric from her shoulders and the gown pooled to the floor, her body now bare before him.

Kicking the dress away, Imogen licked her lips and turned to face him. With anxious fingers, she stroked his cock through his fabric. His buckle was already undone and she unbuttoned his trousers while he hungrily watched. Rav removed his boots, shoved his trousers the rest of the way down, and tossed them to the other side of the room. In one swift swoop, his shirt was lost somewhere too.

Imogen drew him toward the bed by his wrist. "You brought an extra delectable treat to serve us, so I want to return the favor."

Rav smirked as Imogen lowered herself to the bed and scooted backward until she felt the hardness of the headboard against her flesh. With her index finger, she motioned him to come to her. His fists hit the mattress and he crawled his way to her, straddling her body, and she grabbed him by the hips. He knew exactly what to do, what she craved, as he got on his knees, his cock gloriously before her.

The veins throbbed on his hardened length, desperate as much as she was. Imogen brought her head forward, swiping her tongue across the tip. She clenched her hands harder on his hips, her fingernails digging in as she urged him closer. Rav slowly rocked back and forth inside her mouth—low groans escaped his throat as she worked her way up his cock in the way he liked. He tasted salty to perfection as she relished in his flavors, and his skin was like velvet on her tongue.

Rav removed the hat from her hair, then interlaced his fingers through her red locks. With a growl, he gently tugged himself from her mouth. "I'm about to come. Turn over."

A wicked grin spread across her face and she pushed him back by his chest, then did as she was told. Imogen placed both hands on the headboard, gripping it tightly, her body tingling with anticipation, demanding him to fill her.

"Fuck me!" she shouted, knowing the entire palace could hear her. And pleased they had.

Rav's body pressed against hers, his fingers stroking between her wet folds. "We will be doing this all night, my queen." And with one swift thrust, he was inside her, the headboard slamming the wall as she lurched forward.

She moaned, arching her spine into him, the pads of his fingers running down each vertebra.

Again and again, Rav thrust, his hands on her breasts, toying with her nipples in a way that made her body hotter than lava. Then his teeth were at her throat, making her moan even louder. Imogen reclined her head back as her second favorite part of him sank into her. The ecstasy rolled through her veins as her blood filled his mouth. Each roll of his hips, each suction at her throat, had the desire building until a rush of crimson colors rocketed within her, the pleasure seeming as if it wouldn't end.

Then he ripped his fangs free of her flesh and with her name on his lips—the sound filling the room in a violent, exquisite way—he erupted too. His chest heaved against her body, hers inflating and deflating just as savagely.

When Imogen finally caught her breath, she glanced over her shoulder, giving him a devilish smile. "We're not done yet, Rabbit. Lay on your back."

Rav chuckled, uncaging her, as he flipped to his back, his head resting on Ferris's pillow. Imogen's fangs lowered while she cradled his hips with her thighs and leaned forward, inhaling his musky scent. Her tongue swiped the vein of his throat, his pulse beating rapidly.

Imogen sank her teeth into his soft, delicious flesh. She drank and drank until he was hard once more, desperately growling her name.

And now, she would ride her king.

CHAPTER FIVE

RAV

The sun never shone in Wonderland. If it did, vampires would be trapped inside nearly half their lives to avoid turning to ash. So, instead, time was told by how dark the sky was: pitch black at night, ash gray at midday, and varying shades between. Judging by the deep charcoal, Rav had spent the entire night with Imogen in the Knave's bed. Ferris had undoubtedly attempted to sleep at some point, and Rav hoped the fool had heard the queen screaming *his* name.

Fucking shitbag. He'd never understand why, out of all the servant's Imogen killed, it had never been *that* one.

Alice, on the other hand, would be interesting. A mortal who wanted to be a vampire and thought them to be romantic instead of ruthless… What would she do now that her wish had been granted? Over the centuries, only a handful of humans had wanted to be turned, but this was different. Humans no longer truly believed in the existence of Rav's kind. He couldn't help being curious about how she would react. Would parts of this world live up to her expectations, or would she mope about because it was so vastly different? And the first feeding—would that intrigue or repulse her? There were so many questions that he wanted answers to.

"What are you thinking about, Rabbit?" Imogen asked as she stepped into her gown.

Rav slipped his shirt over his head. "Hmm?"

"You look as if you're ready to cause trouble."

Rav ran a hand through his tumbled hair. "No trouble. I'm just thinking of the girl."

Imogen's gaze took on a hard edge. She raised an eyebrow, silently letting Rav know he needed to elaborate.

He stepped forward, buttoning the back of her dress without her having to ask. "I'm curious how similar we are to what this new … vampire culture thinks. Do you suspect that it will affect her change at all?"

"I don't see how similarities between her expectations and reality would have any impact." Imogen bent and grabbed one of her shoes from under the bed. "It's not their mental strength that's tested."

Rav nodded, though he already knew that. The change could be brutal. A vampire—one stronger than Ferris or any of the dungeon guards—sometimes had to coax them through it. Even then, there was no guarantee they would survive. Some bodies were simply not equipped. Humans called it survival of the fittest.

"You want to study her," Imogen said with a roll of her eyes.

Studying things was a habit of his, not that he always knew what he was searching for. Just … *something*. And it gave his life a touch of focus. After centuries, living could become dull without a purpose. Even a meaningless one. Rav shrugged. "Let me have my fun."

"Fine." Imogen swiped her second shoe from the floor and crossed the room, running a finger down his cheek. "Conduct your little experiment, quench your thirst for useless knowledge, then come back to me. I'm going to bathe."

"I'll join you after," he promised.

The queen sauntered past him, swatting his naked ass. Rav chuckled and quickly pulled on his trousers. If things had gone well, Alice would have already finished transitioning into a vampire. It took less than thirty minutes, ideally, and he'd spent six times as long fucking Imogen.

Rav left the bedroom, skipping down the stairs, and smiled to himself. When he saw Ferris sitting on the bottom step, his smile widened. The Knave stared straight ahead at the wall, his lips pursed, with his hands in fists.

"What's wrong, Knave?" he asked, smug.

Ferris shot him a look hot enough to burn. "Nothing."

"Nothing?" Rav laughed at the obvious lie. "Enjoy the new scent all over your sheets."

One second, Ferris was sitting, then the next he was standing, his face an inch from Rav's. "Remember, *my king*. Those with the most, have the most to lose."

Rav pushed Ferris away with a single finger to his chest. "Is that a threat?"

"Who am I to threaten you?" he asked, feigning ignorance.

Rav groaned. He didn't want to deal with Ferris, not even to taunt him. He wanted to see how Alice was progressing. "One day, Knave, your disrespect will get you killed."

At that, Ferris smirked.

Rav smirked back, though rage boiled within him. He couldn't let the pathetic bastard see how he was getting under his skin. The Knave knew what he was doing, the fucker, but Imogen clearly wanted him alive. It was hard to find loyal servants and, to her, that was exactly what Ferris was. Rav had to respect that, just as she respected his interest in Alice. So, he hurried to his own room to change into a clean outfit more befitting him.

Once in a comfortable pair of black linen trousers and a plain red shirt with a black jacket, Rav made his way past the throne room, and down a winding stone staircase to the dungeons.

A muscular male vampire stood watch at the front of the room wearing the queen's crest on a crimson tunic. The tang of old blood hung in the air, mixing with the damp, musty scent from the straw sprinkled across the floor. Six-by-eight cells stretched down the long, dark passageway, separated with metal bars. Shackles hung from the walls to help keep the prisoners from breaking free. At the other end of the room was a door that led to the *interview* room. All the fun toys were kept in there.

The only guest today was Alice and, judging by the silence, the change had gone well. Or killed her already. Rav peered through the rows of metal bars, not catching a glimpse of Alice's white dress.

Brows lowered in confusion, he turned to the guard. "Where is the girl?"

"Girl, Your Majesty?" he asked.

"Yes. The girl the Knave brought down hours ago to complete the change." He flicked a hand at the cells. "Where is she?"

The guard's throat bobbed. "The Knave didn't bring anyone here today."

Rav blinked, sure he'd misheard. "White dress, dark makeup, about this tall," he said carefully, holding his hand up at roughly Alice's height. "The queen's bite mark on her neck…"

The guard shook his head, his expression wary.

Rav's rage stirred, foaming at the brink, threatening to spill over. "That motherfucking piece of shit!"

The guard blanched as Rav spun on his heel and stormed out of the dungeons. He would kill Ferris. Chop him into tiny little pieces and scatter him from the balcony. Except his head. His head, he would stick on a pike outside the palace as a warning.

"Imogen," he shouted once he hit the main floor. He would deal with the Knave after they found Alice. "We have a problem!"

CHAPTER SIX

IMOGEN

The water was warm against Imogen's skin as it lapped at the edges of the bathtub. She spread the soap up and down her pale breasts, then sank her head below the water.

A shout came from somewhere within the palace and Imogen jerked forward, creating waves along the bathtub walls. Her eyes narrowed as she cocked her head, listening for the sound to come again, wondering if she'd imagined it. Then it reverberated through the palace walls. Rav calling her name. If it had been anyone else, the interruption would have irritated her. But for him to yell for her meant something was important.

Imogen didn't bother wiping the liquid droplets from her skin as she stepped out from the cast iron bathtub. She flicked her wet hair over her shoulders and grabbed a raven-colored robe from the hook on the wall beside the sink. She shoved the silk on as she opened the door, her nipples pebbling from the cool air. With the robe still open, she stepped into the hall.

Furrowing her brow, she looked both ways into the empty

area. "Rabbit?"

Footsteps thumped against the stairs and Rav raced toward her, his face red with fury.

"What is it?" she asked, staring at his disheveled hair. The last time she'd seen her king this furious was when one of their servants had attempted to stab Imogen through the heart with a dinner knife. That servant lost his head and heart before the blade could even touch her flesh.

Rav struck his fist against the wall. "I told you the bastard wasn't trustworthy."

"Who?" Imogen wrinkled her nose.

"That fucking Knave of yours."

Ferris. Her eyes turned to slits as she thought about him, replaying every single interaction between them. He never once disobeyed her, and if he truly did deceive her, she would rip his heart out and crush it. She and Rav could always detect the untrustworthy ones right away, and she didn't see how she could have missed it.

"What did he do?" Imogen asked, while tying her robe. She then straightened her shoulders and released her fangs.

"The girl is gone," Rav spat. "I went to the dungeons, and the guard said the Knave never brought in anyone. I saw the smug bastard before I went down there, sitting on the steps outside his room."

Imogen felt her temper rising as her heart quickened. Nothing ever slid past her. Ever. But something wasn't right about this. "Where did he take her then?"

"I don't know, but we need to find them." Rav struck the wall again.

If Rav had just seen Ferris, then he still had to be in the palace. Somewhere.

"Knave!" she screeched, brushing past Rav.

Imogen rushed straight to his room and threw open the door. His drawers were wide open, clothing dumped all over the floor, as if he'd taken things he'd hidden. *That bastard.*

Gritting her teeth, she drew Rav out of the room as soon as he entered. They then went up and down the palace, gathering all the servants to help them search for the traitor. There wasn't a sign of him anywhere. Not a single cabinet, wardrobe, or curtain had been left unsearched. No one had seen him with Alice. No one had even seen him since Rav.

A sinking feeling nagged at her. "Did anyone check your portal?"

"No," Rav growled, already taking off in the direction of it. They turned down several of the red and black checkered hallways, then flew down the glistening steps leading to the lower levels of the castle. A sulfuric scent filled the air, as if a match had just been struck. Someone had used the portal.

Imogen picked up her pace, remaining right on Rav's heels. Just as they were about to reach the last hallway to the portal, a shadow slinked around the corner before she caught sight of the figure.

It wasn't Ferris but her *son*. Chess. He looked nothing like his father besides his chestnut hair. It fell to mid-neck, shorter locks framing his face, his yellow irises matching hers. He wore his usual dark vest, nothing underneath, paired with leather trousers and boots.

"Did you use Rav's portal again?" Imogen hissed, already knowing his answer.

"I did." He smirked, stroking a finger along the wall. His gaze flicked between her and Rav. "I suppose you were too busy fucking each other to notice what's been going on."

"How long have you been lurking around down here?" Rav asked.

"Long enough," Chess said coyly. "My pleasant feast was interrupted when the Knave rushed a girl through the portal."

"And you didn't stop him?" Imogen grabbed her foolish son by his vest.

Chess didn't bat an eyelash. He had so much of her in him that she didn't know whether to be proud or furious.

"Why should I care about a human girl he wanted to feed off and send back?" He shrugged.

"She was turned, Chess." As precious moments ticked by, it didn't matter that he was her son—she wanted to kill him.

"Funny thing." Chess grinned, removing Imogen's hand from him. "Ferris went out the secret door, alone, only minutes ago."

"Chess!" No one should have known about the hidden door besides the three of them.

"I don't think Ferris realized he sent the girl up the portal just as the sun was rising." He bit his blood-stained lip. "Oops."

Imogen wrapped her hand around Chess's throat. "Find the Knave and bring him back here. You know better than anyone how to get around Wonderland without being seen. If you screw this up, you'll meet the same fate as your father."

"You don't have to be so dramatic, Mother. I'll bring your little toy back so we can be one big happy family again."

He'd better.

Imogen removed her hand from Chess's throat and watched him saunter toward the hidden panel in the wall. For now, they would have to seal it up to make sure Ferris couldn't slip back inside on his own.

"I think there's more to this than you refusing to bed Ferris again," Rav finally said when the door shut behind Chess.

Imogen thought about the way Ferris had always been watching her. His lust-filled gazes now seemed as though they could have been false, as if he'd been using the tactic to spy on her instead. For something… Or for *someone*.

"Chess will bring him back"—her gaze connected with Rav's—"then you'll pry the Knave's fangs from his severed head. As for the girl, if the sun doesn't kill her, we have to find her. A newly-turned vampire can't be allowed to run around the mortal world. And, if she *is* dead, then we need to collect another human to take her place."

TIN

CHAPTER ONE

TIN

Tin picked absently at the dried blood on his iron-tipped gloves. Day had turned to night with no sign of his target. Lord save the ugly bastard if he was off killing the brownie who'd hired him. She still owed Tin half his money, payable only when the dwarf's head was delivered. The dwarf was as good as dead either way, if only because Tin was stuck perched in the damn tree for so long, but he was a professional.

And professionals got paid.

With an exaggerated huff, Tin pried his iron axe from where it was imbedded in the tree near his head. An unusual weapon for a faerie, but he had long ago embraced the pain of iron. He had no choice, really—it was that or go mad. Almost as mad as this dwarf was making him. It was no wonder someone wanted the miner dead.

A light-skinned sprite landed on the branch just above him, all spindly limbs and unkempt hair. She seemed oblivious to Tin's presence as she plucked delicate white leaves from the otherwise-green foliage and tucked them into a little basket on her arm. Her wings shook, golden pollen raining down.

Tin jerked away from the shimmering powder before it landed in his long silver hair, and snatched the sprite in a blindingly fast motion. The tiny creature shrieked inside his closed fist, then fell silent as he tightened his grip until bones crunched.

"Nasty creature," he spat, though sprites weren't particularly bothersome, and unfurled his fingers. Bits of sprite coated his gloved hand. He brushed it off the best he could, wiping the remnants on his pants.

The sprite's innards weren't the only relic of a kill to adorn his clothing. Kelpie scales were artfully sewn into his dark clothing for extra protection, and the small rings holding the right side of his hair back were whittled from their blackened bones.

A low whistle sounded in the distance, the tune cheerful and carefree. Tin gripped his axe tighter and leapt lithely from the tree, landing silently in the grass. He edged around the wide trunk and peered in the direction of the lighthearted song.

The dwarf he'd been waiting for crested the hill with a massive pack strapped to his back. Over his shoulder, a pickaxe was visible in the moonlight, the handle tucked safely away. His hands were empty. Good. It was annoying when they fought back.

Tin held his breath and watched his mark close the distance between them. The dwarf had a gnarled beard, ratty, knotted black hair, and a bulbous nose, all of which were coated in dark powder from the mineral mines. Suddenly, Tin regretted not bringing a bag to carry the head in. Mineral powder was even harder to wash from around the kelpie scales than pixie dust. Alas…

The dwarf was still whistling his merry tune when Tin leapt from his hiding place, axe swinging. His mark flailed and his heavy pack pulled him backward where he landed in a heap. "Wait! I—"

His eyes went wide and he sucked in a breath as the moonlight flashed over Tin's face. The mark of shame—or as Tin thought of it, his badge of honor—was known in every corner of Oz. The Wizard had taken *pity* on him after Tin's heart turned back into stone. Instead of being sentenced to death for assassinating eleven fae lords, he'd been branded. Shackled and bound, he'd been unable to escape as liquid iron was dripped slowly onto the side of his face. Each drop had landed at the edge of his cheekbone where it scalded a path across his skin. By the time it was finished and the iron cooled, Tin had been left with a design of wild, twisting silver lines that covered nearly half his right cheek.

"Have mercy," the dwarf begged.

Tin grinned savagely. The Wizard should've killed him. "There is no mercy in this world."

"Why?" the dwarf asked in a cracking voice. "I've done nothing!"

"Everyone has done *something*."

Tin swung his axe, severing the target's head before he could scream. He bent, fisting the dingy hair. Bright red blood gushed from the neck as he lifted the proof of his work. As he sauntered back toward the brownie's house to collect the rest of his fee, leaving a red trail in his wake, he whistled the end of the dwarf's song.

Firelight and music reached the brownie's cave from the nearby village. When Tin arrived, he found the old female atop a rock outside the opening, swaying to the song as she waited for him. Thin wisps of white hair floated around her molting head. Toenails curled over the ends of her feet. Age spots marked her olive skin, just as red stripes decorated her loose dress.

"You're late," she snapped.

"What do you care? He's dead." Tin threw the bloody head at the brownie, nearly knocking the portly faerie off the rock. This job was too far below his skill-set—and his pay grade—for him to put up with snide comments.

"I hired you to kill him *before* sundown."

Tin cracked his neck. It would be more profitable to kill the brownie and take whatever valuables she owned. She was ancient and barely came to his knee—it would be easy—but if he began killing his clientele, no one would seek him out. It was already hard enough finding work outside of the Emerald City. Country folk weren't much in the way of intrigue like those in the capital, but they made up for it with their ruthlessness. If the fae here didn't take care of their own problems, no one would.

The brownie must've sensed the shift in Tin's thoughts because she made a show of checking the validity of the head. "Fine. It's done." She reached down the front of her dress for a small bag. She pretended to weigh it in her hands before tossing it at his feet. "This concludes our business, assassin."

He caught the bag with the toe of his boot just before it landed in the dirt. It took every ounce of his meager self-control not to lunge for her throat. Tin opened the bag to be sure it was full of diamonds and not pebbles, though he was confident the brownie wasn't stupid enough to swindle him. The last person who'd tried that ended up impaled.

Satisfied, he turned on his heel and walked toward the town for a well-deserved drink. If he could find a room for the night, and someone to buy the gemstones off him before he moved to the next town, all the better.

Glimpses of fae flashed through the trees as he neared the edge of the clearing. Vivid, gem-colored fabric swirled around their lithe bodies. The firelight caressed exposed skin, some pale, some dark, some flecked with scales and others with feathers. Ribbons tied to posts lifted and fell in time with their flawless movements.

It seemed a nightly ritual in this part of Oz to greet the dawn with dance, which meant they would be at it all night. He'd never stepped foot in this particular town and wasn't sure what their reaction to him might be. Sometimes they called for his head, other times they hid inside and bolted the doors. Often it was a mixture of both. Whatever the response to his iron scars, Tin didn't much care unless it created extra work for himself.

Tin touched the rings in his hair without meaning to. He refused to hide his face, even if it made things easier, so he dropped his hand and strode straight into the town and through the party. The dancers faltered as they noticed him. Hooves ceased stomping, wings stilled, and soon the music sputtered out as well.

Tin made an exaggerated bow and held his breath. When no one screamed or made to attack, Tin dodged the decorative floating balls of light on his way to the tavern. It was better to hurry before they made up their minds on how to respond. The sign for the Peppered Pike hung crooked over the door in elvish writing. He steeled himself for the owner to give him the boot the moment he stepped inside, but he could really do with a night in an actual bed. Right after a drink.

Inside, the tavern was empty save for a female wiping down the bar. Two ribbed horns circled the sides of her head and her dark hair was styled to run parallel with them. "Welco—" Her words cut off as her gaze met his, recognizing him immediately.

Tin did his best to give her a reassuring smile but the iron distorted half of it. "Do you have any rooms?"

The girl shifted back warily. "We're … closed … during the…"

He didn't mention that she'd started to welcome him before she looked up. Instead, he pulled out one of the larger diamonds and held it in the center of his palm. Her eyes grew impossibly wide at the sight of all the fresh blood on his glove.

Shit. Diamond or no diamond, he knew she was five seconds away from bolting.

"Give the man a room, sweetmeat."

Tin froze at the familiar voice—one he blissfully hadn't heard in years—and eyed the alcohol behind the bar. "What are you doing here, Lion?"

"Good. You remember who I am," he said with a chuckle. "Join me."

The last time Tin saw the bastard was at his hearing, when Lion was called as a witness against him. For all the courage Lion gained, it had only made him a fool. Tin ground his teeth together and turned to face the other fae. Lion was exactly as he remembered: coarse golden hair tied in a low ponytail, bronze skin, and piercing golden eyes. The tuft at the end of his tawny tail skimmed the floor beside his boots. A fur cloak wrapping around Lion's broad shoulders made him appear even larger.

But, no matter how much bigger Lion was, Tin was certain he wasn't a threat. Lion had a heart, after all, even if it was darker than most, and that bloody organ made all creatures weak.

"What are you doing out of the South?" Tin growled.

Lion smirked arrogantly and flicked a look at the tavern girl, who let out a sharp gasp from behind the bar. "Another drink, if you wouldn't mind, and one for my friend."

"I asked you a question."

Lion rolled his eyes. "Stop being an ass and sit down."

Tin drew a slow, steady breath and reached for the axe at his hip.

"You're going to scare the lady," Lion warned coolly.

The hell if he cared. "I warned you. If I ever saw you again—"

"We're immortal, Tin. There's plenty of time to kill me. I have a job for you, so you may as well make your fortune first."

Fortune. Tin kept his hand on his axe but didn't wield it. He didn't kill people because he needed money—he *liked* killing—but that wasn't to say that he didn't recognize its usefulness.

The horned female sat the drinks down on the table with shaking hands. Some of the foam splashed over the sides, landing on Lion's sleeve. He growled at her and she hurtled out the back door.

Once they were alone, Lion continued. "You remember Dorothy, don't you?"

Tin narrowed his eyes, his grip tightening on his weapon. It was rather hard to forget the little human girl who'd crashed into his life and set him on the path to self-destruction.

"Of course you remember the little bitch." Lion took a long gulp of his drink, studying Tin over the rim of the glass. He nudged the empty chair across from him with his boot. Another invitation to sit.

This time, Tin accepted.

ALSO FROM CANDACE ROBINSON

Wicked Souls Duology
Vault of Glass
Bride of Glass

Marked by Magic
The Bone Valley
Merciless Stars

Cruel Curses Trilogy
Clouded By Envy
Veiled By Desire
Shadowed By Despair

Faeries of Oz Series
Lion (Short Story Prequel)
Tin
Crow
Ozma
Tik-Tok

Demons of Frosteria
Frost Mate (Prequel Novella)
Frost Claim

Cursed Hearts Duology
Lyrics & Curses
Music & Mirrors

Immortal Letters Duology
Dearest Clementine: Dark and Romantic Monstrous Tales
Dearest Dorin: A Romantic Ghostly Tale

These Vicious Thorns: Tales of the Lovely Grim

ALSO FROM AMBER R. DUELL

The Dark Dreamer Trilogy
Dream Keeper
Dark Consort
Night Warden

Forgotten Gods
Fragile Chaos

Faeries of Oz Series
Lion (Short Story Prequel)
Tin
Crow
Ozma
Tik-Tok

Darkness Series: Temptation
Darkness Whispered

The Prince's Wing
When Stars Are Bright

Vampires in Wonderland Series
Rav (Short Story Prequel)
Maddie
Chess
Knave

Once Upon A Wicked Villain
Spindle of Sin

Acknowledgments

This was the most emotional journey out of all the Wonderland books, seeing as Ferris and Mouse have both been through so much. We hope you enjoyed their journey and Mouse thanks you with a Shakespeare reading after Ferris plays you a song on his drums.

Wonderland has been such a cool thing for us to take on, and there have been lovely people along the way to help us! Thank you to Brandy for helping us make this story even better.

To Amber Hodges, who brings the proofing circle to a close with things we've missed! Jerica, for your wonderful sentence structure help! Elle, for supporting these books from the beginning! Hayley, who helps us so we get the British things right! Ann, Vic, and Lindsay, who always find little fixes we desperately need!

Our families who continue to stand by our sides through the happy and frustrating writing times.

Ferris also needed a band name, so thank you to our winner, Diedre, for giving him a cool one!

About the Authors

Candace Robinson spends her days consumed by words and hoping to one day find her own DeLorean time machine. Her life consists of avoiding migraines, admiring Bonsai trees, watching classic movies, and living with her husband and daughter in Texas—where it can be forty degrees one day and eighty the next.

Amber R. Duell was born and raised in a small town in Central New York. While it will always be home, she's constantly moving with her husband and two sons as a military wife. She does her best writing in the middle of the night, surviving the daylight hours with massive amounts of caffeine. When not reading or writing, she enjoys snowboarding, embroidering, and snuggling with her cats.